THE
PENDRAGON
LEGEND

ANTAL SZERB

THE
PENDRAGON
LEGEND

Translated from the Hungarian by
Len Rix

PUSHKIN PRESS
LONDON

English translation © Len Rix 2006

First published in Hungarian as
A Pendragon legenda 1934
© Estate of Antal Szerb

First published in 2006 by

Pushkin Press
12 Chester Terrace
London NW1 4ND

Reprinted 2006
This revised edition published in 2007
Reprinted 2010

ISBN 978 1 901285 89 5

Cover: *Knebworth House, Hertfordshire* Simon Marsden
© The Marsden Archive UK/The Bridgeman Art Library

Frontispiece: Antal Szerb

Set in 10 on 12 Baskerville
and printed in Great Britain on Ensobelle 70 gsm
by Cox & Wyman Ltd Reading Berkshire

Pushkin Press acknowledges with gratitude
a translation grant towards publication from the
Hungarian Book Foundation

www.pushkinpress.com

THE
PENDRAGON
LEGEND

"MY WAY IS TO BEGIN at the beginning" said Lord Byron, who knew his way around polite society.

Strictly speaking, I suppose all my stories begin with the fact that I was born in Budapest and that soon after—though it escaped my notice at the time—I was given the name I still bear today, János Bátky.

I pass over the events of the next thirty-two years—which include the Great War—between my birth and my first encounter with the Earl of Gwynedd, for he rather than myself is the hero of this remarkable tale.

So, to our first meeting.

Early one summer, with the London season drawing to its close, I was at a *soirée* at Lady Malmsbury-Croft's. This kind lady had taken me under her wing ever since my time as Donald Campbell's scientific secretary. I should explain that my occupation is to assist elderly Englishmen in the pursuit of their intellectual whims. Not to earn my living, as it happens: I have a small inheritance from my mother on which I can get by in whatever country I choose. For some years now that country has been England. I am extremely fond of its noble landscapes.

During the course of the evening the hostess seized me and led me off to a tall, grey-haired gentleman with the most wonderfully impressive head. He was seated in an armchair and smiling silently to himself.

"Your Lordship," said she, "this is Mr John Bátky, the expert on medieval British insectivores—or was it old Italian threshing machines?—I really can't remember at this moment. But whatever it is, I know you'll find it absolutely fascinating."

And with that she left us.

For some time we smiled benignly at one another. The Earl had a remarkably handsome head, of the sort one sees wreathed in laurel on the frontispiece of old books: a kind you don't often see nowadays.

At the same time, I was rather embarrassed. I felt the noble lady's somewhat inexact description had made me appear mildly ludicrous.

"Allow me, if I may," the Earl began at last, "to ask what our hostess actually meant."

"My Lord, the sorry truth is that the good lady was to some extent right. I am a Doctor of Philosophy, specialising in useless information, with a particular interest in things a normal person would never consider important."

This was a facetious attempt to fend off a more serious topic, namely, what I actually do. I have found that the English do not approve of displays of intellectual curiosity.

A strange smile crossed the Earl's face.

"Not at all. I am quite happy to talk about serious topics. I am not English. I am Welsh. That makes me, apparently, fifty per cent more like a Continental. No Englishman, by the way, would ever ask you your occupation. However, for my own intellectual satisfaction, I must insist on an answer to the question."

He had such an intelligent-looking head that I blurted out the truth.

"At the moment I'm working on the English mystics of the seventeenth century."

"Are you indeed?" the Earl exclaimed. "Then Lady Malmsbury-Croft has made another of her miraculous blunders. She always does. If she gets two men to sit with each other thinking that they were together at Eton, you may be sure that one of them is German and the other Japanese, but both have a special interest in Liberian stamps."

"So My Lord is also a student of the subject?"

"That's a rather strong term to use, in this island of ours. *You* study something, *we* merely have hobbies. I dabble in the English mystics the way a retired general would set about exploring his family history. As it happens, those things are part of the family history. But tell me, Doctor—mysticism is a rather broad term— are you interested in it as a religious phenomenon?"

"Not really. I don't have much feeling for that aspect. What interests me within the general field is what is popularly called "mystic"—the esoteric fantasies and procedures through which people once sought to probe nature. The alchemists, the secrets of the homunculus, the universal panacea, the influence of minerals and amulets ... Fludd's Philosophy of

Nature, whereby he proved the existence of God by means of a barometer."

"Fludd?" The Earl raised his head. "Fludd shouldn't be mentioned in the company of those idiots. Fludd, sir, wrote a lot of nonsense because he wished to explain things that couldn't be accounted for at the time. But essentially—I mean about the real essence of things—he knew much, much more than the scientists of today, who no longer even laugh at his theories. I don't know what your opinion is, but nowadays we know a great deal about the microscopic detail. Those people knew rather more about the whole—the great interconnectedness of things—which can't be weighed on scales and cut into slices like ham."

The fervour in his eyes was certainly un-English. The subject was clearly close to his heart.

Then he was overcome with embarrassment. He smiled, and assumed a more casual tone.

"Yes, Fludd is a bit of an obsession with me."

At that moment a pretty girl joined us, and chatted away at great length, rather inanely, while the Earl, with true good breeding, generously encouraged her. I writhed with frustration, desperate to resume the conversation. Nothing interests me more than the way people relate emotionally to the abstract—why Mr X is a convinced Anglo-Catholic and Miss Y is devoted to Gastropoda. And why an Earl should be so enthusiastic about someone so distant and thoroughly dead as Fludd—that justly-forgotten quack and sorcerer—was a particularly interesting question.

But once again, Lady Malmsbury-Croft descended on me, and this time her blunderings proved less inspired. She led me to a distinguished old dame who would not have looked out of place in a museum and who quizzed me about animal rights in Romania. My protests were in vain: she insisted on regaling me with shocking examples from her last visit to Armenia. Apparently some lapdogs had become separated from their owner and been forced to fend for themselves.

Luckily a friend of mine, Fred Walker, suddenly appeared before us, with a sleekly-groomed young man in tow. He seated this person beside the lady, gathered me up and whisked me away. The old dowager failed to notice the change.

"Who is this Earl?" I asked him.

"You don't know him? Why, he's the one genuinely interesting person in the room. Owen Pendragon, Earl of Gwynedd. A thoroughly fascinating crank—just the chap for you."

"So what's his story?"

Gossip was one of Fred's strong points.

"Well, then—this is years ago now—he had a mistress, a woman of rather dubious reputation, as you will see. She began her career in Dublin, walking the streets. He was going to marry her—people were quite outraged—but she had second thoughts, dumped him and married an old millionaire called Roscoe. Roscoe was the Earl's father's best friend.

"The amusing bit in all this," he went on, "is that the Earl is otherwise a convinced, if rather quixotic, aristocrat. The story goes that while he was up at Oxford he joined a society that was so exclusive there were only three men in the entire university of sufficient rank to belong. Then the other two went down, and he stayed on as the one and only member. For two years he pondered who to take on as Vice-President, but couldn't find anyone. Finally he went down himself and the society folded. For similar reasons, he has never once set foot in the House of Lords."

"I'm sorry, Fred, but I don't see anything special in this. Your stories are usually a lot better. From a man with a head like that, I expected something much more interesting. For an aristocrat to marry a woman of the lowest class is only natural. His social rank is enough for two."

"True, János. But that's not why I described him as an odd character. He really is odd. Anyone will tell you that. But the other stories I've heard about him are so absurd and nonsensical I'd better not repeat them."

"Let's hear some of this nonsense."

"Well ... for example, what should I make of the story that he buried himself like a fakir, and after two years, or two weeks—I forget which—they dug him up and found him in perfect health? And in the war, they say, he went around during the gas attacks without his mask on and suffered no ill effects. He's supposed to have magical healing powers. The most incredible of these stories is that he revived the Duke of Warwick a day after his doctors

12

had pronounced him dead. There's a rumour that he has a huge laboratory in Wales where he carries out strange experiments on animals. And he's created some new creature that comes alive only at night ... He doesn't make any of this public because he loathes the democratic nature of the sciences. But it's all nonsense. All I know is that, in company, he's always extremely kind, and no one ever notices anything at all strange about him. But he isn't seen very often. He doesn't leave his castle for weeks on end."

With that, he leant over towards me and whispered in my ear: "Mad as a hatter!"

And he left me there.

In the course of the evening I successfully contrived a second meeting with the Earl. I sensed that he found me not uncongenial. He told me my eyes reminded him of a seventeenth-century doctor, one Benjamin Avravanel, whose portrait hung in his castle. The man had been murdered.

I won't transcribe the long conversation we had, particularly since I did most of the talking while he asked the questions. And though I never did discover why the Earl was interested in Fludd, the discussion was not unproductive. I seemed to have gained his sympathy because, as we parted, he said:

"There are some old volumes on your subject in the possession of my family. If the mood takes you, do call in at my little place in Wales, and spend a few weeks there, looking them over."

I felt the honour keenly, but am so idle by nature I would never have taken it seriously. However a few days later I received a written invitation that actually specified a date. That was how it all began.

I mentioned the invitation to one of my friends, Cecil Howard, an employee of the British Museum working on a subject related to my own. When he heard the news, the colour drained from his face.

"Bátky, you're a lucky dog. In this country it's only foreigners who get that sort of chance. Wonders are spoken of the Pendragon Library. But since Sackville-Williams was there to catalogue it, eighty-five years ago, no one with any expertise has been allowed in. The Pendragons have been reclusive for centuries. If you work up the material they've got there you'll be the leading authority on the history of seventeenth-century mysticism and the occult.

"My God," he sighed, sounding utterly deflated. "You'll write the Life of Asaph Pendragon. You'll get telegrams of congratulation from America, and five PhD students will come on annual pilgrimage from Germany to consult you. You'll even get a mention in the French journals. And apart from all that, it's quite something to be invited to Llanyvgan. It's the finest and most exclusive castle in Wales."

I left him to his envy. A colleague's envy, when all is said and done, is the scholar's one reward on earth. I didn't tell him that in all likelihood I wouldn't be publishing anything. My nature is to spend years amassing the material for a great work and, when everything is at last ready, I lock it away in a desk drawer and start something new. I had in fact revealed my horror of writing for publication to the Earl and had met with his full sympathy. I think the confession may well have led to the invitation. The Earl felt sure that the outcome of my researches would not be any sort of masterwork.

I also concealed from my colleague one fact he would have sneered at from the dizzy heights of his learning: that it was the living Earl of Gwynedd rather than the dead Robert Fludd that had seized my imagination. The Earl's face, his person, his whole being, together with the tales Fred had told me, had set my mind racing. He seemed to embody an historical past the way no book ever could. My intuition told me that here was the last living example—and an exceptional one at that—of the genuine student of the arcane in the guise of the aristocrat-alchemist, the last descendant of Rudolph II of Prague, and one for whom, as late as 1933, Fludd had more to say than Einstein.

I tell you, the invitation thrilled me. To pass the intervening time—and what else could anyone like me, seeking spiritual adventure, do in my position?—I set about researching the family history. I found a mass of material in the *Dictionary of National Biography*, and enough references to occupy me for a month of full-time work.

The Pendragons trace their origin—though I notice the line isn't exactly clear—to Llewellyn the Great. This is the Llewellyn

ap Griffith who was beheaded by Edward I, the king whom János
Arany immortalised for the young reader in Hungary as riding a
pale-grey horse. The old Welsh bards who went to their death in
the flames singing like the doomed heroes of their own tragic art
were in fact being punished for praising the house of Pendragon.
But all this is in the mists of the past. These are the medieval
Pendragons, living with their half-savage tribes among the great
mountains: in their wars against the English there is something
redolent of the hopeless struggle of the American Indians.

Then a strange incident disturbed the tranquillity of my studies.

I was smoking my pipe in the foyer of the hotel one evening, in
the company of Fred Walker, when I was called to the phone.

"Hello, is that János Bátky?" a man's voice asked.

"Yes."

"What are you doing at the moment?"

"I'm talking on the phone. Who are you?"

"Never mind. Are you in an enclosed booth?"

"Yes."

"János Bátky … you would be well advised not to get involved
in other people's affairs. You can be quite sure that the people you
are working against are aware of your movements."

"I'm sorry, there must be some mistake. I've never worked
against anyone. This is János Bátky speaking."

"I know. Just bear this in mind: everyone who pokes their nose
into the Earl of Gwynedd's little experiments comes to a sticky
end. Dr McGregor died in a road accident. The same thing could
happen to Dr Bátky".

"Who is this McGregor?"

"Your predecessor."

"My predecessor? In what way?"

"I can't speak more openly. The less you know about this, the
better for you. All I can tell you is: stay in London."

"But why?"

"The air in Wales won't do you any good. You must sever all
connection with … "

He was trying to articulate something.

"Hello, hello … I can't catch what you're saying. Can you speak
more clearly … ?"

But he had hung up. I went back to Fred, thoroughly agitated, and told him what had passed.

"Strange … " he said, and tapped the ash from his pipe into the fireplace, seemingly lost in thought.

"Fred, for God's sake, don't be so damn English. Say something. Can you think of no explanation?"

"Well, I did tell you the Earl of Gwynedd is an odd fellow. Everything to do with him is a bit weird. You'll certainly have some unusual experiences at Llangyvan."

I leapt to my feet and began pacing rapidly back and forth. The mere thought of travel upsets me at the best of times, even without this sort of mysterious threat.

"Who could this Dr McGregor be? How could I find out?"

"It won't be easy. In parts of Scotland every second person is called McGregor, and there are plenty of doctors up there."

My pacing became even more erratic.

"Tell me, Fred, what do you advise? You know how impractical I am … Would you go to Llangyvan, after this?"

He looked at me in surprise, but gave no answer.

"Well … say something!"

"What can I say?" he asked. "It would never occur to me for a moment not to go. I'd be ashamed to let a thing like that influence me."

Now I was ashamed. 'If you're a man, be a man … ' All the same, it isn't every day you get a phone call like that … and everything to do with the Earl was so very strange …

"Tell me," asked Fred, "who have you spoken to about this trip?"

"Only to Howard, at the BM."

"Oh, Howard? Surely the whole thing is just one of his jokes? He knows about your … Continental temperament … "

"Or perhaps … "—I found myself shouting it out—"he wants to stop me going, because he's jealous!"

"I'd expect no less from an academic. Well, that's it, then. Don't give it another thought, old man."

I took his advice, and did my best to forget the peculiar phone call.

The next day I resumed my studies in the British Museum Reading Room.

The Pendragons entered English history when a Welshman, in the person of Henry VII, ascended the throne. A Gwyn Pendragon had fought at Bosworth Field, side by side with Richmond, the white-armoured Champion of Truth. Perhaps he even saw the gory ghosts flitting prophetically between the camps of Richard III and the challenger; perhaps he heard the evil king rush howling onto the field of battle, promising his kingdom for a horse ... at all events he moved as familiarly among the sainted heroes and monstrous villains of Shakespeare's pentameters as I did among the readers in the British Museum. In 1490, as a reward for his services, he was given the title of Earl of Gwynedd—which had remained in the family ever since, and now graced my future host—and he built Pendragon Castle, which was to be the family seat down the centuries. The name in Welsh means 'Dragon's Head'.

The pseudoscientific volumes upon which my fancy lit were brought to me by blank-faced young assistants moving about on silent feet. The only sound to be heard under the great dome was the pleasing murmur of turning pages. From the bearded black doorman with the stove-pipe hat, who looked for all the world as if he'd been there since the official opening in the last century, to the swarm of elderly eccentrics who teem in all the libraries of the University of Life, everyone was in his or her place.

Or not quite everyone.

For a full month now the chair on my right had been occupied by a flat-chested old lady with a look of permanent disapproval on her face. She was researching the love-life of primitive peoples. But today she was nowhere to be seen, and there was no umbrella signifying her occupation. Instead, an elegant, athletic-looking young man sat there, reading a newspaper and glancing around from time to time with a troubled air. I quickly diagnosed his condition: it was his first time in the Reading Room, and he felt like a man on his first day in the madhouse.

The young athlete filled me with a mixture of pity and malicious amusement. As a sportsman he deserved no better, and anyway, what on earth was he doing in this place? Clearly he would have felt the same about me on a golf course.

I continued reading.

I learnt that the era when rough ancestors hewed castles from the cliff face had finally given way to more halcyon days, a prolonged springtime. Successive Earls of Gwynedd were courtiers of Henry VIII, attendants upon Elizabeth and ambassadors to the brilliant Continental courts of the Renaissance. They wrote verses and commanded fleets; they roasted Irish rebels on spits and commissioned paintings from the Italian masters; they fell in love with ladies-in-waiting and plundered monasteries; they made spectacular bows before the Virgin Queen, and poisoned their wives, as the custom was, unless their wives had managed to poison them first.

I looked up dreamily from my book. Before me rose a pile of another ten. On my neighbour's desk there was still not a single one, and his discomfort was visibly growing. Finally, with an air of decision, he turned towards me:

"Excuse me … what do you do, to get them to bring you all those books?"

"I simply fill in the title and catalogue number on a slip, and put it in one of the baskets on the circular counter."

"That's interesting. Did you say catalogue number? What's that?"

"Every book here has one."

"And how do you find it?"

"You look in the catalogues. Those big black volumes over there."

"And what sort of books do people here read?"

"Whatever they like. Whatever they're working on."

"You, for example, what are you working on?"

"Family history, at the moment."

"Family history: that's wonderful. So … if I wanted to study family history, what would I have to do, then?"

"Please, would you mind speaking as quietly as you can—the superintendent is staring at us. It depends on what sort of family you want to study."

"Hm. Well, actually, none. I've had nothing but trouble from mine since I was little."

"So what does interest you?" I asked, sympathetically.

"Me? Rock climbing, most of all."

"Fine. Then I'll order you a book that really should appeal to you. If you would just write your name on this slip."

He wrote, in a large, childish hand: George Maloney. I requested Kipling's *Kim* for him, and my new acquaintance buried himself in it, with great apparent interest. For some while I was left in peace.

Everything I read about the Pendragons was lent a mysterious perspective by the tales Fred Walker had told me, by the telephone call, and by the Earl's character and imposing presence. By now James I was on the throne, and studying the natural history of demons. Previously scholars had pursued the noble and the beautiful, but now they were starting to turn to the world of the occult, in search of the Ultimate Wisdom.

Asaph Christian, the sixth Earl, was not a courtier like the fifth. He wrote no sonnets, did not fall in love or leave fifteen illegitimate children, or even a legitimate one, and after him the title passed to his younger brother's son.

Asaph spent his youth in Germany, in the cities of the old South, where the houses stooped menacingly over the narrow streets, and the scholars worked all night in their long, narrow bedrooms whose cobwebbed corners were never pierced by candlelight. Amongst alembics, phials and weirdly-shaped furnaces, the Earl pursued the *Magnum Arcanum*, the Great Mystery, the Philosopher's Stone. He was a member of the secret brotherhood of Rosicrucians, about whom their contemporaries knew so little and therefore gossiped all the more. They were alchemists and doctors of magic, the last great practitioners of the occult. It was through Asaph that the cross with the symbolic rose in each of its corners was added to the family coat of arms.

On his return to Wales, Pendragon Castle became an active laboratory of witchcraft. Processions of visitors, in coaches with darkened windows, came from far and wide. Heretics arrived, fleeing from the bonfire. Ancient shepherds brought the accumulated lore of their people down from the mountains. They were joined by bent-backed Jewish doctors, driven from royal courts for seeming to know more than is permitted to man. And they say that here too, in disguise, came the King of Scotland and England, the demon-haunted James, to probe his host's secrets in nightly conference. Here the first English Rosicrucians initiated their believers, and Pendragon Castle became the second home of Robert Fludd, the greatest student of Paracelsus the Mage.

This was the Fludd through whom I had befriended the Earl. Truly speaking, I owed the invitation to him. At this stage I had no idea that all this ancient material, and all these names that had meant so little to me—Pendragon Castle, Asaph Pendragon—would come to play such an extraordinary part in my life.

From a collection of North Wales folklore I learnt that the legend of Asaph Pendragon began soon after his death. It speaks of him as a midnight horseman, never leaving the castle by day, setting out only at night, with a carefully chosen band of followers, to gather plants with magical properties by the light of the moon. But such prosaic purposes were not enough to satisfy popular imagination, and the story grew that the terrifying night horseman had been out dispensing justice, an attribute he retained even after his death.

By night he would catch robbers sharing out their booty in secret dens, and next morning, to their utter amazement, the victims would find their treasures returned. The felons had been so astonished by the apparition that they kept every one of the undertakings extracted by him, and died soon after.

The most gruesome of these histories concerns three murderers. The volume I held in my hands tells it rather well.

Once, in a Welsh mountain inn, three young noblemen killed and robbed a Jewish doctor on his way to join the Earl in his castle. The court, which in those times might well be suspected of anti-Semitism, acquitted the men, and they set sail for France. That night some peasants watched with awe as the night rider and his retinue turned to the south, galloped up the rocky slopes of nearby Moel-Sych and soared into the sky in a southerly direction. The next day the three noblemen were found in the castle moat, their limbs crushed and their necks broken. The Earl had meted out the justice due to his intending visitor.

At eleven I went for a coffee. My neighbour tagged along.

"Jolly good read," he said of *Kim*: "amazing book. Chap who wrote it must have been there. Really knows the place."

"You've been to India yourself?"

"Of course. There as a kid. Grew up there. And in Burma. Then South Africa and Rhodesia. Not a bad place, Rhodesia."

Once again I felt that deep sense of awe I always experience when I come up against the British Empire. These people nip over to Burma the way we do to Eger. Only, they're less curious about it. They know that wherever they go in the world they will be among exactly the same sort of people as themselves.

"Actually, my old man was a major in an Irish regiment," he continued. "Stationed all over the place. That's why I missed out a bit on my education. Things to do with books and so forth. But it's also why I did so well in the tropics."

"You were a soldier too?"

"No. I never quite made it into the army. I have this bad habit of failing exams. Some of them I must have had five goes at … But I never got lucky. But forget about that. What's done is done. We Irish live for the future. I didn't become a soldier; not everyone can be a soldier. I just loafed around wherever I wanted in the Empire. Not a bad place to be. Have you heard of the East African Uwinda expedition?"

"Yes, as I recall … " I said, scrambling to salvage my self-respect.

"I was in it. We were over nine thousand feet up. Fantastic climbing. There was one mountain, I tell you, with sides like glass. You moved up three feet and slid back five. We slithered around for two whole days and got nowhere. I said to the Colonel:

"'Look here, sir, are we from Connemara, or are we not?' Because you know, that's where I'm from," he explained, with deep reverence. Then he continued:

"'True,' says the Colonel (a typical patronising Englishman): 'we've even had one or two chaps from there who were sane.'

"'Well,' I said to him, 'I'll show you who's sane.' I fitted one of those lightweight climbing ropes on to the camp cat, round its waist. I fixed the doctor's surgical clamps tight on its tail, made the blacks stand in a ring around the base of the slope, and the cat shot off, all the way up to the top. Amazingly good at that sort of thing, cats.

"Up at the top, there was a tree. The cat skimmed up the tree and thrashed around among the branches. Then it stopped, because the rope had got thoroughly tangled up and was holding it fast. I tugged for a while on the rope to see how firmly it was attached to the tree. Then I climbed straight up, removed the clamps from the cat's tail—no point of inflicting unnecessary pain on poor dumb animals—and hauled the whole party up after me."

I gazed in wonder at this Münchausen and began to question whether he'd ever been near the tropics. But he was an agreeable young chap. He was practically chinless, his arms were uncommonly long, and he moved with the ease and grace of an animal. Altogether he seemed somewhat closer than most to our primal nature.

By the time we got back to the British Museum the usual old madwoman was already centre stage in the garden outside the entrance, giving the pigeons their midday feed. As ever, her face was transfigured with the joyous smile of a Franciscan saint soaring up to Heaven. Around her you could see nothing but pigeons. Her whole person was smothered in pigeons. Three sat on her head, five on each shoulder, and countless numbers clung to her dress. I could tell that she fancied herself as saintly as Francis himself, and she filled me with loathing.

"I'd like to shoot her," I said to my new friend, as we ascended the stairs.

Almost as I said this, he spun round and hurled a large pebble—I didn't even see him pick it up—which hit her a glancing blow on the nose, a full fifty metres away. She uttered a powerful scream and dropped the pigeon feed, the birds took flight and the woman collapsed. She had clearly never reckoned on being hit by lightning while performing the great good deed of her life. Her sense of a moral universe must have collapsed with her in that moment.

Maloney continued walking, very calmly. The whole thing had happened so quickly that, apart from myself, no one had seen who did it.

"What was all that about?" I asked in amazement when we got inside the foyer. We were standing in the half-light, under the bearded heads of Assyrian kings some four thousand years old.

"Why do you ask? You yourself said you could shoot her. But all you can do is talk. You aren't from Connemara."

From that point on, and after what followed later, I became inclined to believe about half of the impossible yarns Maloney spun. And I could see that Connemarans weren't quite like anyone else.

We returned to our reading for a while.

The seventh Earl, and those following him down the century, were relative nonentities. It was as if the memory of the great Asaph had cast a shadow of dullness over them. The tenth Earl moved away from the ancestral seat at Pendragon and built the castle at Llanvygan, the family home since 1708, which has been so much praised for its beauty.

With the move away from dismal Pendragon, the family history took a brighter turn. Throughout the eighteenth century, like every other noble house, it produced distinguished admirals, diplomats and minor poets, and the enigmatic shadow of Asaph appeared to have been lifted. Or not entirely. The thirteenth Earl requires a mention.

This gentleman, despite his unfortunate number, was the most convivial and thoroughly human character in the whole saga. He was the only Earl who had affairs with actresses, the only one who knew how to drink, and the only one who could crack a good joke in company.

One of these jokes was considered particularly witty in its time, though it is difficult now to see exactly where its humour lies. He was told one day, while at cards, that his mistress—whom he had raised from the level of a simple orange-seller—had run off with the fencing master, taking a significant quantity of the family baubles with her. His sole response was, "Every good deed gets the punishment it deserves," and he carried on with the game.

His Christian name, incidentally, was John Bonaventura, his mother having been Italian. This odd combination of names stopped me in my tracks. I had the feeling that I had come across it, or one very like it, once before. But the memory escaped me, and did not come back to me until much later, in connection with some very odd occurrences.

To the remaining pages I gave only a cursory glance. They dealt with the nineteenth-century Pendragons, who flourished peacefully and with honour in the never-ending reign of Victoria. The present Earl's father had been caught up in the fashionable imperialism of the day and was seldom at home. He served in various colonial regiments, held high office over subject peoples and died, in 1908, as governor of one of the provinces of Indo-China. His death was due to some sort of tropical disease that had broken out in the area at the time.

My limited information about the present Earl, the eighteenth, is provided by *Who's Who*. Born in 1888, he was thus forty-five at the time of my tale. His full name was Owen Alastair John Pendragon of Llanvygan. Educated at Harrow and Magdalen College, Oxford, he served in various colonial regiments, distinguished himself in several different ways and belonged to a great many clubs. *Who's Who* usually goes on to give details of hobbies and interests—these being of the greatest importance to the English—but the Earl seemed not to have provided any response to this question.

Lunchtime was upon us. I returned my books, along with Maloney's, and was about to leave.

"Well, this is something else I've learnt," he remarked. "So now I know what goes on in a library. I'd rather be in a nice little swamp. My God! I haven't read so much in ten years. Where are you eating, by the way?"

"Greek Street. In a Chinese restaurant."

"Would you swear blue murder if I joined you? I hate eating on my own."

Even by Continental standards this was a rapid beginning of friendship—or whatever you might call it—and I was taken by surprise. But there was something rather touching about him, like a chimpanzee on the loose in the London streets, misunderstood by everyone but full of well-meaning.

"I'd be delighted," I said. "But I ought to warn you, I'm lunching with a Chinese friend. I don't know how developed your sense of colour is, or how you feel about yellow gentlemen."

"I've nothing against Chinks if they aren't cheeky. We Connemarans make no distinction between one man and another. Only if they give cheek. I once had a kaffir boy who didn't clean my boots properly, and when I spoke to him about it he answered me back. So I grabbed him, stuck some kid's shoes on his feet and made him walk in them for three days in the Kalahari Desert. It's a pretty hot place. I tell you, by the third day the kaffir's feet were half their original size. You could have used him as a fairground exhibit."

We had reached the restaurant. Dr Wu Sei was already waiting for me. When he saw that I'd brought a stranger with me he retreated behind his most affable oriental smile and fell silent. But Maloney simply chatted all the more, and won my heart by proving not just a lover of Chinese food like myself, but a real connoisseur. Normally when I ate there I would let Wu Sei do the ordering, then enjoy whatever was brought without bothering to find out whether the finely-chopped delicacies were pork, rose-petal soup or bamboo. Maloney conducted himself like a man discriminating between veal escalope and *boeuf à la mode*; he could distinguish seventeen flavour gradations of chop suey, and he won my unstinting admiration.

"Which way are you going?" he asked me after lunch.

I told him.

"Would you curse me if I went part of the way with you?"

Now I was really surprised.

"Tell me," he asked, with some embarrassment, as we strolled along: "you're a bloody German, aren't you?"

"Oh, no. I'm Hungarian."

"Hungarian?"

"Hungarian."

"What's that? Is that a country? Or are you just having me on?"

"Not at all. On my word of honour, it is a country."

"And where do you Hungarians live?"

"In Hungary. Between Austria, Romania, Czechoslovakia and Yugoslavia."

"Come off it. Those places were made up by Shakespeare."

And he roared with laughter.

"Alright, so you're a Hungarian … Good country, that. And what language do you Hungarians speak?"

"Hungarian."

"Say something in Hungarian."

It was some years since I had last spoken the language and, strangely moved, I recited some Ady:

Mikor az ég furcsa, lila-kék
S találkára mennek a lyányok,
Ó, be titkosak, különösek
Ezek a nyári délutánok.
(Under a strange, lilac-blue sky
The girls stroll to their assignations;
Mysterious, enigmatic
Summer afternoons.)

"Very nice. But you don't fool me. That was Hindustani. It means: 'Noble stranger, may the Gods dance on your grave in their slippers.' I've heard that one before. However, since you're the first Hungarian I've met, let's do something to celebrate this splendid friendship. Come and have dinner with me tonight. Please, I'm asking you. If you find me a bit mad, don't worry—you'll get used to it, everybody does. And anyway there'll be three of us. I'll introduce you to a very clever chap, just down from Oxford, nephew of some Lord or other. He's a scream. He can get his mouth round five-syllable words you've never even heard of, easy as you could say 'hat'."

After a little hesitation I accepted. I love meeting new people, and as it happened I had nothing else to do. To tell the truth, I was rather bowled over by the fact that he was inviting me to the Savoy, a place so grand I would never have been able to afford to go there at my own expense. I even began to see Maloney in a new light. Mad, I said to myself, but a gentleman.

We met that evening in the bar.

I found him there in the company of a young man: a tall, very slim young man with a remarkably engaging, delicate and intelligent face; rather effeminate, perhaps, with the athletic sort of effeminacy that characterises so many interesting Oxford men.

"Allow me to introduce you to the Hon Osborne Pendragon," said Maloney.

"Pendragon?" I exclaimed. "Would you perhaps be related to the Earl of Gwynedd?"

"As a matter of fact, I have the honour to be his nephew," he replied, in a curiously exaggerated and affected drawl. "What's your cocktail?"

My least concern just then was a cocktail.

26

"Might you be spending your summer vacation at Llanvygan?" I asked.

"That is absolutely correct. I'm off to the family home in Wales the day after tomorrow."

"I'm going there myself, fairly soon."

"Bathing no doubt in the sea off Llandudno? I prefer a private bathroom, myself. Fewer people, and rather more select."

"No, no."

"Or perhaps you're off to climb Snowdon?"

"Not at all."

"Where else does one go in North Wales?"

"Llanvygan, for example."

"Excuse me?"

"The Earl has very kindly invited me to his place at Llanvygan."

At this point Maloney gave vent to an ancient Irish battle cry.

"Man, man!" he roared, and almost dislocated my arm.

"Well?"

"So we can travel together! Osborne has invited me too. What a coincidence! First of all, I ask myself, how did I end up in the Reading Room of the British Museum? Well, we all have our moments. And of all the five hundred freaks sitting there, it happens to be this gentleman I start to pester, and go on badgering, until it turns out we'll soon be staying in the same place. Magnificent. Let's drink to it!"

And indeed it was a strange coincidence. I felt truly exhilarated. It was as if the mystical power of Llanvygan Castle had projected itself all that distance. I felt the hand of Fate upon me, and was once again seized by the old, pleasurable angst that had so often haunted me, the feeling that once again things were stirring around and above me; that the Parcae were teasing out the threads of my future.

But then again: neither the half-wit Maloney nor this thoroughly affected young aristocrat carried the mark of destiny on their brows, unless it were the mocking destiny of a degenerate and cynical age such as our own.

Through all this, the young Pendragon had remained perfectly impassive. Then:

"These days even Fate has become debased," he remarked, his voice rising towards the end of the sentence. "In Luther's time, for example, the notion of Chance consisted of no more than a bolt of lightning striking the ground before him. It didn't even have to hit him. And the result was the Reformation. Nowadays it means nothing more than two chaps going off together on the same holiday. Where now is *ananké*, where is Destiny? Or the *amor fati* Nietzsche praises, if I remember correctly, as the noblest thing a man could pursue?"

"Osborne is amazingly clever," said Maloney.

"Yes, but only because it's so unfashionable in England. If I'd been born in France I'd have become an idiot, just to spite them. So what do we say to getting stuck into that dinner?"

The dinner was superb. Over the meal, Maloney did most of the talking. His adventures became more and more richly-coloured with each glass of Burgundy.

His first story concerned a routine tiger hunt, but he went on to set entire Borneo villages aflame to make the point that Connemara men could light their pipes even in a stiff breeze, and he ended by tying the tail of a king cobra in a knot while its head was held by his tame and ever-faithful mongoose William.

"I envy our egregious friend," observed Osborne. "If only a quarter of what he relates in the course of a dinner is true, his life could be described as decidedly adventurous. It seems things do still happen, out there in the colonies. A merry little tiger or king cobra might produce a pleasurable *frisson* even in the likes of me. My one wish is to go there myself. To some place out in the back of beyond, where missionaries remain the staple diet of the natives."

"So why don't you?"

"Sadly, since my grandfather of blessed memory died of some wonderful tropical disease my uncle has concluded that the air in those parts doesn't agree with us. I have thus to spend the greater part of my time in Wales in our electrified eagle's nest, from which every self-respecting spook since the time of the late lamented Queen Victoria has been driven out. Sir, three years ago, the last remaining ghost in Wales was assaulted with tear gas: the poor fellow—an elderly admiral—was sobbing like a child. But for me, belief in these things would be extinct in the region. However

I have some interesting plans for the summer, and I hope you'll assist me in them. I've had terrific success at Oxford with my supernatural recordings on the portable gramophone. I can produce heartfelt sighings in the most improbable of places, together with the rattling of chains and lengthy prayers in Middle English. But of course this is just sport. Real adventure is dead and buried. It couldn't take the smell of petrol."

"You're eighteen, are you not?" I asked.

"I am."

"On the Continent, young men of your age have a quite different idea of adventure."

"I'm not sure I follow you."

"I was thinking of women."

"I don't even think of them," he replied, faintly blushing. "I'm very fond of them, at a distance. But the moment they approach me I feel a mild horror. I feel that if I took hold of them they would somehow fall apart in my hands. You are a Continental … have you never had that sensation?"

"Not at all. I can't recall a single woman who might have disintegrated in my hands. Why, has it ever happened to you?"

"To be perfectly frank with you, I've never risked the experiment."

"Permit me to observe that I think it precisely on account of this seclusion that you feel your life to be uneventful. On the Continent, relations with women are considered to be what life is all about."

"Then I must repeat the words of Villiers de L'Isle-Adam: 'Living? Our servants will do that for us.'"

As we left the Savoy I found myself, under the influence of a great quantity of Burgundy, in a thoroughly buoyant mood. It just wasn't true, I said to myself, that London is boring, and I congratulated myself on having met two such splendid young men. It was ridiculous to pass my days surrounded by books. One should live! And I meant this word in its Continental sense. A woman … even in London … would be good occasionally.

At Maloney's prompting we went on to a night club. These are places where you can actually drink all night, and we availed ourselves of the privilege. One whisky followed another, each with less and less soda. Osborne was sitting rather stiffly. The general ambience of the place clearly made him uncomfortable, but he was too proud to show it.

Maloney had reached the high point of a yarn in which he had roped a Malay girl to a tree when, just at the crucial moment, ten of her uncles appeared brandishing their krises.

We never discovered what followed, because he spotted a woman at a nearby table, roared out a loud greeting and abandoned us. I watched ruefully as he chatted to her on the friendliest of terms. She was very attractive.

"Strange fellow, this Maloney," said Osborne. "If I came across any of his stories in a book, I'd throw it away."

"Do you think any of it is true?"

"Oddly enough, I believe a lot of it is. I've seen him do some quite unpredictable and crazy things—things that completely defy logic. If I may say so, this whole evening has been entirely typical, though I suppose I shouldn't talk like this."

"Tell me, all the same. We Continentals are relatively so much less discreet, we reckon an Englishman can afford to let his hair down once in a while."

"Well, take this example. Yesterday, Maloney had no more than thruppence ha'penny in his pocket. For weeks, I am quite sure, it's all he had in the world. And this evening he's treated us like lords. It seems to me quite probable that last night he knocked someone down in a dark street. No harm intended, of course—he just wanted to prove that Connemarans can knock a man down with the best of them. Then he helped himself to the chap's money, as a way of combining business with pleasure."

Maloney returned.

"Would you gentlemen mind if my very old friend, Miss Pat O'Brien, joined us? She's also from Connemara, which tells you all you need to know. She's in the chorus at the Alhambra. A supreme artist."

"Delighted," I said, perhaps too readily.

But Osborne's face was stiffer than ever.

"Well … er … Much as I admire your compatriots—I'm a Celt myself, of the same stock—wasn't the general idea supposed to be that this evening was for men only?"

"My dear fellow," said Maloney, "you're the cleverest chap on earth and, upon my word, it brings tears to my eyes to think I have such a friend; but it really wouldn't hurt you to spend ten minutes in female company once every few months. You'd certainly make some surprising discoveries. Not so, Doctor?"

"Without question."

"Well, if you gentlemen insist," returned Osborne, with a gesture of resignation.

Maloney had already brought her.

"Merry Christmas and a Happy New Year," she proclaimed, and sat herself down with the smile of someone confident of having contributed her share of witty conversation. Given that it was still summer, I smiled dutifully at the remark. Osborne made no such effort.

"Cheer up, young fella," the girl said to him, raising her glass; and she sang a little song conveying the same basic idea.

"I'll do whatever I can," Osborne solemnly declared.

This Osborne is an idiot, I said to myself. The girl was simply stunning, in the innocent, rosy-cheeked way which, together with the manly British character, is the finest ornament of these islands.

She certainly enlivened me, and she listened in respectful silence to my fumbling compliments—not something Englishmen lavish on their women. With us, if we are even slightly drawn to a woman, we tell her we adore her. An Englishman hopelessly in love will merely observe: "I say, I do rather like you".

"Come away with me to the Continent," I urged her in my rapture, stroking her bare arm. "You should live in Fontainebleau and glide three times a day up the crescent staircase of Francis I, trailing your gown behind you. The moment they set eyes on you, the three-hundred-year old carp in the lake will find they are warm-blooded after all. Miss France herself will panic and give birth to twins."

"You're a very sweet boy, and you've got such an interesting accent. But I don't understand a word you're saying."

This cut me to the quick. I am very proud of my English pronunciation. But what could a Connemara lass know of these things?—she spoke some dreadful Irish brogue herself. I left her to amuse herself with Osborne while Maloney and I made serious inroads on the whisky.

By now Maloney was looking, and sounding, rather tipsy.

"Doctor, you're a hoot. We certainly hit the jackpot when we met. But this Osborne … I'd be so happy if Pat could seduce him. These English aren't human. Now we Irish … back home in Connemara, at his age I'd already had three sorts of venereal disease. But tell me, dear Doctor, now that we're such good friends, what's the real reason for your visit to Llanvygan?"

"The Earl of Gwynedd invited me to pursue my studies in his library."

"Studies? But you're already a doctor! Or is there some exam even higher than that? You're an amazingly clever man."

"It's not for an exam … just for the pleasure of it. Some things really interest me."

"Which you're going to study there?"

"Exactly.

"And what exactly are you going to study?"

"Most probably the history of the Rosicrucians, with particular reference to Robert Fludd."

"Who are these Rosicrucians?"

"Rosicrucians? Hm. Have you ever heard of the Freemasons?"

"Yes. People who meet in secret … and I've no idea what they get up to."

"That's it. The Rosicrucians were different from the Freemasons in that they met in even greater secrecy, and people knew even less about what they did."

"Fine. But surely you at least know what they did in these meetings?"

"I can tell you in confidence, but you must reveal it to no one."

"I'll harness my tongue. Now, out with it!"

"They made gold."

" Great. I knew all along it was a hoax. What else were they making?"

"Come a bit closer. Homunculi."

"What's that?"

"Human beings."

Maloney roared with laughter and slapped me on the back.

"I've always known you were a dirty dog," he said.

"Idiot. Not that way. They wanted to create human beings scientifically."

"So, they were impotent."

We were both thoroughly tipsy, and found the idea hilarious in the extreme. In my hysterics I knocked over the glass in front of me. Maloney immediately sent for another.

"Now tell me, Doctor, how did you get to know the Earl of Gwynedd? He's very unsociable."

"I've not seen that. I met him at Lady Malmsbury-Croft's, and he immediately invited me."

"How did you manage that?"

"I suppose, with all this stuff about alchemy—making gold."

But I was no longer enjoying the conversation. It was too much like the sort of conversations I remembered from Budapest. I'd lived in England too long. I'd got out of the habit of being quizzed in this way. Interrogated, in fact.

Suddenly I smelt a rat. Drink always brings out one's basic character, and in me it reinforces my most fundamental trait: suspicion. Wait a minute. What if Maloney was talking advantage of my drunkenness to winkle some private information out of me? True, I hadn't the faintest idea what sort of secret I might be hiding, but there must have been one. The man on the telephone had also behaved as if I had.

However, I might be able to turn the tables on him. Maloney wasn't too sober himself: he'd drunk a lot more than I had. Perhaps I could prise out of him what the secret was that he wanted to prise out of me.

With a spontaneous-seeming gesture I knocked my glass over a second time, exploded into a loud drunken laugh and stammered out:

"These glasses … When I grow up I'll invent one that stays upright. And a bed that automatically produces women."

I studied him. He was looking at me with unmistakable satisfaction.

"You speak true, oh mighty Chief! The only problem is, it's all gobbledegook."

"I? What do you mean?"

"All this miraculous Rosicrucian stuff—it's a load of old cobblers."

"Never say that!"

"I know perfectly well that you're a doctor."

"Maloney!" I exclaimed. "How did you guess?"

"You've only got to look at you. And anyway, you say you're a doctor. You see … you're not even denying now that you're an expert on tropical diseases."

"Well … that's true. I'm especially fond of the tsetse fly and sleeping sickness."

"But even more, of that disease with the long name that the Earl of Gwynedd's father and William Roscoe died of."

"Roscoe?"

"Roscoe, Roscoe the millionaire. There's no point pretending you've never heard the name. Let me remind you about him."

"Please do."

"I'm talking about the Roscoe who was financial adviser to the old Earl, when the gentleman in question was Governor somewhere in Burma."

"Ah, you mean the old Roscoe? Of course, of course—my brain is a bit fuddled; it always is when I'm drinking. You mean the Roscoe who, later on … who went on to … "

" … to marry the lady who was engaged to the present Earl of Gwynedd."

"That's it. Now it all comes back to me. But why aren't we drinking? Then the poor chap died of the same disease as the old Earl, which was very strange."

"Extremely strange. Because it was a disease with a very long name, and, for a start, old Roscoe had been back in England for years and years."

"Yes, true. And yes, that is the reason I'm going to Llanvygan. But for God's sake don't tell anyone. But can you just explain this—I've never been clear on this one point: what exactly is the link between the Earl of Gwynedd and old Roscoe's death?"

"Well, it's not something they're likely to let you in on. But since you've been straight with me, I'll tell you a secret. Come a bit closer, so Osborne can't hear."

"Let's have it."

"In his will, Roscoe stipulated that, in the event of his dying an unnatural death, his whole fortune should go to the Earl of Gwynedd and his successors."

"That's nonsense, Maloney. They don't make wills like that in England."

"It certainly isn't nonsense. Old Roscoe became obsessed with the idea that his wife wanted to poison him. That's why he made this secret will."

"And why the Pendragons?"

"Because he owed everything to the seventeenth Earl. And also, because he'd stolen the man's fiancée from under his nose he had a bad conscience all his life and he wanted to make amends."

"So that's why the Earl is taking an interest in tropical diseases. He thinks there was something fishy about Roscoe's illness, and that he has a claim on the estate."

"I think so."

I had found my bearings. My profound attachment to things out of the ordinary had led me to a great mystery which, who knows, I might be destined to solve—though it rather pained me to think how much I knew about everything but tropical medicine. I sensed that the whole business was intimately connected with the telephone call. Something was afoot. The Parcae were spinning their threads.

By now Osborne's conversation with Pat had come to a complete full stop. They were just sitting there, solemnly and in silence. Her face conveyed mild irritation, his total boredom. I got up and went over to the girl, while Maloney started to chat to Osborne.

"So," I asked her, "how did you find the honourable gentleman?"

"Honourable or not, all I can say is that he's a very odd bloke. I don't give a toss for titles, but I do expect a man to be polite."

"Why, was he rude?"

"He certainly was. He went on the whole time about some German called Dante who sent people to Hell. And this colleague of mine, called Lais—Dante wrote that she would be floating about in … I really can't tell you what. Journalists shouldn't be allowed to write that sort of thing about a nice girl. But that's the type he mixes with."

"I adore nice girls," I said, taking her hand. "You're a thoroughly nice girl, I'm a thoroughly nice boy. In this wicked world we should stick together."

"Yes, I saw at once that you had a good heart," she replied. To reinforce this judgement I sat even closer and put my arm around her waist.

"I'm as true as bread and butter," I proclaimed with feeling.

"Yes, I can tell from your eyes you'd be very nice if we got even closer."

This emboldened me to kiss her shoulder.

"I've no idea what you would be like close up. We should find out."

The rest of my wooing was conducted through actions rather than words. Oh, the miraculous, electric suppleness of these island girls! Only a poem could express the joy of caressing one after midnight.

But such is my deplorable character that even as I busied myself with these amorous gymnastics I was listening with half an ear to the conversation Maloney was having with Osborne.

And what I thought I heard shocked me deeply. He appeared to be suggesting that I'd done everything I could to get myself invited to Llangyvan, and had only gone to Lady Malmsbury-Croft's because I'd known the Earl would be there.

Meanwhile Pat was busy telling me something, and I lost concentration. They could have been talking about an entirely different matter and, with my usual hypersensitivity, I'd simply been imagining things.

I pulled away from Pat. She stared at me in astonishment. Everything had begun so well between us.

But why on earth did Maloney tell that lie? Because he was incapable of telling the truth, or because he just couldn't understand what people told him? Or was it … that there was a purpose behind it, something to do with the conspiracy my troubled intuition had warned me about?

For a while Osborne listened to Maloney without interest, then stood up.

"Sorry, I must be off. See you again at Llanvygan."

And without even shaking hands, he vanished like the Cheshire cat. Clearly he couldn't bear to sit a minute longer beside a woman.

Maloney went over to another table, leaving me alone with Pat. Forget about Maloney, I thought: I'm going to take this girl home. A philologist is a man, after all. How wonderful her white body would be, at full stretch on a bed. I could spend an hour just gazing at her.

"Are you fond of music?"

"Awfully. You should see me dance."

"Do you know what? I think we should move on. Come and have a cup of tea at my place. I'll get the gramophone out and we'll dance."

"The very idea! I've only just met you!"

"That's no problem. We'll make up for lost time later."

"If you were an Englishman I'd slap your face."

"But since I'm not, why not kiss me instead?"

"There are too many people watching," she said, encouragingly.

Everything would have been fine if I'd got up and left just then. I would have had a magnificent night, in London, where the great Casanova endured six weeks of celibacy. But fate decreed that at just that moment I should glance across at Maloney's table.

I don't know whether it was in fact or in my imagination—I can't always tell them apart—but I had the distinct impression that Maloney was signalling to the girl.

And suspicion welled up in me even more strongly than before: not ordinary suspicion, it was more like some ecstatic, primeval, almost metaphysical terror. She was clearly working with them. Our chance meeting with her had been prearranged. And if I now took her home, God knows what might happen.

But what could happen? What was I afraid of? How could anyone be afraid of such a beautiful, delicate creature? I really couldn't explain my feelings. Murder and robbery I could easily associate with Maloney, but they would have been the very last thing …

My mind was filled with shadowy, convoluted imaginings, the thought that I was about to become inextricably entangled in the dark enigma that surrounded Llanvygan. The threat over the telephone, the midnight rider, the death of William Roscoe were all bound up in that fear. And the fear was stronger than I was. Fear is a passion.

"Darling," I said to Pat, "not this time. I've just remembered that my nephew has arrived from the country and will be sleeping in my flat tonight. But all is not lost that is delayed. Promise me we'll meet again."

She gave me a look of undisguised contempt.

I took my leave of Maloney, arranged to see him the following day, and trudged off home.

The next morning I was of course deeply upset by what had happened, and I cursed the morbidly suspicious character I had been born with. Where others are made bold and carefree by drink, it just fills me with black bile. But it was too late. I never saw her again.

Over the next few days I continued my intellectual preparations for the Welsh adventure. I leafed once more through the folios containing Fludd's literary legacy. I found the Latin text hard going, thickly interspersed as it was with cabbalistic Hebrew, but I don't think I would have understood much more had it been in Hungarian. As I scribbled my notes the feeling never left me that the Earl would make everything clear.

From Fludd's *Medicina Catholica* I learnt to my surprise that all diseases can be attributed to meteors, winds, the various regions of the earth and the archangels who blow the winds. And furthermore, that the soundest method of understanding a man's character was through his urine, following the principles of the little-known science of uromancy.

I read his biography by Archdeacon Craven, and re-read Denis Saurat's excellent *Milton and Christian Materialism*, which devotes an extremely interesting chapter to Fludd.

According to Saurat, the intellectual circle that included Fludd and Milton did not view the soul as independent of the body. As committed Christians they had not a moment's doubt about its immortality, which forced the conclusion that the body too must be immortal. I was reminded of the Pendragons' motto: *'I believe in the resurrection of the body.'*

What, I wondered with a dismaying sense of superstitious confusion, would that have meant to people of past centuries, inclined as they were to take things literally? Who knows, they might even have thought that they too would rise from their graves in some not-too-distant future. According to the legend, the night rider did just that, when impelled to deal out justice on behalf of the murdered physician.

Maloney had cancelled the meeting at which we were to decide on our precise travel arrangements. I had by now more or less assumed I would be travelling alone, when, on the very last day before we were due to leave, he suddenly appeared.

"Hello, Doc! Well, are we going to Wales?"

"I certainly am. What about you?"

"I dithered about it for a couple of days. I got a very tempting invitation to Cuba—they're going to stage these amazing cock-fights, a sort of Olympic Games for cocks. But then I thought, I can't leave Osborne in the lurch, and I can't let you wander round this crazy country peering out through your specs. You might even get lost and end up in Scotland, and God preserve you from that!"

"So, we're off tomorrow on the one-fifteen."

"No, no—that's what I wanted to tell you. A very kind friend of mine, Mrs St Claire, has offered to drive us to Chester. From there we take the train to Corwen, where Osborne will be waiting for us in his car. Is that alright?"

By now my attack of distrust had passed, and in fact I had something of a guilty conscience as regards Maloney, so I was happy to accept the offer.

"I'm very grateful to Mrs St Claire for her kindness. But what sort of person is she? Won't she mind travelling with a complete stranger?"

"On the contrary. I told her you're Hungarian and, would you believe it, she said Hungarians really do exist, and she's extremely fond of them, because their history is so much like ours, we being the Irish. You never mentioned that. She said she absolutely insisted on meeting you, so you could talk about Hungary. She's going there in August."

The story seemed plausible enough. Maloney's lies generally involved a greater element of fantasy. We arranged to meet the following day at the Grosvenor House Hotel, where the lady was staying.

When I arrived, Maloney was waiting for me in the foyer.

"I wired Osborne yesterday to tell him we were coming, and to be there waiting for us. I've just had his reply to say that's fine. The lady will be down in a jiffy."

And indeed, a few minutes later a tall, elegant woman in a motoring jacket approached us with a dazzling smile. Once she was close enough for my myopic vision to take in the striking beauty of her face and form, she seemed strangely familiar, and by the time we had shaken hands and exchanged greetings I had recognised her, and remembered what a remarkable person she was. My heart was beating wildly.

Three years earlier I had spent the summer at Fontainebleau with my friend Cristofoli, an archaeologist and poet. My poor aunt Anna had recently died and I was flush with money. We were lodging, in great style, at the Hôtel de l'Angleterre et de la France, beside the Park.

One day Cristofoli, who by the way was the most sensitive creature on earth, became much more animated than usual, and announced that he was in love.

The object of his favour soon arrived. I had actually seen her in the dining room the previous day. She was always alone. And she really was beautiful, not merely by the uniform standards of the age of film but in her own, highly individual way. She was absolutely distinctive.

Cristofoli was himself a fine-looking young man and extremely enterprising by nature. He had ascertained that her name was Eileen St Claire, a British subject who had arrived from Paris by car. Nothing more was known about her. She appeared only at meal times, after spending the entire day driving her Hispano through the forest, alone.

Cristofoli passed the day reciting Petrarch's sonnets while he waited for evening to arrive. He hoped to introduce himself to her during the ballroom dancing session, but she failed to appear there. That night he slept not a wink, nor did he allow me to, and I began to feel a certain antipathy towards the lady.

The days that followed were more exciting than a hunt. Cristofoli was resourceful and difficult to shake off. As a poet he felt himself above the usual social conventions. Whenever her car arrived at the hotel he would open the door and help her out. Eileen St Claire would give him a friendly nod and move on without so much as a word. This was done so coolly and so quickly he was unable even to begin reciting the prose poem he had spent so many days devising.

His last hope was the 14th of July, the national holiday whose cheerful anarchy always brings people together. The entire town was out on the street, dancing, drinking and exchanging familiarities. I was afraid that the lady would keep aloof from this popular event. We were out celebrating, not far from the hotel, and had befriended all the showgirls and coloured people, when suddenly we caught sight of her tall figure.

In a flash, Cristofoli forced his way through the protesting crowd to present himself before her and, in the heat of the moment, offered her the first thing that came to hand—a cheap toy trumpet.

"Thank you," she said, with a smile, and miraculously vanished, like a rabbit from a conjuror's hat. Cristofoli ripped off his necktie and tore it to shreds.

His only hope now was to rescue her from some major conflagration, carrying her out of the flames in his mighty arms.

Then one day she was no longer alone. There was a man at her table, a hideously degenerate-looking man with a distinctly green complexion. He spoke in a low, rapid voice while she listened with a look of exasperation. Cristofoli was beside himself, and calmed down only when he learnt from the head waiter that the man was her doctor. Eileen St Claire and the doctor then spent the afternoon in her suite of rooms.

"Of course it's a medical examination," I told my unhappy friend, in an attempt to cheer him up.

That night the surprising and inexplicable denouement took place. First, the doctor left on the evening train. What happened next I have had to put together from the few incoherent words Cristofoli let fall.

He had left the ballroom at around eleven and was on his way up to the room when he met her in the corridor. He stopped in his tracks and just stared at her in silence. In silence, she took him by the hand and led him to her suite.

I was woken, at five a.m., by his return. His face was glowing with an unearthly happiness and he was quite incapable of conversation. He simply declaimed poetry and wept. I told him to take a sedative and let me get back to sleep.

In the morning he dressed as fastidiously as a young girl for her first ball. I had been ready half an hour earlier, and by the time he came down for breakfast I had already heard the dreadful news and was at my wits end how to break it to him. In the end, I had to tell him: Eileen St Claire had left earlier that morning.

We set off at once for Paris. We went to the police, to detective agencies, everywhere. All efforts to trace her were in vain.

Then Cristofoli's delicate nerves gave way. I was forced to take him to a sanatorium, where they nursed him for three weeks. Even after his recovery, he was never quite right again. He broke off relations with me, but also with poetry and archaeology. I lost all contact with him, and for many years thought he had committed suicide. Only recently however someone mentioned that they had seen him in Persia, where he was now Minister for Air Transport in the revolutionary government.

And now here was I, sitting face to face with the same woman. I could hardly feel neutral towards her, and briefly considered whether I should mention that I already knew who she was. But in the end it seemed wiser to say nothing.

We got into the car, Maloney in the driving seat and the two of us in the back. The memory of Cristofoli served only to deepen the mystery that seemed to surround her like a birthright.

There was little conversation, and its tone was somehow rather distant, without genuine interest. At last the topic that Maloney had mentioned cropped up, and she expounded her views on the similarities between the Hungarians and the Irish.

"Both nations spent hundreds of years under the oppressive 'protection' of a more powerful neighbour. Both showed real greatness when they had to fight against tyranny, and somehow both fell into confusion and lost their way the moment they won their independence."

She then spoke of the blighted centuries endured by the Irish, their national martyrs, and Kathleen-ni-Hoolihan, the immortal hag who, in her own ghostly way, symbolised the ghost-haunted land of Ireland.

She described these beautiful and touching things—which of course I had heard before from Irish patriots—in such a remote and ethereal way it was like a lesson being repeated. I found myself wondering, to my surprise: was there any aspect of life on earth she wouldn't take as a source of instruction, or a call to duty?

We took a light lunch at Birmingham, then continued on our way. We had by now exhausted our fund of general topics without establishing any real personal contact. This saddened me, I must admit. I felt it would all be in vain: I would never succeed in penetrating her hinterland.

We were not far from Chester when she turned to me:

"I would like to ask you a favour. You're going to Llanvygan, to the Earl of Gwynedd. The Earl was once a very good friend of mine—perhaps the best I ever had. Later, we became estranged, irrevocably estranged, as the result of a misunderstanding. But I am still very fond of him, and wish him well: from a distance, of course. And now I feel the need to remind him of my existence, after all these years."

So! A lyrical confession! But the manner, the tone in which it was delivered, was such as she might have used to tell me her new butler was proving satisfactory. When this woman opened her heart she became even more enigmatic than when she remained silent.

"I wonder if you would give him this ring? Perhaps you'll think it odd that I should ask you rather than Maloney, whom I have known all these years ... but you know Maloney. He's a thoroughly nice boy, from an excellent family, but somehow not a person you would trust with a florin. That's why I'm asking you. I hope you don't mind."

"I should be delighted to be of service."

"And I must also ask you not to tell the Earl from whom you received it. Tell him it was sent to you in an anonymous letter requesting you to pass it on to him."

"Excuse me, but surely you want the ring to remind him of you?"

"Oh yes, but I would like him to work out for himself who sent it.

43

If he can't manage that, then he doesn't deserve to be so much in my thoughts. And you will give me your word of honour that you will never, in any circumstances, tell him that you got it from me."

This was not a request, or even a command. It was a simple statement of fact, delivered in the same colourless tone as her previous speech, a simple assumption that I would now give her my word. She spoke as if the possibility never occurred to her that one might not accede to her wish.

I gave her my word.

Yet something inside me protested fiercely. Quite apart from the malign aura that clung to her from the association with Cristofoli, I could not forget that Eileen St Claire was Maloney's friend. All this might well have been arranged in advance, a conspiracy. Every suspicious circumstance seemed to be aimed at Llanvygan, entangled ever deeper in this unfathomable mystery. Her personal secret was part of the greater secret surrounding the Earl, the one that my intuition warned me so strongly against, the one that attracted and repelled me so intensely. And yet, I had given my word. Why? Because Eileen St Claire was so extremely beautiful, and I am so helpless.

I put the ring away.

And thus we arrived at Chester. Maloney and I got out at the station and took our leave.

"So you will do what I asked you," she said. "When you get back to London, tell me what the Earl said. Goodbye."

She looked at me, smiled, and took off her glove.

"Yes, you may kiss my hand."

We were sitting on the train, continuing our journey. At one point Maloney asked if I would put a package in my suitcase, as it was too large for his. Nothing else of note occurred on the way.

Soon we were winding in and out among the mountains of North Wales. There was a change of train, after which the landscape became even more picturesque, and by the time we reached Corwen it was distinctly rugged. Osborne was waiting for us, and after a brief exchange of greetings we set off again.

The road ran through a narrow valley between precipitous mountains. Osborne slowed down.

"The track on the left leads directly up to the old family seat, Pendragon Castle. As you can see, the surface has been rather neglected. Only tourists use it now; the peasants avoid these parts. They're still worried about old Asaph, the sixth Earl. That was where he practised his black arts."

The valley widened out, and we could now see the ruins of the castle, high on the mountain peak, perched on the barren edge of the cliff and looking for all the world as if it had grown out of the rock itself. Huge, black birds circled round the derelict Norman tower. Maloney expressed exactly what I was feeling when he remarked:

"It must have been damned uncomfortable, living up there."

After that, the landscape became rather more friendly. In no time at all we passed through the village of Llanvygan and caught sight of the opulent iron railings of the park. A mighty avenue of trees led to the castle, a large, bright, inviting construction, altogether different from what I had been imagining. Once inside, however, the poor lighting in the vast rooms, the ancient furniture and the immense silence left me feeling properly subdued once again.

As I dressed I composed a little speech with which to greet my host. We were shown into a spacious hall, across which the Earl, with a young girl at his side and three liveried footmen behind him, approached us with rapid steps. It all had the air of a princely reception. His severe, distinguished countenance wore an expression far removed from that of the amiable scholar-aristocrat I had met at Lady Malmsbury-Croft's. He did not even wait for us to greet him. He simply shook my hand and began speaking, as if issuing the orders for the day.

"So you're Maloney? Very good. I hope you will enjoy your stay. This lady is my niece Cynthia, Osborne's sister. Rogers—the butler—has instructions to show you to the library in the morning, Doctor. Regrettably, I am unable to dine with you tonight. Do you have any questions?"

"Yes. I've received a ring, sent to me in an anonymous letter, asking me to give it to you. I think I should let you have it straight away."

The Earl took the ring, and his face became even bleaker.

"You say you don't know who this ring is from?"

"I have no idea, My Lord."

The Earl turned on his heel and left us without another word.

"Interesting man," Maloney remarked.

But my astonishment and dismay were too much for me. I felt absolutely disconsolate. It was impossible to deny: my premonition had not deceived me. Eileen St Claire brought men nothing but trouble. And now, it was quite clear, she had caused me to lose the Earl's goodwill. What a fool I am! I always come to grief when I do favours for other people. John Bonaventura Pendragon was right: "Every good deed gets the punishment it deserves."

I took a bath, changed again, and went down to dinner. The lady of the house was seated next to me, in a magnificent gown. I cannot have amused her greatly. I was too nervous and feeling sorry for myself, and with good reason.

On the other hand, she was very good-looking. But even if she had not been so very pretty, she was also the Lady of the Castle, the descendent of Pendragons, and I felt too unworthy to do so much as open my mouth. The reader might think me a snob: let him think so. I admit that I do privately believe that an Earl is different from other men.

The things she was telling Maloney intimidated me even more. Two years earlier she had been presented at court; she spent the London season with her aunt, the Duchess of Warwick, who lived in Belgravia in a street so superbly exclusive that tears came to my eyes whenever I walked down it. And garden parties with Lady This, and evening parties with Lady That, and bazaars with someone else … The names of her girl friends, all resonantly historic names that tripped so lightly off her tongue, fell on my head like hammer blows.

If every meal is to be taken in such an aristocratic milieu, I thought, I shall waste away. I should mention that during my time in England I had quite often been in 'good society', but almost invariably as a hired secretary, not as a guest. But these Pendragons were something above 'good society'. And, last but not least, a distinguished young woman was in my eyes even more exalted and formidable than, for example, a distinguished old gentleman.

To all this was added the oppressive sense that, through Eileen St Claire's intrigues, I had permanently forfeited the right ever to be made a welcome guest at Llanvygan. In my misery I drank a great deal of the full-bodied wine of the house, hoping it might help me sleep. Such was the introduction to my first night at Llanvygan, the start of my supernatural and inexplicable adventures.

I was lying in my oppressively historic bed (no doubt dating back to Queen Anne), reading and reading. It was a philosophical work. Philosophy nearly always calms my mind and sends me quickly to sleep, perhaps as a refuge from boredom. The subjective and the objective, whose particular mutual relationship had been the topic in question, began to take on human characteristics in my half-waking, half-dreaming state.

"What a wind!" said Subject to Object.

"Don't worry about it, it's blowing from windward," replied Object to Subject, the way the left half of the brain will chat to the right half when one is half-asleep ... Then I found myself most thoroughly awake.

What was that?

I became aware that I had been hearing the noise for quite some time—that human-inhuman, indefinable something of a noise. Now, in the darkness, nothing else seemed to exist. First it went tap, tap; then something like tree-ee; and then came something that could never be recorded in writing—a long drawn-out sigh, like a terrified gasping for air. It was deeply unnerving.

And the whole sequence was repeating itself at intervals of about three minutes, though the timing cannot have been entirely regular—it was more a question of when I noticed it.

Anyway, I switched the light on. The room was now at least two hundred years more historic than when I had gone to bed. I had seen rooms like it in London museums and French chateaux, but then there had been guides and written inscriptions to direct one as to what to imagine—Napoleon strutting back and forth with his hands behind his back, or a slender woman seated at her spinning wheel. But none of the elaborately carved wardrobes in this room carried any such source of enlightenment. Nothing tied the imagination to what was merely informative and comforting. For all I knew, some ancestor might have died in here, repenting his unspeakable crimes amid horrific visions ... And all the while, there came this unceasing sound: tap, tree-ee, and the terrible sigh. Not a pleasant sensation.

I lit a cigarette. The dance of smoke from my Gold Flake drifted across the room but failed to make it any more congenial. I was desperately tired. The wind was howling down the open fireplace like an uncontrolled blast of interference on the radio. And, time and time again, tap, tree-ee, and the inexpressible sigh.

Of course I realised it must be a window, or something of that kind, producing the noise. On many a windy night the same battle had been waged between an unsecured window and my fevered imagination.

I knew that, whether I wanted to or not, I would have to go and investigate. I knew my habits of mind: until I did that, I would have no rest.

I got out of bed, donned my dressing gown and quietly drew back the door.

It opened on to a corridor. The corridor was in pitch-black darkness, draughty and thoroughly unfriendly. Like a man who has tested the icy water and drawn back his foot, I went back into my room.

At times like this I arm myself with a revolver: they are what I keep one for. It might seem a little too much like something in a film, that a man should sleep with a loaded revolver, especially one like me, living such a peaceable life, but I had no choice: it was a long-established habit.

I pulled out the drawer of my bedside table—and thought my eyes must be playing tricks on me. If in place of the revolver I had found a tortoise, I could not have been more amazed. It was no longer in the right-hand corner, where I had put it, but in the left. There could be no question of error. I had even counted my cigarettes as I put them in, one by one.

No cinema fantasy was required for the next step. I opened the cylinder. It was empty. Someone had removed the cartridges.

As a general rule, only three things are stolen from me: cigarettes, razor blades and handkerchiefs. Never before a revolver cartridge. The distressing thing was that I now had none left. I had loaded it with six when I bought it ten years earlier and it had carried five ever since, after I fired one off to test it. I reckoned they would last me a lifetime. I never seriously thought I might use a single one in anger.

If I tell you I was not enjoying the situation, I am using a degree of understatement.

Meanwhile the noises off were rising in crescendo, as was my nervousness. It was as if loudspeakers were booming away in all sixty rooms of the house: tap, tree-ee, ahh … h … hh. Charming hospitality, when your windows roar like this. No—it couldn't be a window. Here at last was the great and terrible adventure my anxieties had been leading me towards for ten long years.

In place of my revolver I took a torch. I drew a deep breath and leapt out into the corridor.

The window facing my bedroom door was shut. The sound seemed to be coming more from the left, so I headed in that direction. The next window was over ten paces away, and before it the corridor made a slight bend. The ancients hadn't bothered much about lighting.

And then, to my immeasurable satisfaction, I came face to face with the culprit. Of course it was a window. It wasn't properly shut. It swung to and fro like a corpse on the gallows. I immediately set about trying to close it.

I say trying, because this was no simple task. The window had a fiendishly historic lock. It now dawned on me how very clever I was to have once perused an excellent standard work on old English locksmithery. This was one of those very rare occasions, crosswords apart, when the knowledge I had acquired would be put to some use. I slammed it shut with a flourish that no Shakespearean chambermaid could have bettered.

The tension in my nerves eased. Wearily, but immensely reassured, I staggered back to my room. Through a combination of sheer courage and technical skill I had seen off my major fear. I would take a sedative and at last get some sleep. The business of the revolver could wait till the morning.

But fate willed otherwise. The window was merely a gentle prelude.

The moment I reached the bend in the corridor I saw a light outside the door of my room. I stepped two paces closer, and then, forgetting all sense of geography in my fright, began shouting in three languages at once. In front of the door, with a flaming torch in his hand, stood a gigantic medieval figure.

Just to be clear on this: not for a moment did I think it could be any sort of ghostly apparition. While it is a fact that English castles are swarming with ghosts, they are visible only to natives—certainly not to anyone from Budapest.

In fact the astonishing thing was, that it wasn't a ghost. If the spirit of some elderly Englishman appears in a castle by night, there can be no complaint. It is something we have all been prepared for by literature. We solemnly vow to give his bones a decent Christian burial, and that is that.

The single most eerie thing about our planet is that there are no such things as ghosts. For this, as for everything else, there must be a rational explanation, but it has always escaped me. What, for example, is one supposed to do, at midnight, when a giant medieval figure that is not a ghost is standing before your bedroom door? It is in fact in excellent health, and though it stares at you in a slightly hostile way, it politely enquires:

"You have perhaps mislaid something?"

"Would you be so kind as to explain who on earth you are?"

"My name is John Griffith, sir."

"Pleased to meet you. The Earl, I think … "

"Yes, sir. I am in the service of the Earl of Gwynedd. Would you have mislaid anything?"

I related the story of the window. My new acquaintance listened to my tale with typical British impassivity. I had the distinct feeling he did not believe a word I said. We were silent for some time. Then he added:

"So all is well. Good night, sir … But if I were you … I would avoid going out into the corridors at night … These old corridors are somewhat … draughty. I mention this just in case."

And he strolled away, torch in hand, a truly medieval vision.

Perhaps it was my imagination, but the advice seemed to carry some sort of threat.

Back in my room, I began setting things straight. John Griffith had not been wearing medieval costume but, so far as I could be sure in my rather peculiar state of mind, garments from the early seventeenth century—a black doublet with puffed sleeves and padded black trunk hose. His collar was turned down as in the later portraits of Shakespeare. But enough of that.

I felt like the old Israelite in the Bible—I forget his name—who went in search of his father's asses and found a kingdom. The window I had been driven towards by my nervous false alarm had proved to be only a window. On the other hand, it was an undeniable fact that cartridges had been removed from my revolver, and that I was under surveillance from a giant in period costume. All this required some thought.

I decided to lock the door, only to discover, with an astonishment greater than any I had experienced earlier that night, that while it had a lock, there was no key.

Nonetheless I went to bed. I was exhausted, and managed somehow to put all these worrying concerns from my mind. I was just drifting off when I heard the door quietly open.

The wind poured in again, and all the terrors of the night came flooding back. My heartbeat stopped, my brain ceased to function, but my instincts were still working—a bit like St Denis strolling away from Montmartre after his decapitation.

I flicked the light on, aimed the empty revolver at the intruder, and said:

"Stop!"

I seemed to be acquiring a sort of sleuth-like nonchalance.

With confidence, and consciousness, returning, I realised it was Maloney. He wore a black, skin-tight outfit which I immediately decided must be for rock-climbing. He closed the door carefully behind him and whispered:

"Hullo-ullo-ullo."

"Hullo-ullo-ullo," I returned, with a slightly interrogative intonation.

"I hope I'm not disturbing you," he went on.

"Optimistic as ever," I replied. "How did you get here? And

more to the point, what are you doing in that outfit? Do you always dress up for your constitutional?"

"My dear Doctor, we haven't time for your witticisms. Some very odd things are going on in this building."

"They certainly are."

"If I wasn't from Connemara, I'd swear the place was haunted. But as things are, I don't know what to say. Tell me, have you by any chance come across … er … what shall I call it … an apparition?"

"It depends what sort of apparition you mean."

"A huge great fellow, in a sort of Christmas pantomime outfit. With a torch in his hand. He stares at you and then moves away. Not a nice experience."

"I've actually spoken to him. He's called John Griffith."

"Well, not a very ghostly name. In Wales every other person is called Griffith. But what's he up to, prowling round outside our rooms?"

"I haven't the faintest."

"I can't help it, but I am not happy with bogey-men like that lurking outside my room. And have you noticed anything else? For example, have you a key in your door?"

"No, I haven't."

"Same with me. And were your belongings searched while we were at dinner?"

"Well … the cartridges have been removed from my revolver."

"Hm. The thought occurs to me … Doctor, would you just check that the parcel we put in your suitcase is still there?"

Though the idea that anything might have been taken out of my luggage seemed improbable, I stepped out of bed, opened my second suitcase—the one I hadn't yet unpacked—and searched through it, again and again. There was no trace of the parcel.

"Interesting," Maloney observed. "There are either thieves, or ghosts, walking this house. What do you make of it all?"

But I didn't see the matter as quite so simple. Had there been thieves on the prowl they would have taken my money, or my cigarette case at the very least, not my revolver cartridges and Maloney's mysterious little parcel. Once again, my suspicion of the man was strongly aroused.

"Tell me, Maloney—if you don't mind my asking—what exactly was in that parcel?"

He gave me a searching look.

"So you opened it?"

"Are you mad? Are you suggesting that I am responsible for the loss of your package? Tell me right now: what was in it?"

"Just various rock-climbing things: they wouldn't mean anything to you. The powder you saw was a kind of resin. To rub on the rope before I use it."

The next instant he dashed to the door, pressed his ear against it and listened. Now I too could hear footsteps approaching. He stepped back into the middle of the room and, without any introduction, burst out into "Happy days are here again", beating time with a paper knife on a glass. He made a terrific noise. The footsteps faded into the distance.

"Sorry about that," he remarked. "I suddenly feel more cheerful. Life is great. This house is almost as good as the jungle. I remember when I was in Labuan, enjoying a quiet game of poker with the major, and this native policeman burst in to say that a band of orang-utans were approaching and had already sacked three houses. Orang-utans can be very nasty when they gang up in this way. There's always a dominant female with them, and if she gets killed, the rest all run away. Fine, but how does a chap know which of those hairybacks is the old lady? I said to the major: 'Just leave this to me. I know their little ways.' I went out, and there they were, a pack of grinning apes ... "

But by then I wasn't in the mood to wait for Maloney's story to finish. I was quite convinced that his manic behaviour was deliberate, that there was some purpose concealed under this cloak of idiocy—as with the Brutus we read about at school.

It's true I am prone to suspicion, but I was certain that he had begun singing when the footsteps approached in order to establish an alibi: to show that he was with me and not making any trouble, not getting into any mischief; he was just having a little sing-song ...

"Sorry," I said. "Can we leave the dominant female for some other time? Would you kindly explain why you're in climbing gear at this time of night? In the films, by the way, it's what the hotel thieves wear … And in any case, you haven't explained how you got to my room."

"Oh, that's simple. You know, as we arrived I noticed that there was a balcony up here on our floor, with carved figures taking the weight of the one above on their heads. I immediately felt I just had to climb up there. I've never done bearded stone statues before. And then I couldn't get to sleep, I was so upset by the unfriendly reception we got from the Earl. Anyway, night climbing is my speciality. So I togged up and went out on to the balcony."

"And climbed up?"

"No, that's my point. I got out on the balcony, and found that the whole castle was surrounded."

"What?"

"Oh yes. A horseman was standing at the gate, with a torch in his hand. He spotted me, and started shouting at me."

"What was he saying?"

"I've no idea. He spoke some really strange local dialect. Actually, he only said one word, but I didn't understand even that. But just that one word was pretty unpleasant. So I came back inside."

"And then?"

"Then I tried to get back to my room, and met this thingy … this apparition … in the corridor. I started to get curious. I thought I'd come and ask you. You're such a clever person, I was interested to see what you'd make of it all. So, what do you think?"

"What do I think? 'There are more things in heaven and earth, Horatio Than are dreamed of in your philosophy'."

"Why do you call me Horatio? Is that a compliment or an insult?"

"Whichever you choose. And now I must wish you a more peaceful good night."

"Good night, Doctor. And don't dream about strange figures in fancy dress."

He left, and I went back to bed, absolutely exhausted. I felt like a shipwreck victim finally washed up on the obligatory desert island.

But I couldn't sleep. Too tired even to think, I lay in a sort of comatose restlessness, if there is such a thing, for what seemed hours on end.

Something was happening. Something was definitely happening. The Parcae were spinning their threads. The fate of the House was alive and active in one of the rooms; a serious crisis in the history of the Pendragons was about to unfold.

And there stood—or rather lay—I, János Bátky from Budapest, with my endless premonitions and fears, helpless, not knowing a thing, confused and defenceless, at the very heart of the plot.

Suddenly I heard such an extraordinary noise I virtually flew out of bed and rushed to the window.

Maloney had not lied. Outside the window, with halberd and torch, a horseman in black galloped away into the darkness.

Next morning the sun shone so benignly on the fabled green lawn of the park that I thanked God once more that I was in Britain. The sun rarely shines in these islands, but when it does the effect is so wonderful it is as if it were smiling down on a new-created world.

I was still shaving when Osborne entered my room. After the dismal night I had passed his appearance was almost as refreshing as the sunshine itself. His whole being radiated that special quality of youth that is the greatest treasure of these islands, and unique to them. Surely nothing ill can dwell in a house where a young man like that can feel so contented.

"Hello, Doctor. I trust you had a good night. The saying is, whatever you dream about on your first night here will come true."

"Well, as far as that's concerned, I had a most interesting night. I'm not even sure what was dream and what was reality. I'm glad of the chance to speak to you about it in private. I tell you, some very strange things took place."

"Strange things? We've had none of those here in two hundred years, unfortunately. I can't speak for the time before that, especially when we were still up in Pendragon. Llanvygan is the most petty bourgeois place in the whole United Kingdom."

"My notions of the petty bourgeois are somewhat different."

"Well, you'd better tell me about your little adventures, then."

"Where shall I start? First of all, didn't you feel the Earl received us, how shall I say, rather coolly?"

"Oh no, not at all. In England, as you know, it's a point of principle that a guest should be received with the least possible fuss, to make him feel at home. But perhaps my uncle did overdo it slightly."

He was deep in thought.

"But you are right, up to a point," he continued. "My uncle practically never invites anyone, and you must have made a great impression on him to be asked. Cynthia and I were delighted when he told us—we hoped he might be abandoning his habitual reclusiveness—and we were surprised that he wasn't more pleased to see you."

"Could you suggest a reason for it?"

"Of course. He is completely—as it used to be called—of a melancholic humour. At times he is immensely benign, the kindest man on earth. Then he draws back into his shell. There've been times when the three of us have been here and he hasn't spoken to us once in six weeks, and he certainly wasn't angry with us. He locks himself away in his rooms. We aren't allowed in there. The whole of the second floor is his."

"And what does he do up there, during those times?"

"I believe he works on his special animals. My uncle is a sort of amateur zoologist. But he never talks about it. He does sometimes go out for a stroll, but he never speaks to anyone; in fact I don't think he even recognises people. And you're not allowed to speak to him. On one occasion, you know, after the episode when he is said to have revived the Duke of Warwick, he chased a journalist up a tree because he asked for an interview. It seems yesterday was another of his bad days. But you mustn't take it amiss. You must make yourself at home here, as much as you possibly can."

"Thank you. But what would you say if a giant in fancy dress patrolled outside your bedroom door at night?"

Osborne roared with laughter.

"My dear man, you are far too sensitive. At night all Llanvygan servants are giants in fancy dress. An ancient ruling requires the Earl of Gwynedd to maintain thirty night-watchmen, complete with halberds, wherever he resides. Even their garments are prescribed. There's nothing unusual in that. Britain is full of these old medieval statutes. Anyway, thirty men with halberds are a great deal more practical than the knights in armour Lord Whatsisname has to keep permanently at the ready. Or the trumpeter who has to play non-stop whenever the king hunts in the vicinity of some peer or other. Not to mention the fistful of snow one Scottish lord has to supply to the court every year. Does that reassure you?"

"Not completely. But while we're on the subject, I'll tell you what else has been going on."

"What, more horrors? I begin to envy you, Doctor. You foreigners have all the luck. I've lived here for three years and not one table has danced the tango in my honour."

"Please, you must take me seriously. The cartridges were removed from my revolver. A packet Maloney entrusted to me has vanished from my suitcase. At night, a horseman stands outside the house with a flaming torch. Is that what usually happens here?"

Osborne was again deep in thought, and did not reply until urged to do so. Then, very quietly and with a look of self-importance on his face, he said:

"Tell me, Doctor, do they teach Geography in Hungary?"

"Of course they do," I answered, somewhat irritably. "And much more thoroughly than in England."

"Then you should have learnt that all Welshmen are mad. In England, every primary schoolchild knows this. I have no idea what has got into my uncle, nor do I bother my head about it. One fool can't fathom the thoughts of another. Possibly he doesn't even know about these things. The butler is just as crazy; none of the staff is completely sane. A certain mild abnormality is required of anyone who crosses the threshold of Llanvygan. It's the tradition. It's why I felt free to invite Maloney."

"And the Earl me. Thanks very much."

"If I were you, I wouldn't concern myself with these trifles. You can be sure that by tonight your cartridges will all be back in place. The butler probably made a bet with the cook. It's happened before. But the horseman you must have dreamed. I would have known about him too, don't you think?

"Please believe me," he went on. "For the last two hundred years nothing remarkable has happened to anyone living here. At best, a few minor eccentricities, little incidents of no consequence, much to my regret."

Slightly reassured, I went down to breakfast. I found Maloney already at the table. He made no comment on our nocturnal encounter.

Cynthia Pendragon, now dressed rather more casually, seemed to me altogether less formidable than she had the night before. This time I studied her rather more calmly. Even setting aside Pendragon, Llangyvan and several centuries of glorious English history, she was very attractive.

The loveliest of her features was her forehead. A high, clear brow dominated the face, lending it a certain piquancy. It was a broad, rational, honest face, with large blue eyes. The upper lip, with a touch of aristocratic grace, protruded slightly forward over the lower.

After the meal, Osborne and Maloney went off to play golf, and I prepared to head up to the library. The stony-faced butler, with his Franz Joseph whiskers, was already waiting for me.

To my great surprise Cynthia had not gone with the golfers, as I had expected in view of her background. Instead she fell in with me, announcing that she would show me round. I cannot say I was entirely delighted. The Mohammedans excluded women from Paradise, and I would exclude them from libraries, especially the pretty ones. Their mere presence obstructs my reading.

"Are you fond of books?" I asked, foolishly.

"Books are my hobby, indeed my obsession. And Welsh folklore. In fact, I've always wanted to be schoolteacher in a mountain village and spend my life doing ethnographical research. But my uncle thought it unsuitable. I mean the schoolteaching, not the research."

This was not exactly the image I had formed of the Earl's niece. Somehow I would have preferred her to have confessed to be unable to spell. But it seemed intelligence was yet another sobering Pendragon legacy.

We had reached the library.

It was an extremely long and narrow room, with countless books lining the walls, the majority in the uniform binding embossed with the Pendragon-Rosicrucian coat of arms.

I was filled with the tenderness I always feel—and which nothing can match—when I encounter so many books together. At moments like these I long to wallow, to bathe in them, to savour their wonderful, dusty, old-book odours, to inhale them through my very pores.

With genuine pride, Cynthia pointed me to the finest treasures of the library, the illuminated Welsh codices. She was proudest above all of those few written not in Latin but in the native language.

"You can see what a life's work this could be for me," she said, "to edit and publish these manuscripts—which exist nowhere else—with commentaries. It would be a major contribution to Welsh literature."

"It certainly would. But can you imagine the work it would entail? It's a job for elderly professors, not for young—and beautiful—patrician ladies."

She blushed.

"You obviously take me for one of those English girls who answer 'yes' and 'no', and love dancing, and have winsome, empty smiles."

"God forbid!" I said. "One has only to look at you to see how intelligent you are."

But in truth, I lied. She was far too pretty for me to suppose any such thing. However, since it seemed her foible to be intelligent, I would have to woo her from that angle. For me, as it happened, this promised to be easier than if she had been interested only in sport.

Next she showed me the Persian codices, collected at the end of the last century by one of the Earls who had been in the tropics. I knew a little about them, having seen them at the great Persian Exhibition at Burlington House. There were some twenty of them and I stumbled from one ecstasy to the next. Little did I imagine what an active part they would play in my own personal history. In my excited bibliomania I forgot the first rule of English good manners, which strictly bars the didactic, and lectured my hostess on everything I knew about Persian books and illustrations—not that it was very much.

Cynthia listened with rapt attention. I don't think she was

actually much interested in all the technical details I chattered on about, but she seemed to enjoy the performance.

It probably wasn't often that anyone talked to her about these profound, and rather dull, things, and she was immensely flattered.

Cynthia was a fairy on a magical island, and our friendship was progressing with the sort of speed you'd expect at a well-attended party, after champagne, and after midnight.

But what is champagne beside a really old tome? In one hand I held an original Caxton, in the other two Wynkyn de Wordes—not to mention the Continental *incunabula*, and two Aldines enthroned on a separate shelf.

What a wonderful thing is a book! It simply sits there on the shelf, looking like nothing in any way special, and saying not a word. You open it, and you still know nothing about it, because *incunabula* have no title-pages. Then you glance at the back, at the colophon, and discover that you are holding a Caxton in your hands—an archduke, a Pope. Is there any human being who can carry self-effacement to that level of perfection?

I spent the morning familiarising myself with the more noteworthy volumes. Then the gong summoned us to lunch. In my overflowing happiness I sang Cynthia a Hungarian folksong about ripening ears of corn.

"You Continentals … you're so … different," she murmured dreamily.

"I've known English people who loved books."

"That's not what I mean. With you there's still … passion."

And she blushed scarlet.

Over lunch Maloney and Osborne talked golf, and we planned various excursions. The Earl did not appear.

We were sitting over our coffee and brandy when the local vicar, the Rev Dafyd Jones, was announced. He was extremely frail, and very nervous, with a hunted look in his eye.

"Excuse me for intruding. In point of fact I was hoping to speak with the Earl, but he won't see anyone."

"Not even you?" Cynthia asked with surprise.

"I don't think he's in," said Osborne.

"He was seen this morning, walking in the direction of Pendragon," said the vicar. "I thought he might be back for lunch. I'm very, very sorry. I shall be off now."

And with a great sigh, he sat down.

"Is there something amiss in the village?" asked Cynthia.

"Amiss ... well, no, strictly speaking, there isn't. Only superstition, the ancient curse of our people. It seems nothing can drive it from these mountains," he intoned.

Osborne pricked up his ears.

"Well, tell us about it! Do please join us in a drink, Vicar, and tell us the story. Is that table at your sister's dancing about again?"

"That's not superstition; that's a serious scientific experiment. You may come and observe it any evening you like. No, it's something else. The whole village has gone mad."

"I'm delighted to hear it. Perhaps we might have some details?"

"You know old Pierce Gwyn Mawr?"

"The prophet Habakkuk? But of course I do. He belongs with my favourite childhood memories. I hadn't heard of him lately: I assumed he was dead."

"He isn't dead. On the contrary, if you please. This morning he began to prophesy again."

"Excellent. I'll go and listen to him straight away. But what's the problem?"

"The problem is, that the entire village has assembled, and they are completely beside themselves. All work has come to a standstill."

"And what is Pierce telling them?"

"Mainly, that the end of the world is at hand, and they should repent."

"And what is his source of information? Are there perhaps omens in the sun and the moon?"

"He says there are none yet, but there soon will be. Only, in the mean time ... "

"Well ... ?"

"The four horsemen of the Apocalypse have appeared. He watched them all night, circling around Llanvygan House, and then they rode off towards Pendragon."

"I saw them myself," said Maloney. "But how do you know they're eucalyptic?"

"This is becoming interesting," said Osborne, rising from his chair. "The doctor also saw them, and there isn't the slightest tendency to the prophetic in him."

The vicar's already pale face showed increasing signs of unease:

"And my sister, too, heard the clatter of hooves ... She had a terrible night, poor girl, as she always does when the wind is up. I thought she had just imagined it. What explanation can you offer for all this?"

"None at all, for the moment. But is it so surprising that someone should be riding around the house?"

"So in fact ... in fact ... " stammered the vicar, firmly gripping his chair, "you too think there is something in what old Pierce is saying ... ?"

"Of course," replied Osborne. "But don't you think, vicar, that it might be a little parochial to assume that the Horsemen of the Apocalypse might begin their European tour at Llanvygan? Wouldn't they be rather more likely to open in London, or Paris, somewhere more central? Or in Rome, where the Antichrist himself sits on the papal throne?"

"That's not the issue, sir ... I'm thinking about something rather different ... about something that might be quite specific to Llanvygan. But it's rather difficult for me to mention."

"Why?"

"In view of ... with regard to ... the family."

"Which family?"

"The Pendragon family."

"I cannot imagine what you are thinking," said Osborne, after a protracted silence.

The vicar stood, wringing his hands. At last he began, in a mournful voice, like someone reciting a lesson.

"We are all aware of the family legends, and other local traditions and stories attaching to Asaph Christian, the sixth Earl of Gwynedd. These stories, moreover ... "

"The midnight rider!" exclaimed Cynthia, jumping up.

"Indeed," said the vicar, with a bow. "Miss Pendragon and I have for some years been trying to collect all the folkloric data connected with him. According to the superstitious notions of simple people, the same deceased gentleman appears whenever some great turning point is about to occur, either in the country as a whole, or in the house of Pendragon. He was last seen in 1917, when the Germans began their submarine offensive against Great Britain."

"Yes," interjected Cynthia, "but we've since then more or less concluded that it could have been a mounted patrol on its way to the coast."

"Oh yes, we've concluded," the vicar mused … "the devil we've concluded!" he burst out, and turned crimson. "Ten years I've been vicar here, and never yet have we concluded anything; in fact … I beg your pardon; I humbly beg your pardon. These days my nerves are in shreds. I really am terribly sorry … "

And he gestured like a man about to sink with shame.

"At any rate, I'm off to see old Habakkuk," said Osborne. "Won't you join me?"

And we made our way down to the village.

The prophet was seated in an armchair outside his house, surrounded by a large throng of people, all straining to catch his disconcertingly quiet utterances. With his flowing beard, he certainly looked the part.

This was not the wild and hysterical ranting I remembered from Hyde Park Corner or from charismatic Salvation Army rallies. He neither rolled his eyes nor spoke in tongues, like his transatlantic colleagues who have developed prophecy into a successful line of business. His speech was as regular and deliberate as that of any elderly peasant recounting his experiences.

"And this is how it will be, unless you change your way of life. I don't wish to accuse any individual: you all know I am speaking in the common interest. You can see for yourselves how it is across the whole of Wales. They have shut down the mines in Pembroke and Caernarfon. Tens and tens of thousands are unemployed, and the Devil finds work for idle hands. Someone from Rhyl told me that the sea is very different from what it used to be. Anglesey fishermen have caught a fairy-child who declared that a famine is on its way ...

"But I had no idea what all this meant until two weeks ago, when I met the Dog myself.

"I had climbed Moel-Sych, and night was falling. I was sitting on a rock, when suddenly I saw him, up on the meadow, at about a hundred paces. His coat was snow-white, his ears blood-red, just as in the old tales I heard from my grandfather, Owain Gwyn Mawr. He was digging, digging ... I did not dare to go over to see what it was he was digging ... but of course I knew—he was digging the grave of some important person. Many, many will die, in Wales and in England, people who think now that they will live their full span on earth ... "

He drew a Bible from his pocket and read from the Book of the Apocalypse. He declaimed a chapter as far as the words *'and I shall give him the morning star'*, then continued reciting from memory.

"And they brought forth the Book of the Seven Seals, which no man might open, only the Lamb of Sacrifice. And when the Lamb had broken open the seals, the Angel sounded his trumpet, and behold, the Horsemen appeared. The First Horseman rode a white horse, and in his hand a bow, and on his head a crown. The Second Horseman rode a red horse; to him was given the power to take away the peace of the world. The Third Horseman sat on a white horse, and in his hand a pair of scales. The Fourth Horseman sat on a horse that was mortally pale, and his name was Death. And those who do not bear the sign on their brows will be trodden in the dread winepress of the wrath of God. Every island shall vanish, and the mountains will be no more.

"Last night, I saw the Horsemen. The horses' heads were the heads of lions, and from their mouths came forth fire and brimstone. For the day of reckoning is at hand.

"Repent ye, therefore, before it is too late. Except ye do this, woe unto ye, oh people of Wales: your days are numbered."

My second night got off to a better start than the first. There was no wind, and after dinner I went for a moonlit stroll in the park with Cynthia. My thoughts had become decidedly more positive than they had been the day before.

Cynthia told me about her childhood—all very boring, but I took it as a good sign. If you wish to attain intimacy with members of the opposite sex, you make an effort to share your past with them, to make them no longer strangers, newcomers to your life.

I fell asleep early, and remained that way until one in the morning, when I was woken by loud voices in the corridor, both male and female. At first I was very angry at having been disturbed. "Do they really have to stage their little folk festival outside my door?" I wondered, still not fully awake. "The Singhalese hold it a crime to wake a sleeping dog. Next time I'll go there."

But further sleep was out of the question. The din was becoming louder and more agitated. They were talking, I gathered, in Welsh: I couldn't understand a single word.

I got up, got more or less dressed, and went out into the corridor. There I met my acquaintance from the previous night, John Griffith, with two more giants in fancy dress and two housemaids, in very little dress at all. But the scene was no cheerfully amoral idyll. John Griffith was no longer a figure to strike fear. His Shakespearean doublet was unbuttoned, revealing his nightshirt. His colleague had a halberd in his hand, but was holding it upside down, like a broom.

"What's the matter?" I asked.

They stared at me, without reply. There was more jabbering in Welsh. Then they all ran off down the corridor.

I ran after them. By now I too was thoroughly agitated.

We stopped in a vast, barely furnished room, and listened. From some distance away, strange noises could be heard—as if someone were praying, in a sort of chant.

" Sir, just now he was speaking English, but now I've no idea what it means."

I listened closer, and understood.

"*Panem nostrum quotidianum da nobis hodie. Et dimitte nobis debita nostra …* "

It was the Lord's Prayer in Latin, intoned as for Mass.

"Who could be saying Mass here?" I asked.

"Mass? Oh my God!" one of the girls exclaimed, and promptly began to sob. For the Methodist Welsh, Roman Catholicism is still the work of Satan.

"It's been going on all night," said Griffith. "Praying and wailing, and speaking in tongues. Earlier on, it started humming, like this:"

And he hummed the *Marseillaise*.

"But who is it?"

"We can't find him. We've searched everywhere. We just can't find him."

Suddenly we heard footsteps approaching. The girls fled, shrieking, into a far corner. The man with the halberd levelled his weapon at the door.

The door opened.

In stepped Cynthia, clad in some sort of riding costume, with a revolver in her hand. She was obviously enjoying the role of intrepid Amazon.

"Hands up!" she shouted at us.

We raised our hands. She recognised us, and we lowered them. She blushed, and apologised.

"So you heard it too? What is it?"

But the noise had gone quiet. Griffith told Cynthia what he knew, while she stared uncomprehendingly.

"Singing the *Marseillaise*, and intoning Mass? These motifs are unprecedented in the history of the house. In fact, quite alien to the folklore of these parts. We really must note them down."

Again footsteps could be heard, more rapid this time, and another footman burst in.

"He's in the library. Definitely the library."

We hurried off towards the library. At the great oak door Griffith and his companions stopped and stood, awe-struck. There is something thoroughly daunting about a closed door.

By now the voice was clearly audible.

"And when the Lamb shall break open the seal, the angel shall sound his trumpet, and the Horsemen will appear … The First Horseman shall ride a white horse, a bow in his hand, and a crown on his head … "

The visitation spoke in a sonorous, if somewhat nasal voice, with a distinct Welsh accent. It was rather like the way Swabians speak Hungarian, saying 'b' for 'p', and 'd' for 't'. And it was having trouble with the 's' as well, lisping, as Welsh peasants often do.

"Why, it's Pierce Gwyn Mawr," exclaimed Griffith.

And indeed it was. It was repeating what the prophet had said earlier, word for word.

"Impossible," said the man with the halberd. "Every entrance is locked. There's no way he could have got in."

"Oh my God," cried one of the girls. "Ghosts can pass through keyholes."

"How could it be the ghost of old Pierce?" said another. "He's still alive."

"It could be his double. It happened to my uncle. It went and got completely drunk down at the Elephant, and the next day he had to pay the whole bill."

"Let's just go in," I suggested. It had dawned on me what all this was about.

But only Cynthia and I dared enter. We switched the light on, and the voice immediately stopped. Cynthia's face was extremely solemn, and a little fearful.

"The moment has arrived," I said. "You may be present at the birth of a new family legend."

We searched the library high and low. We looked behind every curtain. One by one the others came and joined in. But in vain. Half an hour went by, but the voice remained silent. Then I had an idea.

"Let's move on," I said. "He isn't here, he's in the room above. The sound is coming down the chimney breast, through the open fireplace. That's why it seems to be coming from here."

Griffith and his entourage rushed out of the room. I manoeuvred the situation so that Cynthia and I lingered behind. By the time we reached the door the others were well down the corridor. I pulled Cynthia back into the library, gestured for her to keep silent, and turned the light off.

The moment darkness returned, the apparition resumed its chanting. It continued reciting the Book of the Apocalypse from exactly where it had left off.

Cynthia gripped my arm in fear. It made me feel like a strong, protective male, and I put my arm around her. Then I stroked her hair, to give her courage. She did not protest.

I blessed the worthy domestic ghost for providing me with that one moment of closeness, which was to lead to far greater intimacy and tenderness. Now we were linked together: we had a shared memory, and a shared secret.

I took her by the hand and led her on tiptoe to the fireplace. There was no longer any doubt that this was where the sound was coming from.

I bent down and pointed my torch upwards. It was just as I had thought. Squatting in the chimney, in the foetal position, was Osborne. From the gramophone on his lap the voice of Pierce Gwyn Mawr continued to declaim the Book of the Apocalypse.

"Hide and seek, Osborne?" I said. "We've found you. Down you come, little boy."

He climbed down, showering soot everywhere and looking very pleased with himself. "Pretty good, hey, Doctor? I'm particularly chuffed with the old man's solo. I recorded it this afternoon. If you can keep mum, it'll be the start of a new legend. Tomorrow the Reverend and his sister will reveal their metapsychic explanation of how the prophet managed to say his piece at Llanvygan House, and a hundred years from now the Cynthia of the day will pronounce it yet another fascinating bit of lore, to be collected and posted off to *The Brython*. Now come on up to my room and let's drink a Hennessy to the terrors of the night."

We followed him up. It was the first time I had seen his room. It was fantastic. I think the intention was to recreate a tropical bungalow. There was no bed, just a hammock. Every bit of furniture was made of bamboo, and suspended from the walls. At their foot, a little ditch ran right round the room, filled with water.

"To keep snakes out," he explained. "Cynthia, you must drink to sibling love. Properly speaking, we are co-workers. I create the legend, you record it. Doctor, you are perhaps not aware what an eminent folklorist my sister is. She has published two articles."

"Oh, shush!" Cynthia exclaimed.

He took down a journal from the wall. It was entitled *The Brython*. He opened it at a short item of twenty lines on 'Christmas country dances of Merioneth'. It was signed: 'Hon Cynthia Pendragon, Llanvygan.'

I congratulated her warmly. She was highly embarrassed, and immensely proud. I don't think she would have given it up for forty ancestors. That's women for you.

"I cannot approve of what you've been up to, Osborne," she said solemnly. "If you go on like this you'll completely undermine folkloric research. After this I can never again be sure what is genuine and what is humbug."

"That's just it," he replied. "That's how it must have been in the olden days—half miraculous happening and half practical joke."

"Were you perhaps the midnight horseman as well?" I asked.

At that precise moment a loud report was heard.

"What's that?" cried Cynthia. "A revolver!"

"Never," said Osborne. "A revolver at Llanvygan? Someone must have slammed a door."

"No, no, that was a revolver," she yelled. "Come on. Let's go and see what's happening."

We dashed out into the corridor and raced wildly through several rooms and hallways. And how different they looked, in the terror of night. The furniture seemed curiously elongated, and black hooks protruded from beneath the carpets, tripping you as you ran. Footsteps were heard approaching, and terrified servants burst in from all sides—there were at least two hundred in the building.

We found nothing on the first floor. But we did encounter Maloney, coming out of his room in his pyjamas, looking extremely dishevelled.

"You heard it too? Like someone being shot ... "

Then Rogers, the butler, appeared, and took charge of the situation.

"Quite possibly the shot was fired upstairs, on the second floor. We will have to break into the Earl's apartments."

The same thought was forced on everyone ... Cynthia had turned a deathly pale. The Earl ... perhaps he had taken his own life, after reaching the nadir of depression, with no hope of relief? Had the omens and prophecies been correct?

We hurriedly climbed the narrow staircase, the only way up to his suite of rooms, and stopped before a vast iron door bearing the Pendragon-Rosicrucian crest.

"How do we get in?" asked Osborne. "This door is always locked."

Rogers pulled out a key.

"The Earl's instructions are, sir, that I may enter at any time."

He opened the door and went in.

But after passing through a second room, he stopped.

"Household staff must remain here. It's quite sufficient if only we go in."

The next room must surely have been part of the Earl's secret laboratory. It wasn't so much dark as filled with a greenish light, like an underwater cave.

And in fact we were in just such a cave. The walls were lined with immense glass tanks, filled with water and adorned with artificial rocks, between which strange aquatic plants grew on long, ungainly, wandering stems. And among the rocks and the flowers swam creatures so horrific they are burned into my memory: they still haunt my dreams. And they are even more horrific when I wake in the dark, remembering them.

They were shaped like lizards but were very much larger, a metre or more in length; and they had no eyes. Their soft, gelatinous bodies were palely translucent or whitish, like those of huge molluscs. From their temples sprouted fantastically shaped and coloured feelers, and two legs grew at the front of their eyeless heads. They circled slowly among the artificial rocks with a ghostly motion.

The next room was ice-cold, like a refrigeration chamber. The walls were lined with chests of drawers made of lead. In the middle was a white operating table, with three of the same animals lying motionless on it, together with a collection of surgical instruments, scalpels, rubber gloves, glass bottles and syringes. The Earl must have been using them just minutes earlier.

The next moment a door opened on the other side of the room and in he stepped, wearing a white operating gown.

He stared at us in a most unfriendly way, and did not say a word.

At last Rogers summoned up the courage to speak.

"I beg your pardon, My Lord ... we heard a gunshot."

"Yes," he replied. "But that is no reason for you all to come flocking in."

Then, filled with embarrassment, he said, with a hint of a smile:

"Forgive me … I'm not used to receiving visitors here. Would you mind if we went somewhere a little more congenial?"

And he led us to the room next door, which was furnished rather more conventionally.

"Do take a seat."

"What's been happening?" asked Cynthia. "I was terrified."

"Well, to tell the truth, someone took a shot at me."

Cynthia screamed. The Earl went over to her and stroked her head.

"As you see, I've come to no harm. At the precise moment I bent over to retrieve an instrument I'd dropped. I think, if I had remained upright … but no matter."

But by then we were all on our feet and shouting in confusion at him, forgetting the deference due to his rank.

"Who was it? How? Where?"

"Do please sit down. I can't tell you anything. I've searched the entire floor and found no one. Was the iron door locked?"

"Yes, My Lord," replied Rogers.

"I don't understand any of it. Unless the shot was fired through the open window … But that's impossible. How could anyone get up there—unless he could fly? But Cynthia … and the rest of you … please calm down. No harm has been done; there's no damage, not even to the building. Now if you will excuse me, I'm going to lie down."

"But for Heaven's sake!" cried Osborne. "Whoever did this is clearly still here on the second floor, hiding. Please, allow us to search your apartment."

"No, my boy, that's out of the question. Rogers, and perhaps Ifan, will remain here, and we'll take another look through everything. Now go to bed, and don't let anything trouble you. We Pendragons have nine lives … "

As he spoke, I had the distinct impression that he cast a meaningful glance at me and Maloney. Surely he didn't think that we … ?

And thus, very graciously, he dismissed us.

That was the second night. We stayed up for hours, discussing things. Maloney in particular had some wonderful proposals for solving the mystery, and an equal number of tropical yarns. As for me, I had abandoned all hope of a good night's sleep at Llanvygan.

The next morning, all was revealed to me—or at least, a fair bit. Maloney and Osborne had been indulging themselves in the role of amateur detectives and had established the possibility that while the staff had been diverted by the 'supernatural' gramophone a door could have been left unlocked, allowing someone to slip into the house, who could then have opened the iron door with a skeleton key, and locked it behind him as he left.

Cynthia and I went off to the library. We browsed among the books, but without the enthusiasm of the previous day. I lacked sleep; I was melancholy and restless. And I was no longer in any doubt. My forebodings had been fully justified. I was up to my neck in a dark and dangerous escapade, in the thick of a siege. My greatest desire was to get away from a situation where earls were shot at in my presence. Back to the British Museum, to the impregnable calmness of books …

"'*Inter arma silent musae*,'" I quoted. "I feel I've come here at a very bad moment. I'm an intruder, a reluctant witness of the trials and tribulations of this house. The Earl hasn't honoured me with a single look since I arrived. He obviously isn't happy about my visiting … I must go back to London. I only hope that our friendship—may I call it that?—might continue."

"If you truly are my friend," said Cynthia, "don't leave us now. If for no other reason … if you feel the atmosphere isn't appropriate for your research … then stay a few more days for my sake."

I made an involuntary movement as if to caress her. She drew back in alarm.

"I'm sorry, I'm afraid you misunderstand me. But you are needed here. I need someone, shall we say, whom I can completely trust."

"Then I shall stay until you throw me out. But excuse me … I can't think how I can possibly be of help to you. To be perfectly honest with you, I know very little about folklore."

"I'm not thinking of folklore. It's another matter entirely. My uncle's life."

"How do you mean? Do you think what happened yesterday will be repeated?"

"I don't think it. I know for sure."

"My dear … you're still suffering from the shock of yesterday."

"Doctor, you don't know all the facts. I wouldn't normally have spoken about these things, but now I've no choice. This is the third time in a month that someone's tried to kill my uncle."

"Do you really mean that?"

"I do."

"How?"

"The first time I was there. I was nearly killed myself. My uncle and I went to the seaside—Llandudno—and we were on our way home in the Delage—it's an open-top tourer. I was driving. Suddenly my uncle shouted at me to stop—but he didn't wait for me to brake, he pulled the lever himself, so violently we were both nearly thrown out. We got out, and there—about ten yards ahead of us—was a wire stretched across the road at head height for someone sitting in a car. At that speed, if we hadn't stopped, we would have both been beheaded."

A shudder went through me.

"The strangest thing about it was … that my uncle saw it coming. It was dusk, I tell you, and no one, however keen their eyesight, could have spotted it. He himself can't explain how he did it. He says it was the family fairy, Tylwyth Teg … but that's only his little joke, teasing me about my obsession with folklore."

"And the second time?"

"That I can't tell you exactly. It wasn't here, it was at Pendragon House in London. A few days after my uncle met you at Lady Malmsbury-Croft's he arrived home unexpectedly—much earlier than planned. I'm the only person he's told that someone is trying to kill him … But the whole thing is so very strange … "

"In what way?"

"Well—make of this what you will—he says that poison gas was somehow pumped into his room. But … I'm not sure how to say this … gases don't affect him. In the war … "

This second story I naturally did not believe. The Earl, like so many other people who suffer from nerves, seemed to be obsessed with the notion that someone was out to kill him with poison gas. It was just luck that he had a complementary delusion that he was immune to its effects.

"Well, it certainly explains why he doesn't feel like chatting to me about seventeenth-century mysticism. I think anyone else would have withdrawn the invitation."

"But that would have been ungentlemanly."

"And something else is becoming clear,"—it came to me in a flash. "Do you know that Maloney and I are under constant surveillance?"

"You're imagining things," she replied.

"Of course. I frequently do. But this time there are facts. The cartridges were taken from my revolver. My suitcases were searched. I ought in fact to have left immediately. But somehow … it was all so improbable I couldn't believe it was really happening."

She gazed at me in despair.

"My God, that's dreadful. But please, do try to understand what an extraordinary situation we are in … and who knows what dangers the Earl has been forewarned about …

"All the same, I beg you to stay," she went on. "I know what a sacrifice it will be for you to remain in a place where you could be under such a horrible suspicion … but it's for my sake. Let it be enough for you that I, a member of the family, would unhesitatingly trust my life to you. I have complete faith in my intuition. And my uncle says anyone who loves books cannot be a bad person. You'll see—he'll understand everything soon enough, and make it all up to you.

"But until that time," she continued, holding out her hand to me, "please, please, don't leave me alone. I have no one. My uncle has gone back into his shell. Osborne is completely unreliable. Doctor … this place frightens me."

I stroked her hand, and promised to stay by her side.

I knew I was not in the least like the young heroes of American movies, who would take on and destroy the entire New York underworld if the girl of their heart were in danger … but this was primarily a matter of moral support. Cynthia could not be left to face her fears alone, and she needed help in solving the mystery.

"Cynthia," I asked. "Do you have any idea who could possibly want him dead?"

"None at all, absolutely none."

"What about the Roscoe heirs?" I asked, in another flash of inspiration. I had remembered the murky tales I'd heard from Maloney, during that evening full of suspicion in the London night club.

"Who?" she asked, in surprise.

"What, haven't you heard of William Roscoe?"

"Of course I have. He was a friend of my grandfather's—a very wealthy man. Wait a minute—now I remember—my aunt, the Duchess of Warwick, once warned me never to mention the name in my uncle's presence … but I don't recall why. What do you know, Doctor? Tell me at once."

"I know nothing for certain, just a few words dropped by an unreliable source."

"Still, you must tell me everything."

"Apparently this Roscoe stipulated in his will that his fortune, which would otherwise go to his wife, should pass to the Earl of Gwynedd in the event of his dying an unnatural death. He believed his wife wanted to kill him."

"And?"

"Some time later, he died of a tropical disease—the same one that killed your grandfather, the seventeenth Earl. So the money went to his wife, and I don't know who else. Now the heirs have the notion that your uncle wants to prove that the disease that killed Roscoe was artificially induced by them. If he succeeded, the entire fortune would be his. They imagine that his secret laboratory experiments are directed to this end. And that fear could be behind their attempts on his life."

Cynthia weighed this up.

"That's ridiculous," she said at last. "His biological work is purely theoretical. He's explained it all to me. He's grappling with the fundamental questions of biology—the nature of life, the difference between what lives and what doesn't, and what transitional stages might possibly exist between the two."

"But that isn't enough to reassure the Roscoe heirs."

"True. But I really can't imagine … I cannot think of a single possible reason why he would want to lay hands on all that money. I mean, we're not exactly paupers. It would be quite out of keeping for an Earl of Gwynedd to take active steps to increase his personal wealth. It's simply not in his character. Wealth can only be inherited, and then only from family."

"There may of course be other motives … revenge, retribution … or God knows what."

"That's totally improbable. There's some other secret business here, Doctor. Who knows what ancient blood-feud? … It's as if every single one of our ancestors has been gathering here, these last few days … Pierce Gwyn Mawr is prophesying death and destruction, and the midnight rider has been seen … "

"Does the Earl have any enemies?"

"I've no idea. The fact is, I don't know very much about him. Osborne and I have only lived here for three years, since our mother died. Before that, I hardly ever saw him. All I know is that he's the most magnificent being on earth. The great aristocrats of the past must have been like him. They didn't have to do or say anything remarkable: their mere existence revealed a finer form of life, above and beyond this one. It's impossible to say why everyone holds him in such high esteem. But if noble blood does stand for anything, he's the living incarnation of it. I just can't believe he could have enemies. He's too far above everyone else for there to be any serious differences; though of course, by the same token, he hasn't any friends."

I confess I too felt that the Earl was as she had described him. Some people are born to be served willingly by others.

It isn't easy to explain these unprovoked sympathies, the whole complex magic that made Llanvygan so deeply attractive to me. No doubt there was an element of snobbery in it, a degree of intellectual curiosity, and a bit of love too. And there do exist in the soul such feudal passions as service, respect and devotion.

Had I been a knight errant, I should have offered my services to the lord of the castle, and asked the lady for a ribbon to wear on my shield. Oh to be that happy man, a knight errant!

I kissed her hand. She stood in the gothic arch of the window gazing at me, transfigured by emotion. She was the maid of the castle, I her knight. I mouthed a few incoherent words, in which there was not just a declaration of love but a blessed revival, from under the rubble of years, of my better self. What a shame that those moments when man is noble and pure and akin to the angels are so transient, so fleeting, while that complicated nonentity the Ego is always with us—of which one can speak only in terms of protective tenderness and gentle irony.

By some miracle, the next few days passed calmly and agreeably. Nothing remarkable happened, and I was able to sleep at night. There was no more talk of midnight riders.

The summer was still magnificent, the park as beautiful as parks always are when one walks in them with a girl. I played a great deal of tennis, swam and sunbathed. In short, I was spending my summer holiday in the shadow of danger every bit as calmly as the rich who disport themselves below snow-laden mountains of deadly height.

In time I even came to feel at home in the Llanvygan library, and picked up my studies where I had left off in the British Museum.

The library was particularly rich in seventeenth-century material. Mystical tracts which I knew of only from bibliographical references, things that were not even in the British Museum, I now held reverently in my hands.

The number of German works of the period was very striking. With singular emotion I turned the pages of Simon Studion's unpublished *Naometria*, and first editions of Paracelsus, Weigel and Johann Valentin Andreae, volumes which Asaph Pendragon must have brought back with him after his early years in that country. Over these texts he would have mused and deliberated with his friend Robert Fludd: their cabbalistic symbols were still visible above the archaic gothic script. As I sat there in the gathering dusk, an insignificant mortal in the shadow of the vast ranks of books, the centuries passed before me in procession, in reverse order. Where are the Stuarts, and where is Cromwell now? But books live on, as does man's eternal thirst for them.

It seemed as if I had only to open a door to see directly into the era of Asaph Pendragon. Every now and then I was overwhelmed by a strange, disconcerting happiness. I felt preternaturally old, a relic from the age of folios staring out in astonishment at the mankind of today.

In short, I was in a lyrical mood. I kept breaking off to construct, with much labour, a sonnet in English. Let us suppose: I was in love with Cynthia. That might be one way of approaching the truth, at the expense of a double lie. I wasn't in love, and not with Cynthia.

As a rule I don't fall in love, though it did happen to me once when I was very young. Even if the rather pleasing solemnity I now felt pulsing in my veins could really be termed love, it was not Cynthia I was in love with, but the Lady of the Castle, the maid of Llanvygan.

A woman's worth is furnished by her background, her reputation (good or bad), the lovers she has had, and the world of otherness she has come from. Love is like an old-fashioned landscape painting: in the foreground a diminutive figure, the woman who is loved; behind her mountains and rivers, a rich, grand scenery, charged with meaning.

Cynthia's scenery was Llanvygan and Pendragon, Welsh legend and English history. Whoever married Cynthia would find himself related, however distantly, to the deathless pentameters of Shakespeare and Milton.

But the real Cynthia was simple, warm-hearted and natural, as all true aristocrats are when you get to know them. She had no interest in 'society', nor was she self-centred and demanding the way young girls are who have been spoilt. Because of her mother's recent death she had 'come out' rather later than usual, and rarely mixed with people.

She was sincerely and unaffectedly pleased that I was at Llanvygan, where she had passed so many sad and lonely months, and our friendship grew daily more intimate. She was fond of, rather than passionate about, sport, but she was as enthusiastic a walker as I was and enjoyed displaying her knowledge of folklore while showing me round the local places of interest.

She was extremely communicative. By degrees I got to know all about the garden parties she had attended, and all about her friends. Those who did not go in for folklore ranked rather lower in her esteem. There was only one person she really adored, an older woman, whose name she did not tell me. She surrounded this attachment with a element of romantic secretiveness, and I was instantly jealous.

I had good reason, as the tones in which she spoke of this woman were those of love. In her naivety, and as the person in question was a woman, Cynthia did not conceal her feelings. The relationship greatly exercised my imagination and, to tease me, she became even more secretive.

She came on several occasions to seek me out in the library, but never for more than a short time. She was unwilling to disturb my studies, and I did not betray to what an extent they were lyrical in nature. I had a reputation to maintain.

Once however she caught me in the act. I had piled a stack of old books in front of me and was staring in a trance-like half-dream at the coat of arms with its rose cross on the leather binding.

"What are you doing?" she asked in alarm.

"The Rose Cross … " I murmured.

"Doctor, I've always wanted to ask you to tell me about the Rosicrucians. All I know is that my ancestors belonged to the movement."

"That's almost all anyone knows, Cynthia. Every source agrees that a secret society—the forerunners of the Freemasons—took the name, in Germany, in the seventeenth century. They wanted to make gold. The idea spread to England. Robert Fludd and your ancestor Asaph Pendragon, the sixth Earl, were their leaders. They described themselves as invisible and to this day some strange impenetrability guards their memory. Every time you think you've finally pinned them down you discover it's a fabrication or a fable. Descartes, who was alive at exactly that time, scoured the length and breadth of Germany hoping to meet a live Rosicrucian, and never once succeeded … "

"But you, surely, know all about them, Doctor."

"It's very kind of you to say so, but nothing can be known for certain. Look at this: I've a pile here of four books which their contemporaries considered authentic Rosicrucian documents. This massive tome is the *Chymische Hochzeit Christiani Rosencreutz*."

"Good heavens, there's a death's head on the title page. What is this?"

"It's an allegorical novel. The writer claimed later that it was just a bit of mystification, that he only wanted to poke fun at the alchemists. All the same, he might have intended it seriously."

"And this one?"

"In this, there are two short tracts bound together. They are priceless. This is a first edition, printed in Kassel. One of them, the *Allgemeine Reformation*, is without doubt a lampoon: the writer thoroughly ridicules the Rosicrucians and their like. But there's the second, the *Fama Fraternitatis R C*—that is, *Rosae Crucis*—'The Fame of the Brotherhood of Rosicrucians'. These people were in earnest, but who exactly were they? And then there's this third tract here, the *Confessio Fraternitatis R C*. This was also supposed to be a serious text, but it's all nonsense."

"Tell me, Doctor, who was this Rosencreutz—'Rose Cross'? Or have you already told me?"

"He was a miraculous healer and alchemist who, according to the *Fama Fraternitatis*, brought the hidden wisdom from Arabia, from the Hidden City, where the Arab scholars lived. But it's just a legend. We don't even know when he was alive, or if he really lived at all. Then he died, and was buried, and that's where the story starts to become interesting."

"Do tell me! You know I love legends."

"But this isn't a folk tale. It has a rather strange atmosphere—it makes me altogether uneasy, I can't explain why. Listen to this: after his death, his followers took over the House of the Holy Ghost that he'd built. Several years later, the then Grand Master needed to complete some repairs to the building ... But I tell you what, I'll translate this bit of the text for you from the German:

' ... *then he came upon the memorial tablets, which were of brass and bore the names of the entire fraternity and sundry others. These tablets he desired to take into another, more fitting, room. Where and when Brother Rose Cross*

80

had perished, and in what country he was interred, was not revealed to the ancients, nor did we know either. From one of the tablets there protruded a stout nail, and when with much strength we drew it forth it brought after it a great stone, or incrustation, in the narrow wall, over a hidden door, which it revealed to our amazement and surprise, whereupon we, with happy expectation, broke into the wall and caused the door to move. It bore the inscription, in letters of great size:

POST CXX ANNOS PATEBO
(After one hundred and twenty years, I shall open).

Beneath this was the date of its construction. We did no more that night … and in the morning we opened the door. We found a large chamber, which had seven sides and seven corners; each side was the length of five feet and the height of eight feet. And though the sun was never seen in that room, it was lit from a second sun, which had learnt its radiance from the real one and which hung in the centre over a tombstone bearing a round altar covered with a copper slab, which bore the inscription:

A C R C HOC UNIVERSI COMPENDIUM
VIVUS MIHI SEPULCHRUM FECI

(Living, I built this tomb for myself
in the likeness of the universe.)'"

"What does that mean?"

"The floor was divided up to represent the empires of the earth, while the ceiling represented the celestial spheres. In the chamber they found the secret books containing the ultimate wisdom of the Rosicrucians, and the instruments used in their occult trade."

"And?"

"At this point the narrative breaks off and starts to talk about other things. It suggests that it could well go on to say a great deal more, but these things are not for the ears of the uninitiated … However the non-authentic Rosicrucian writings insist that they opened the tomb and found their master—he was extremely old, and immensely tall—but his body showed no sign of ageing. He was lying there as if alive and merely sleeping."

"I believe I understand why this story has such a hold on you … It's one I seem to have heard before. Don't laugh, but it has such a Welsh flavour. The Welsh could never accept the fact that one of their great men might really be dead. There are so many stories of people living on in their graves, waiting to rise up when the destined hour comes. It's King Arthur biding his time on the isle of Avalon, and Merlin sleeping enchanted under a bush, and Bloody-handed Owain waiting, fully armed, for the great battle … "

"My God," I interrupted, "it isn't just the Welsh … it's hard for anyone to believe that a person simply dies."

"Tell me, Doctor, has it never occurred to you that, shall we say, death … or being dead … is just a transitory state, like sleep, or sickness, or youth … that if the body could be preserved, death itself might come to an end, quite naturally? Think of the clavellina."

"That I cannot."

"Why ever not?"

"I've no idea what it is."

"The clavellina is a tiny, transparent water creature, not unlike the sea-lily. When conditions around it are unfavourable to life its organs become progressively atrophied. Its head, its heart, its stomach all regress, until nothing is left of it but a little heap. And when its surroundings improve again, it starts to regenerate its organs once more."

"That's really interesting," I said. "Fludd's metaphysics have a lot in common with this little heap-creature. According to him, from time to time the soul, or life, withdraws from matter. Matter itself came about when God, who in the beginning filled the whole of space, withdrew into himself, and the emptiness left behind is matter."

"Really? Then isn't it possible that life can withdraw into one part of the body while the rest lies dead … until it wakes again? You know our family motto: '*I believe in the resurrection of the body*'. But I can see you don't enjoy this subject. I'm too much of a Celt. They say the Celts are in eternal revolt against the tyranny of facts … Tell me, instead: what were these Rosicrucians really after?"

"Well, from their books it's actually quite hard to say. They promise all sorts of good things to those who join them. They were particularly proud of four of their branches of knowledge: changing base metals into gold, deliberately prolonging the life of the body, the ability to see things at a distance, and a cabbalistic system for solving all mysteries.

"Apart from that, it can't be said they were very much liked," I continued. "In 1623, for example, fear of them spread through Paris like a wave of mental illness. Customers would appear in the restaurants and bars of the time, and when it came to paying the bill, they simply vanished; or, if they did pay, the gold turned to mud as soon as they'd gone. Innocent French citizens would wake at night to find a mysterious stranger sitting beside them on the bed, who promptly disappeared. The people of Paris responded in the usual way to these terrors: they blamed the foreigners. I'm afraid that in many places they beat them terribly."

"Were you ever in France, Doctor?"

"Of course, many times."

"Do you speak French as well as you speak English?"

"About the same."

It was already getting dark, but I could see that Cynthia was looking at me with growing interest.

"Doctor, you're like the *Encyclopaedia Britannica*. You know everything."

"I do know rather a lot," I replied nervously.

"I believe you even speak Sanskrit."

"Fluently," I replied. But she believed that too.

"And you must surely know the Russian novelists. Tell me something about Dostoevsky or Béla Bartók. I've a friend who never stops talking about them."

"I never met Bartók," I said, untruthfully, shocked at her ignorance. "But I knew old Dostoevsky really well. He and my father were at primary school together, and he often came for supper. He had a beard like Pierce Gwyn Mawr's."

"How lucky you are, to have known such famous people as a child. I'm sure you could even tell me why Aix-la-Chapelle is called Aachen in German."

I didn't tell her, partly because I didn't know, and also because I had suddenly seen through her and become thoroughly annoyed with myself. Women take me in all the time. There are moments when they behave as if they were perfectly human. On such occasions a simple philologist like me will hold forth, launching into

serious expositions, in the belief that the woman is actually interested in what he has to say. But no woman has ever yet taken
an interest in an intellectual matter for its own sake. Either she
wants to woo the man by a display of attention, or she is seeking
to improve her mind, which is even worse. The first of these is
after money; the second is in pursuit of edification, but has other
motives which are no less self-interested: she wants to adopt the
pose of a woman of culture, as if it were some sort of cloak to be
worn at the opera.

I got up and paced angrily back and forth. Cynthia sat staring out from her armchair, lost in reverie. Her gaze was distant,
dreamy, noble. She was like the inhabitant of some Welsh fairytale land that would inspire anyone who had been there with the
profoundest yearning.

But the instant I gauged her true intellectual merit something
was released inside me, and I became aware again of how young
she was, and how lovely. I can never feel much attraction to a
woman whom I consider clever—it feels too much like courting
a man. But once I had realised she was just another sweet little
gosling, I began to woo her in earnest.

"Cynthia," I began, "I really deplore the amount of time I've
been spending with these books. Life passes so quickly. You see, I
grew up so quickly I never even noticed, and just as suddenly I'll
be an old man. And it will all have gone. My memory will fail, and
I'll forget everything I've ever read. When I look back over my life
I shall have to face the fact that I've always been alone."

By now it was quite dark in the room. I stood at the window.
Outside an unusually atmospheric sunset was being projected
onto the screen of the heavens. At such moments sentimental
declarations are twice as effective, according to books and in my
private experience. I proceeded to deploy arguments of a more
personal nature.

"I've never met anyone who understood me so completely. You
are the first woman, Cynthia, with whom I can be truly myself. It's
as if you had once been my sister, or my wife."

Old Goethe was writhing in his grave.

Cynthia got to her feet, dreamily, and came up to me in the bay
of the window. It was the sign I had been waiting for. This time I

knew she would not slap my face. But as I stood there summoning up my courage to manage the business in hand, she asked me, in a voice choking with emotion:

"Oh, Doctor … do you even know algorithms?"

"By heart," I replied, and drew her to me.

I kissed her. She clung to me for quite some time, with no sign of resistance. Visions of sunlit springtime days, of dazzling lakes and azure skies flashed by inside me: as if I were sitting in a train. Life was wonderful, after all.

At last she broke free. She stared at me for a moment, deeply embarrassed, then declared:

"You still haven't told me why Aix-la-Chapelle is called Aachen in German."

It was ten-thirty in the evening. I was seated in my room, in the much-celebrated comfort of an English armchair. In fact I wasn't so much sitting as sprawled out almost supine. I felt too idle to go to bed, and in too much of a daydream to read.

The events of the last few days had fused into a sort of golden haze, from which every so often random flashes leapt out, filling me with alarm. Blended into this haze were the centuries-old atmosphere of Llanvygan Castle, the Earl's aquatic monsters, the Rosicrucians, and Cynthia … Cynthia, I mused—goddess of the moon, Queen of the Night, my latest dalliance, perhaps my future love. Poets had bestowed her celestial name on the great Elizabeth. Cynthia, in whose veins flowed the blood of the line of Gwynedd and with it the secrets of centuries, the accumulated nobility of an ancient race of lords of the mountains, the aurora borealis itself. I congratulated myself on having actually kissed the aurora borealis, Queen Elizabeth and the whole tradition of the English sonnet.

There was a knock at the door. Osborne stepped in. I felt the same fondness for him too.

"Forgive me, but I noticed your light was still on."

"Have a seat," I replied. "Is something the matter? You look so serious."

"Well, my uncle hasn't shown himself for several days … but there's something else. If it goes on like this I'll become superstitious myself. Are you aware, Doctor, that old Habakkuk the Prophet disappeared the day after his attack of Revelations?"

"Yes, I heard about that. The Reverend's account of the episode verged on the miraculous."

"Well, I've found the old boy … But why all this talk? What would you say to a little outing? I just can't make head or tail of the whole business."

"I'll get my coat."

"I'll have a word with Maloney, if he's still up. This is just the thing for him."

The light seemed to be on in his room. We knocked and, hearing his positive reply, pushed the door open.

The light was indeed on, but Maloney was nowhere to be seen. I instantly thought of the Rosicrucians' power to make themselves invisible.

"Where is the fellow?" asked Osborne. "He's just told us to come in."

"Coming," said Maloney's voice, from some indefinable place that was clearly not in the room.

Seconds later a pair of legs appeared in the window frame, dangling from above. Then their owner, dressed entirely in black, leapt lightly down onto the floor.

"Training," he explained, nonchalantly.

"But why at night?" I asked.

"We Connemarans always climb at night. When it's too dark to see you have to trust your instincts, and they never let you down. If there aren't any rocks, a good wall will do, or the trees down in the park."

"Right. Well, come and see what old Habakkuk is up to. Bring your rope."

We got in the Delage and drove for about twenty minutes down the main road, under a brilliant moon.

"From here we proceed on foot—don't want to disturb him. He needn't be aware of us. He didn't notice me here yesterday."

For some time we continued along the road. No one spoke. The profound silence, the dark, distant mountains in all their immensity and the silver moonlight held us in their grip. Above us, at a terrifying height, towered the rock on whose peak stood the ruins of Pendragon Castle.

Osborne turned off the road and we made our way through the dense thicket. For some fifteen minutes we struggled on through the trees, slithered down precipitous slopes, and at last found ourselves before a high stone wall.

"These are the remains of the old wall that used to surround the whole of Pendragon," said Osborne. "Now, where's the gap? To the left, or right?"

After some time we found it.

"Look," said Osborne. "You can see this gap has been made quite recently. You used to have to go round the entire wall to get to Llyn-y Castle—the Castle Lake. Who on earth would have made this way through? And why? On we go now: quiet as you can."

Maloney pushed on ahead soundlessly, and at great speed. Under my feet, however, the brushwood crackled and snapped, and I kept getting murderous glances from the others.

We arrived at an almost sheer rockface.

"We have to climb it," said Osborne. "From up there we'll have a brilliant view of the entire lake, and no one will see us."

Before I had even begun to consider how we might make the ascent, Maloney had reached the top. He undid the rope he had around his waist and promptly pulled us up. Osborne went first, with no problem. I followed, with great difficulty.

"You'd make a pretty feeble monkey," Maloney observed, contemptuously.

From the other side of the rock we looked down on to a small lake, glittering in the moonlight. I had never before seen anything quite so unearthly. Across the water, huge trees ringed the shore, watching over the stillness under the soaring peak of Pendragon. It was a lake from a fairytale, with the fairy's coral castle sunk in its depths.

And there, in a strange little boat shaped like a tub, sat old Pierce Gwyn Mawr, quite motionless. With his flowing white beard draped over his folded arms, he stared straight ahead, through half-closed eyes. He might have been sleeping.

"What's the old chap doing?" said Maloney, restless as always.

"I've no idea," replied Osborne. "Perhaps he's waiting for Tylwyth Teget—that's the fairy who lives in the lake. He's obviously waiting for something, or someone. Perhaps we should too."

We waited a very long time, lying at full stretch up on the rock. Maloney became increasingly impatient. Finally he suggested we should either throw something into the water to wake the old boy up, or else go home. The eeriness of the place clearly had the same sort of effect on his highly instinctive nature as a ghost would on a dog.

But Osborne and I continued gazing, enraptured, at the fantastical scene. It was a Hans Christian Andersen illustration come to life, and my dormant child's consciousness was stirring in me, like the soft strains of a distant violin.

Suddenly the prophet raised his arms and began to sing. His strange, senile, whistling voice entirely failed to string the notes together into a tune: each protracted utterance seemed to be individually torn out of him, to be followed by another quite disconnected from it. The overall effect was distinctly weird, not so much song as incantation. The words, being Welsh, were incomprehensible to me.

And then, no less suddenly, the bushes facing us on the far side of the lake parted, and someone came down to the water's edge. The old man ended his incantation, turned towards him and, without getting up, made a profound bow.

By this time the newcomer was standing on a small rock, every contour of his face clearly visible in the moonlight.

He was a powerfully-built man, very old, of almost preternatural size and dressed in black, a close-fitting Spanish outfit of long ago, like those worn by the night guards at Llanvygan. Only the collar was different, an enormous white ruff the size of a millstone. And the face ... was that of a statue, ancient, timeless, quite beautiful in its august dignity, without a trace of humanity: the bleak, unfeeling face of a Northern god.

He began to speak, in a low but penetrating voice. The language was again Welsh. Pierce seized his oars and rowed his coracle swiftly to the shore. He climbed out, secured it to a tree, kissed the stranger's hand, then vanished into the thicket. The stranger remained standing where he was for a while longer.

Slowly but unmistakably he was turning in the direction of our rock. Then he stopped and glared pointedly in our direction, as if he could actually see us. With a face of terror, Maloney gripped my arm. The unwavering stare of those wolf-like eyes produced an unbearable tension in all of us. I was afraid I might leap up at any moment. Maloney was uttering strange, soft cries.

The stranger turned on his heel and vanished into the gloom of the huge trees.

"Time to go," said Osborne.

He let himself speedily down the rock, and we followed him. We took a short cut through the thicket, then went out through the wall and back to the main road.

Maloney wasn't too pleased with this.

"I say … let's at least try and see where they went."

But Osborne warned him against it.

We almost ran towards the Delage. Though we had so carelessly abandoned it, it was waiting for us amiably enough on the road. After the Castle Lake, the wall, and the ghostly old men, there was something very reassuring about the car—the triumph of technology and the comforting familiarity of the twentieth century.

We were driving home at considerable speed, when Osborne suddenly stopped the car on a bend.

"Take a look at that," he said, and pointed to Pendragon, now clearly visible from where we were.

The old tower, without question or possibility of optical illusion, was filled with light.

"Who's living there?" I asked.

"According to my information, no one has for two hundred years," said Osborne. And he set the car moving again. He was clearly agitated, and unwilling to talk for fear of betraying the fact. We returned to Llanvygan in silence.

"Come to my room and have a drink," he suggested.

After three large tumblers of strong whisky—which we reckoned we had thoroughly earned—Osborne's tension began at last to ease.

"Do sit down," he began. "So, what did you make of all that?"

"What do you make of it?—that's the question," said Maloney. "I can't believe you don't know the old gent. He even looks a bit like you. He must be your uncle, or the ghost of your late grandfather."

"Call me Jack Robinson if I've ever seen him before."

"But, somehow, he knew we were there. He was looking towards us as if he really could see us. I don't know why, but it was a pretty nasty feeling."

"Where could they possibly have gone?" Osborne wondered. "You can't go anywhere from the far side of the lake. Twenty yards from the water the rock face starts, with Pendragon up on the peak. All I can think is that there must be some secret entrance to the castle. By the time we got to the bend in the road they had made it all the way to the top and put the light on in the tower."

"It is possible," I remarked. "I never yet read of an old castle that didn't have a secret entrance. And that's not just in books but in actual reality. It's one of those rare situations where literature shows some sort of connection with real life."

"Then what we have to do is quite straightforward," said Maloney. "Tomorrow, in daylight, we'll take a look at the far end of the lake. Ten to one I'll find you your secret entrance. We Connemarans are pretty good at that sort of thing."

"In any case, we have to go back to Pendragon," I added, "to see who's living up there."

"Well, well," mused Osborne. "Something in me doesn't like the idea at all. Because, you see: just suppose the man we saw is in fact living up there. Whether he's human or a spirit, he's obviously a gentleman. Have we the right to trouble him without an invitation?"

"I take your point," I replied. "An Englishman's home is his castle. All the more, if your home *is* a castle. On the other hand, to some extent Pendragon belongs to you, as heir apparent to the Earldom of Gwynedd. You've more right than anyone to be there—not counting the Earl himself, of course."

"There's something in that," he said. "I'll sleep on it."

"One further question," I went on. "What made you decide to

visit the Castle Lake yesterday? You never mentioned that midnight jaunts were a favourite pastime."

"I don't go in for them at all. I like to sleep at night, however petty bourgeois that may sound. But why I went is a story in itself. Have a look at this."

He opened his desk drawer and pulled out a slip of paper.

"Someone stuck this on the windscreen of the little Rover yesterday morning."

I studied the paper. It was covered in a strange, archaic writing, of the sort you find in seventeenth-century manuscripts in the British Museum. No one nowadays writes with such a flourish. Our hands have altered their shape since then.

It read: '*Pendragon, forte si vellis videre Petrum senem vade ad lacum castelli media nocte ubi et alium rerum mirabilium testis eris.*'

"It's Spanish," declared Maloney, "and, I'm sorry to say, it's not a language I ever learnt."

"Not at all. It's Latin," said Osborne, and translated it: "'Pendragon, if you wish to see old Peter (i.e. Pierce), go to the Castle Lake at midnight, where you will be witness to other miraculous things as well.'"

"If this was actually written by the old boy himself," said Maloney, nodding thoughtfully, " I'd say he'd be a teacher by profession, or why on earth would he write in Latin? Anyway, he's a real show-off."

"Perhaps he doesn't know English?" Osborne observed.

"Or else … " I blurted out, then stopped short. The stupidity of my idea surpassed even Maloney's.

It had occurred to me that the man who had written it—the stranger by the lake—was in fact so old, so truly ancient, that had he written in English his archaic turn of phrase would have been incomprehensible. That was why he had chosen the timeless, unchanging language of Latin. But of course I couldn't utter this daft notion, which could have occurred only to a philologist.

"And did you see the old gent yesterday too?" asked Maloney.

"No," replied Osborne, "only Habakkuk, sitting in his coracle, as he was tonight. The other chap didn't appear. Or he might have, only I didn't wait long enough to find out."

At this point we went off to bed, each nursing his own private theory about what had occurred. Maloney was no doubt wracking his brain for the most spectacular and Connemaran method of catching the old man.

The next morning a boy from the village called on me. He had been sent by the Rev Dafyd Jones. He handed me a letter, the gist of which was that the vicar desired to speak with me urgently and in the strictest confidence. He asked me to meet him in the little graveyard behind the church at ten, adding, with a profusion of apologies, that it was a matter of extreme importance.

I had absolutely no idea what it might be. Against what species of non-existent horror could this excitable visionary be seeking my help? Then I recalled the previous night's events at the lake, and I hastened off, in some agitation, down to the village.

I had no problem finding the little graveyard behind the church, with its lovely trees beckoning to eternal rest. The parson was already there, pacing back and forth, and gesticulating to himself in the restrained manner imposed by his ecclesiastical dignity and by British reserve. I thought he might be rehearsing his Sunday sermon.

When I called out to him he gave such a start that I became alarmed myself.

"Yes, yes, yes, yes," he gabbled. "You, sir, are a well-known physician."

"Sir, I am not a well-known physician," I replied in astonishment. These people had obviously conspired to make me a medical doctor.

"I see," said the priest, "it's a secret. The Earl keeps his activities secret. But in vain. All in vain. Because, you see, it has come to the light of day. What never could bear the light of day. Do you know, sir, what was caught in the Castle Lake this morning?"

"In the Castle Lake? What was?"

He gazed at me in triumph, as at a man exposed.

"Come."

He led me with quick, short steps to a small hut, where the macabre tools of the grave-digger leant against a wall. It was a dark, damp, unfriendly place. In a corner stood a table with something lying on it. Though I couldn't make out what it was, in the darkness it filled me with a most unpleasant feeling.

"This is what was caught," he announced, bringing his torch to bear on it.

One of the Earl's monsters lay there, lifeless.

It was no longer transparent but a shapeless lump of jelly, in the early stages of decomposition. It was revolting.

"Do you recognise it?" the vicar asked.

"I do. It's one of the Earl's miraculous animals. How did it get into the Castle Lake?"

"That's something you ought to know."

"Me?"

"Yes. I implore you, as an immortal soul, to do something about it. This sort of thing cannot carry on. I can't remonstrate with him—I depend on him for everything. You, sir, must take action. He cannot pollute God's pure lakes with these unspeakable monsters."

"How was this one found?"

"I shall tell you. Do you know that Pierce Gwyn Mawr has disappeared? Someone—a half-crazed peasant—told me he'd seen Pierce's ghost rowing on the Castle Lake one moonlit night. He wasn't alone … "

The vicar seized my arm, glanced furtively around, and continued in a whisper:

"He wasn't alone. There was someone with him. A giant, he said, in strange black garments like the ones worn by the night watchmen of the Castle. My first thought was … yes, there was no other conclusion … it was the midnight rider. But now I know who it really was. The monster has betrayed him."

"Who was it?"

"Who else could it be but the Earl of Gwynedd? He was hiding the monster in the Castle Lake. We went there at sunrise. The waves washed it ashore … "

But it was not the Earl of Gwynedd, I said to myself. He might have looked like the Earl, but it was someone quite different. Or, who knows … ?

But I said not a word about my own nocturnal adventures. Stay out of this, don't get yourself involved … Janos Bátky from Budapest. It's no business of yours … Mere scientific curiosity …

"You are a famous doctor," the vicar suddenly began, in a rather different parsonical tone. "The Hippocratic oath requires you to do no harm, but to serve mankind in its suffering. As a physician of the soul I appeal to you, I implore you, I require you with the full weight of my authority, to abandon your horrible experiments forthwith."

" Sir, you are mistaken … "

"I am not mistaken. I know everything. The creature is an axolotl; it comes from Mexico. The Earl brought it back from his travels in America. There it is much smaller. By some secret and unnatural means the Earl has grown it to ten times the size God made it. With an extract of cow's thyroid. It's an abomination."

"Why an 'abomination'?"

"I also know what the Earl does with these animals. He suspends their vital functions. He freezes them. He poisons them. Then he revives them again. Some of his axolotls have died as many as ten times, and are still living."

"That's amazing!"

"And I know why the Earl is doing this."

"Why?" I demanded, seizing his arm.

"The Pendragons' motto—or rather their curse! '*I believe in the resurrection of the body.*' This heresy has led to the ruin of the greatest sons of the house—Asaph Pendragon, Bonaventura Pendragon, and now the present Earl."

"How can a belief bring a man to ruin?"

"The Earl has brooded over it so long it has clouded his understanding. Can you not see the connection? He wants the power for himself to raise the dead … the dead Earls at rest in the vaults of Pendragon."

Now I felt certain I was talking to a lunatic. As Osborne had said: a degree of mild abnormality is essential for anyone who crosses the threshold of Llanvygan.

"Excuse my interrupting, Reverend, but does the Earl ever discuss his experiments with you?"

"The Earl? How could you think it? The Earl considers me an idiot. I owe my parish to that fact. He would never tolerate an intelligent priest in the neighbourhood."

"Then how do you know all these details?"

"From Dr McGregor, poor man."

"From whom?"

"From Dr McGregor."

McGregor … where had I heard the name? Of course, the mysterious telephone caller …

"Who was this Dr McGregor?"

"You don't know? He was the young doctor who was here a few months ago to help the Earl with his experiments. A decent, upright Scotsman, a very good man—apart from his experiments. But … he came to a bad end. A motoring accident. He's dead. He was your predecessor. Think about it, before it's too late. Think, sir, of your immortal soul. I'm sure I can count on you. I see in your eyes that beneath your hardened exterior a human heart is beating, one that is capable of understanding … Give me your word."

Good Heavens, get this madman out of here. What has any of this to do with me—this Castle Lake, these glutinous corpses? … I'm leaving this afternoon.

"Reverend, on my word of honour, I am not a medical doctor. As I live and breathe. My father and mother and all my aunts wanted me to be a doctor, but I had no talent for it whatsoever."

"You aren't a doctor?" he asked, in deep amazement. "Then what are you?"

"Er … it's not easy to define. Let's say, for the sake of simplicity, a historico-sociographer. Or something like it. But by no means a doctor. Upon my word, I've never witnessed a dissection in my life."

The parson clutched his head.

"More complication … Historico-whatever … then why did you let me say so much? About such dreadful secrets? Excuse me … delighted to make your acquaintance, quite delighted … "

"The pleasure is mine."

I took a deep breath and made off rapidly.

That same afternoon we all set off for Pendragon.

Passing through the village, we met the Rev Jones. Etiquette required that we stop for a little chat.

"Tell me, vicar," said Osborne, "when were you last up at Pendragon?"

"Not for ages. Five months ago, when some archaeologists came and I took them up."

"Have you heard any talk of someone living up there now, in the ruins?"

"I have indeed," he replied after some hesitation, and rather nervously. "Several people have noticed lights in the tower."

"Who do they think it might be?"

"We'd prefer not to say, if you don't mind. Lately the Earl has been going up there rather more often. It could be him, spending the night up there. Possibly he has a guest up there. It's not for us to enquire."

He stared straight ahead, clearly embarrassed.

"All the same," continued Osborne, "it seems unlikely that such a strange event wouldn't be discussed in the village. Tell me candidly what people are saying."

"Osborne, please don't think that I pay attention to the foolish gossip of peasants," he replied, colouring deeply. "Besides, the Earl owns the castle, he can do what he likes up there. I for one can't imagine a gentleman such as himself entertaining his lady friends in so bleak a place as the tower."

Osborne roared with laughter.

"Lady friends? That's not very likely. At most, the Pendragons tolerate women within the limits of marriage, and even then without much enthusiasm … Now, we have a notion to go up there. Won't you join us, vicar? We might well need you for a spot of exorcism."

The vicar went pale.

"Osborne … Do you really intend going there?"

"Of course. I see no reason why I shouldn't."

"Oh dear God," … He wrung his hands. "It's impossible, impossible … My dear sister, as you know, is endowed with some remarkable abilities."

"I know."

"Just this morning, she said … "

"Well?"

"That some mortal danger awaited you if you went up to Pendragon."

"Sensational. How would she know that?"

"Don't forget, she foresaw the recent attempt on the Earl's life, which almost succeeded. I didn't mention it then because I didn't fully trust her abilities, I didn't want to cause unnecessary alarm, or be thought superstitious. My conscience has troubled me ever since for my faint-heartedness."

"Tell me, vicar … Could we not discuss this with Miss Jones herself?"

"But of course—that would be best of all. We should be greatly honoured if you would visit our humble abode."

We stepped out of the car. The vicarage was a few yards away, and we went in.

Miss Jones was seated beside the window in the back room. She apologised for receiving us sitting down.

The tiny old woman was almost completely hidden under the pile of blankets. Only her long, narrow and remarkably ugly face could be seen. She had the intense, burning eyes of visionaries and myopics, that seem to gaze inwards rather than out.

"Jane," the parson began, rather anxiously, "Osborne desires to go up to Pendragon."

The old woman's face became convulsed, as if she'd received an electric shock. She voiced some meaningless sounds, regained her capacity for speech with much difficulty, then said:

"Dear, dear, dear Osborne, do not go to Pen-Annwn. Penn-Annwn is the mouth of Satan. A terrible time awaits the whole House of Pendragon. You are every one of you in mortal danger. For you in particular, it would be death to enter the grounds of Pen-Annwn."

"Thank you very much for the depth of your concern for me, Miss Jones. But, as an interested party, and an admirer of the science of prophecy, I'm enormously curious to discover exactly how you can know this with the certainty of something you'd read in a newspaper."

She became completely calm, and deadly serious.

"Do you believe in the power of dreams?" she asked.

"No, I don't," he replied. "If I did, I should long ago have had some terrible experiences with women. I often dream of one who turns out to have no face. Then I need to climb this staircase, but

I always slip back down. But this has never happened to me in real life."

"I believe in dreams," I chipped in.

"Really?" the old woman said.

"In psychoanalytic terms."

"In what?" she asked. She was a little behind the times.

"Well, it isn't the sort of thing one would explain to a young lady."

"Whether you believe in dreams or not … " she began: "if you don't, so much the worse for you."

There could be no more joking. It was obvious that the old woman would be deeply offended if we didn't take her seriously.

"Would you please, Miss Jones, tell us your dream, and explain its meaning," said Osborne.

The old woman's face assumed an expression of satisfaction.

"Pull your chairs up closer and listen carefully. Last night I dreamed I was a young girl, walking outside, along the bank of the river. I was wearing an enormous Florentine hat."

This, for a start, stretched the imagination.

"And Arthur Evans … did you know Arthur Evans? No, you couldn't have known him. But I'm not going to tell you everything, only the most important things. Well, I told Arthur to go on ahead, and I'd follow just behind. And then suddenly there it was, standing before me, the dog … Do you understand? The dog."

The old woman began to cough, expressively and heart-rendingly.

"Forgive me, what dog?" Osborne asked, when Miss Jones had done coughing. "This one here?"—and he pointed to the half-dead Pekinese at her feet.

"Oh no, it wasn't a dog, it was an angel. The dog was standing there, don't you see? The one with the white coat and the red ears."

"Ah."

"I was terribly afraid. But I couldn't run away. Then the dog looked at me and asked, 'What are you having for your tea?' 'Cauliflower,' I said. 'And coffee. Oh yes, and there was a little strawberry cake,' I told him. I didn't want to be less than truthful.

'Young shoots must be eaten,' he said. 'They're very nourishing. It's what I'm having today.' 'And where are the young shoots?' 'In my head,' said the dog. And there was something green sprouting from his head. This frightened me so much I woke up."

"A very interesting and instructive tale," said Osborne. "I particularly liked the bit about the strawberry cake: tell the truth and shame the Devil. It's just that I don't see where I, and Pendragon, come in."

"You don't understand? Truly? But it's as clear as day. The dog—of course you know this, don't pretend otherwise—was Cwn Annwn, the dog of Hell. The young shoot it wanted to eat was you, Osborne, the young shoot of the family. And the dog's head, the head of Cwn Annwn, is Pen-Annwn. Pen is Welsh for head. Pen-Annwn is the true, the Welsh, name for Pendragon. Dreams always speak in Welsh."

"I see."

"Well then … dear Osborne … promise me, a poor old soul, that you will never go up to Pendragon."

For a moment he hesitated. Then, to our great surprise, he gave his word. We took our leave of the vicar and his sister, and climbed back in the car. Osborne drove out of the village, towards Pendragon.

"So what now?" asked Maloney. "We're not going up?"

"Of course we are. But I had to promise. I know the old girl. She'd die of worry. The poor old thing has been on the point of death these three years, anyway. She's particularly fond of me. Besides … what a sensation if I really did die now up in Pendragon. The prophecy would be fulfilled. I'd become a legend, like my ancestors who lived in nobler times. I'd be like one of those Homeric heroes whose death is prefigured three cantos beforehand. Sensational."

At the bend in the road he stopped the car and we debated whether to look for the secret entrance or go on up the usual way. In the end my view prevailed: given that people in those days built secret entrances precisely to be secret, we had little hope of finding it unless we stumbled on it by sheer chance. Much simpler to go up the proper way. And so we did.

The old abandoned track was the one formerly used by

horsemen and was not excessively steep. The car was able to get almost to the top. Just below the ruins we were at last forced to get out and continue up a series of broken steps, overgrown with moss.

Of the old castle, only the walls remained. The roofs and upper storeys had been stripped away by the centuries. The ground had risen above the level of the stone floor and grass had covered it with a green carpet. The walls reared up crazily, like theatrical scenery, with the sky lowering down above our heads in place of the vanished ceilings.

We made our way through echoing squares that had once been halls. Only the window apertures had retained their original outline, defying the bombardment of the ages. Devoid of glass and sightless, they maintained their Gothic contours, in the form of that special English variation the ogee arch, which soars upwards, thinks again, and deviates into a horizontal ridge.

We finally reached the west wing, the best preserved section of the entire castle. Here even the roof remained. We traversed rooms that were more like rocky caves, stirring up the bats as we went, before arriving, to our surprise, in a little courtyard with the ancient tower rising up before us.

The tower was perfectly intact. From all sides, at irregular intervals, narrow windows gazed down without expression. The keep had probably once been a prison, as was the old practice, and interior lighting had never been regarded as a matter of importance. The sheer, almost unbroken expanse of its bleak walls exercised a forbidding power over the viewer.

We walked all round the circular structure, examining everything minutely, but could find no sign of human life. Nor indeed could we find an entrance.

"What's this, then?" asked Maloney. "Did your ancestors fly in through the air?"

"On ceremonial occasions, naturally," said Osborne, "but I believe there should be a pedestrian entrance for working days as well. I seem to remember having been shown it once."

He led us back to the west wing where, after a brief search, we came across some stone steps, in almost pristine condition. We made our way down them and arrived at a corridor lit by holes cut in the roof.

"It runs under the courtyard," said Osborne. "The entrance is at the far end."

We followed it all the way, coming to a halt before a vast oak door reinforced by ancient iron bands that made me think of the Seven Seals.

"I don't remember this door," said Osborne. "Either it wasn't here when I came, or it must have been open."

As we feared, it was locked.

"Well, so far and no further," he went on. "This is where the interesting stuff begins—right under our noses, and it's locked away. The story of my life."

"We should have a go—we might be able to get it open," Maloney suggested. "I've managed quite a few in my time. We Connemarans know about these things. True, this one looks pretty serious. The mechanism looks like the inside of an old clock."

"No, don't bother," said Osborne. "You probably wouldn't succeed, and anyway it wouldn't have been locked if we were meant to open it. Let's do the decent thing."

We made our way back, somewhat downcast.

"Let's take a look at that room next to the stairs. We might find something interesting in there."

The room was vaulted, dimly-lit, and empty. We were just about to leave when, having adjusted to the semi-darkness, my eye fell on something familiar hanging on the wall.

"Look, it's the Rose Cross!"

A finely-carved stone cross, with stylised stone roses at its four points, stood out in relief against the wall.

Suddenly Maloney called out: "Don't you see?—the stone around the cross, and the cross itself, aren't the same stone as the walls."

"Well, of course," I replied. "It's a relief; it was attached at later date."

"Yes, but what if … what if … ?" He said no more but went up to it, fiddled with it for a few moments, and behold, the cross moved. Very slowly, he rotated it.

At the same moment a section of the wall moved with it, drawing inwards like a door opening. The mouth of the secret entrance stood before us.

"Shall we go down?" we asked one another. In the pitch dark we could make out nothing of what lay beyond. Maloney produced a small torch.

"We absolutely must. Who knows, we might even find treasure. Come on, don't worry about it. Trust my instincts as a rock climber."

We made our way along a narrow, damp corridor to an antiquated spiral stairway. We began to descend, going round and round the stout stone column at its centre, for what seemed hours. Finally we reached the bottom.

We found ourselves in a vast, vaulted room, the far end of which could not be seen. From what we could make out by the light of the torch, it contained a row of elongated rectangular tables.

Approaching nearer we realised they were not tables. They were stone coffins, all bearing the Pendragon coat of arms. Rose crosses everywhere. We were in the crypt.

We did a tour around the walls. Oh, how vast that crypt was! Whoever constructed it could have had no doubt that his family would multiply down the centuries, and had provided amply for them when they returned to the womb of the castle.

"Is this crypt still used?" I asked Osborne.

"No. I didn't even know it existed. Since the seventeenth century the family have been buried in the park at Llanvygan.

"I think we should go back now," he concluded. I readily agreed. I'd had enough. The spiral stair and the crypt had exhausted me. My old misgivings had begun to return and I couldn't wait to step into the light of day. Subterranean wanderings of this kind don't entirely agree with me.

"Wait a second," said Maloney. "Just now, when we were going round the walls, I noticed another of those crosses. There could be another door behind that one too. Maybe those old fellows used them for handles."

We located the rose cross, though it was somewhat different from the first. Beneath it was an inscription. The moment I finished reading the inscription I staggered back, and would have fallen had Maloney not caught me.

"What is it? What did you see?" they asked, in some alarm.

"It's exactly what was in the book!" I cried out—in Hungarian—and was surprised they failed to understand me.

POST CXX ANNOS PATEBO
(After one hundred and twenty years, I shall open.)

The very words on the entrance to the grave of Rosacrux.

Maloney had started to loosen my necktie.

"No, no, leave me alone, there's nothing wrong with me," I said, as I came to. "I've read about this place, I know all about it. There must be a door here. And behind it is something really amazing."

A closer look at the wall revealed the faint outline of a door. Maloney manipulated the rose cross for a while, and it swung open. The three of us leapt back in fright, struck by the light that poured through the opening, brighter than any light bulb.

And then ... it was just as in the book.

We entered a seven-sided room. The floor was engraved with mystical figures representing the nations of the world; the ceiling likewise, representing the heavenly spheres. And at the centre of the room floated the indefinable white glow of the luminous body, the other, the subterranean sun, that the old volumes had described.

As if I had been there before, I boldly led my companions deeper into the room, and pointed out to them the altar and the inscription:

ACRC
HOC UNIVERSI COMPENDIUM VIVUS
MIHI SEPULCHRUM FECI
(Living, I built this tomb for myself
in the image of the universe)

We were standing over the grave of the legendary Rosacrux. The story that had been derided for centuries was in fact true. We had come to the House of the Holy Ghost. There stood the altar, inscribed exactly as the *Fama* had recorded it. And over it, the ever-burning flame.

But then ... perhaps the rest was also true? If so, under the altar we would certainly find ... the body of Rosacrux—or the man who had called himself Rosacrux—perfectly preserved despite the passing of centuries.

Could I possibly dare?

But intellectual curiosity, the strongest of all my passions, began to master my superstitious fears.

"Give me a hand," I said to the others. "Let's raise the altar and take a look at the grave itself."

Maloney crossed himself and drew back. Osborne and I applied ourselves to the weight. But it moved as easily as if it had been expecting us. Beneath it lay a stone slab of the sort you see on tombs. Engraved on it was the Rose Cross of the Pendragons, and around it, the family motto:

I BELIEVE IN THE RESURRECTION OF THE BODY

and, a little lower down, the inscription:

HERE LIETH ASAPH CHRISTIAN PENDRAGON
SIXTH EARL OF GWYNEDD

I stood there, deep in intense thought, over the tomb of the midnight rider. What could explain this mystery? It was the tomb of Rosacrux, as described in the ancient books, and it was also the tomb of Asaph Pendragon. There was only one possible explanation. Rosacrux and Asaph were one and the same person. The four letters of the inscription reinforced my conclusion. ACRC could only mean Asaph Christian Rosae Crucis.

This discovery was greater than any I could ever have made had I read my way through the entire Pendragon library. I had found the historical basis of the legend of the Rose Cross. For a brief moment I saw, in my mind's eye, the volume unfolding in which I laid the foundations of my international reputation as a scholar.

Then I remembered the tomb and the body. The real wonder was still to come.

"What do you think: could we manage to lift this stone?"

"I don't think we have the right," said Osborne. "We can't disturb my ancestor's rest out of idle curiosity."

"But, Osborne, you must understand. This isn't idle curiosity; it's curiosity of quite a different kind. If everything else is true to the description, under this stone slab we shall find the body of Asaph Pendragon, uncorrupted and intact."

Maloney interposed:

"Let's just get out of here. I don't like any of this. A grave is a grave and the dead are dead. Better to let them be. The whole place is so creepy I just wish to God I'd never come."

"Now listen, Doctor," Osborne added. "We'll either succeed in opening it, or not. If we do, we'll have two alternatives. Either we'll find a skeleton—which is the more probable—or else everything in your book is true and we'll find Asaph Pendragon's body ... lying there, perfectly intact, with his arms folded on his breast and his finger bearing the magic rings described in the family tradition ... Well, Doctor, forgive me, but I have no wish to see it. Something in me protests against prying into the secrets of the dead."

He was deathly pale, staring at me with eyes of terror.

I realised nothing could be done. I had come up against the timidity, the discretion, the sheer lack of curiosity of this island race. Had I in any way insisted, they would have thought me utterly cynical, or something worse.

While I was locked in argument with Osborne, Maloney was studying the altar. A sudden movement caught my eye, as the slab covering the tomb began to move back, just as the two doors had done. Maloney had found another rose cross and, half-unconsciously, had been manipulating it in the same way that he had before.

The stone slab revealed an opening through which we could see a large, four-sided pit, in the centre of which stood a catafalque, like a bed pillowed with old damask cushions: a bed from which the sleeper had already risen. There was no trace of the body, no bones to be seen, no legendary rings.

"If nothing else, the rings at least ought to be there," I stated. "But in an enclosed space like this bones should also have lasted three hundred years. As you see, the pillows are as new."

"The tomb's been robbed and the bones removed," Maloney said.

"Or, his earthly remains were reinterred somewhere else, in some previous age," Osborne conjectured. "We'll have to ask my uncle: he'll know."

Once more, I took a good look at everything in the vault, closely examining the body of light. But I could form no idea of what it might consist. We turned to go.

We closed the door carefully behind us. I had a moment's concern that I hadn't put out the light as we went; then I reflected that this particular light had been burning for three hundred years, and continued on my way.

We passed through the crypt and laboured up the spiral stairs. Reaching the top, we noticed that the corridor along which we had first come to it led in two different directions. No one could remember whether the entrance lay to the left or the right. We eventually decided it must be to the right, and set off.

But in fact we should have gone to the left, as we discovered only after passing through several underground rooms. In the total darkness, barely penetrated by Maloney's torch, it was hard to find any bearings at all. Finally, with considerable unease, we admitted to one another that we had no idea how to get back. From each of the pitch-black rooms several other rooms would open out, and they were all identical.

"Trust my instinct," Maloney repeated. "Connemarans have good eyes for the dark. I don't say this always applies to me, but I do have my days."

We put our trust in his instinct.

This subterranean wandering had a strangely familiar feel. I had so often dreamed that I was walking down endless dark corridors, not knowing where I was going, and in mounting terror. I knew there was one door I must not open, a room I was forbidden to enter or something unspeakable would happen to me.

Maloney went ahead with the torch. Osborne and I tried to keep close behind, in hopes of at least seeing something. But his instinct carried him along so rapidly, and our way was so meandering, that we finally lost sight of both him and his torch.

I staggered on after Osborne, unable to make anything out, and then, at a bend in the passage, fell somehow further behind, with only my ears now to guide me. From time to time Maloney would give a shout to tell us which way to go.

Osborne, now fully ten paces ahead of me, suddenly cried out in terror. I rushed towards him.

"Doctor, have you a match?"

"No … but my lighter might work … "

I tried it. We gazed around, in its dim, flickering radiance. At first we noticed nothing unusual, then, a few steps along, in the direction we were supposed to have taken, an open trapdoor gaped. Had we gone any further we—or rather Osborne, being the one in front—would have plummeted into its pitch-black emptiness

"Didn't you hear anything?" he asked, struggling to master his shock.

"Only you, when you yelled out."

"Doctor, do you know what happened? … Just as I got there, someone caught hold of my arm and said, 'Stop!' So I stopped. Didn't you see, or hear, anything?"

"No."

"Very strange. If I'd taken another three steps, Miss Jones would have been proved right."

Meanwhile the light reappeared: Maloney had returned.

"Why aren't you coming?" he shouted. "What's going on here?"

"Stay where you are!"

He came to a halt. We closed the trapdoor.

"How come you didn't fall down it?" Osborne asked.

"I suppose I went some other way. That's Connemara instinct for you."

We stood there for a long time, deep in thought. We were all shocked, our minds filled with superstitious notions of fate. Eventually we set off again, and soon found ourselves back in the daylight.

But by the time we got back to Llanvygan one thought was nagging away inside my head with such unpleasant persistence it took all the pleasure from my amazing discovery. Even the crestfallen faces of my fellow scholars were banished from my mind by the idea: Maloney must have found and deliberately opened the trapdoor, so that Osborne would fall into it.

Back at Llanvygan, we found a lot more going on than usual. The Earl had returned.

Over dinner I told Cynthia I had found the tomb of Rosacrux, and explained to Osborne how I had known of its existence.

Osborne listened with unusual seriousness, like a man in the grip of a major spiritual crisis. It was as if he had become truly aware of the remarkable ambience around him.

Hearing the story, Cynthia went pale.

"Didn't I say that the Rosacrux legend had a peculiarly Welsh feel to it? … but how terrible … how unspeakably terrible … "

"What do you mean?"

"I can't put it into words … Can't you sense it? It's like being in another age … and where is the body? Where is Asaph's body?"

After dinner, the Earl summoned Osborne to him, and Cynthia retired to her room. Maloney and I were having a couple of drinks.

"Listen, Doctor," he said, looking directly at me in a way he had never done before. His glance generally wavered, roving about constantly.

"Listen to this. Sitting here as we are now makes me think of the time, about ten years ago, when the IRA took me prisoner. They claimed I'd betrayed their secrets to the security forces. It wasn't in fact true, but appearances were against me. In those days, back home, human life didn't count for much. Thirty minutes stood between me and death. Eileen St Claire saved my life. Those men gave her absolute obedience."

He stopped, and gazed at me expectantly.

"Why are you telling me this, Maloney?"

"Because … had I been smart at the time … I would have betrayed everything to the security forces. By now I'd have a fat job in India, in the Civil Service. But because I was stupid and kept my mouth shut, my only reward was to get out alive. Now you, Doctor, could also be smart."

"I've no idea what you're talking about."

"Just think about what I've said." And off he went.

A terrible nervousness seized me. I got up and went to my room. For some time I paced back and forth at frenetic speed. It was as if my nerve ends were raw and exposed. Everything irritated me: the room I was in, the rough touch of my trousers (which hadn't been properly ironed) rubbing against my knees; the sudden realisation that I should have written to a female acquaintance two weeks before.

After a while these different worries seemed to fuse into a single one, which proved all the more distressing: I no longer knew what I was distressed about—the worst state of mind possible.

I seated myself in the armchair, took out my writing pad, as I always do in times like this, and began jotting down a list of causes for alarm.

1   Who tried to shoot the Earl, in whose interest?
2   Who left the trapdoor open?
3   Who held Osborne back in the darkness?
4   Rosacrux' tomb.
5   Any connection between the above, the old man beside the lake, and the Earl's monsters?

The answer to the third question was probably 'no one'. The instinct for self-preservation can lead us to do things which might easily be thought miraculous. I knew a man who shot himself in the heart, having first made certain where it was under his ribs. He's still alive today (if he hasn't died of something else). According to his doctors his heart jumped aside at the very last minute.

Instinct warns us of mortal danger. Some organ we haven't yet discovered senses the approach of death. In the Pendragons this organ must have been particularly well-developed. The Earl pulled his car up just a few yards from the cable, and Osborne stopped before the trapdoor. The inner command was so urgent he imagined someone had actually seized his arm and spoken: a momentary division of consciousness.

And to the second question—who left the trapdoor open?—the same answer might also apply: no one. It could well have lain open for three hundred years. However you could not say the same for the shot taken at the Earl ...

Now, if anyone had deliberately left the trapdoor open, it could only have been Maloney. He'd been no more than a few steps ahead of us and, by some miracle, hadn't fallen through it himself. And then the shot ... Maloney could nip up the ancient, fluted walls and their buttresses like a scalded cat. I'd seen it with my own eyes.

At that moment the door opened and Maloney was standing at

my side. He glanced rapidly all round the room, clearly searching for something, then tore the pad from my hand and rushed with it over to the lamp.

"Are you mad?" I shouted at him, jumping to my feet.

"What have you written here?" he demanded. "I don't know your lingo, but I can read the word 'Roscoe' here."

He pointed to the paper, where my crabbed hand had written '*Rózsakereszt sírja*'.

"That's not 'Roscoe'; it's '*Rosacrux*'. But what's it to do with you?"

Suddenly he burst into a gabble:

"Doctor, don't be angry … you're so incredibly clever, you know everything anyway … But you must sit down … we may only have a minute or two."

He rushed to the door, glanced along the corridor, and returned.

"Tell me, Doctor," he began, seizing my arm in a fever of excitement, "have you seen the documents?"

"What documents?"

"We haven't time for games. Old Roscoe's letters, the ones he wrote about people wanting to kill him. And the alleged proofs. You should know … "

"Well … ?"

In that moment a hundred possibilities were racing through my head.

"I've seen them," I said, with sudden decision.

"And what was your opinion?"

"My opinion?" I echoed, momentarily at a loss. "What's that to do with you? I shall give my opinion to the Earl and the Earl alone."

"What can you lose by telling me? Do you believe the illness old Roscoe died of can be artificially induced?"

"It certainly can."

"Can you prove it?"

"I can," I replied, remaining in character.

"Then listen to this. And think about it carefully. What's the most you can expect from the Pendragons? Only the fee you've earned. Why should you get anything more? If you're smart, you'll join us instead. I've no time to explain, they'll be here any moment … We've got an incredible amount of money, you know.

You wouldn't even ask what we'd be prepared to pay. You must get in touch with Morvin. If you say the word, I'll give you his address."

At that moment there was a knock at the door. Osborne entered. His face was flushed, and he looked extremely ill at ease.

"Excuse me," he said to Maloney, "but I'm obliged to ask you for a word in private. Perhaps you'd come with me to my room?"

"I've no secrets from the doctor. The doctor is my friend."

"As you wish, Maloney. But what I have to say is not perhaps something you would want others to hear. I have a message for you from my uncle."

"Well, well. At last the noble lord deigns to speak with me."

"This is very difficult," said Osborne, and sat down. Then he stood up again, and lit a cigarette. He was clearly at a loss where to begin.

"During my uncle's absence," he began at last, "there were more strange happenings in the house. His writing desk and bedroom cupboards were forced open. He tells me that while the burglar was pretty skilful, he did leave traces."

"And he took money?"

"No, nothing was taken."

"Then there's no problem. So, where do I come into this?"

"The Earl asks me to inform you that the documents relating to the Roscoe business are not kept in the castle."

Maloney leapt to his feet.

"Do you mean to say I ... ?"

Then he suddenly fell silent.

"I have something else to tell you, Maloney," Osborne continued, with a new purposefulness. His awkwardness had vanished and a grim irony had taken its place. "The person concerned could only have got into the chamber through the window. The door was locked and permanently guarded. Now the Earl is fully aware of your talents as a rock climber ... "

"That'll do!" Maloney yelled. "I've had quite enough of your insinuations. In five minutes I'll be out of this house, and the Earl will have to answer for ... "

"And furthermore, the Earl asks me to return this to you. It seems you left it behind."

He handed over a small, bow-shaped knife, of a type common in South India. I had seen it before, in Maloney's possession.

"Damn!" he exclaimed. It was his last word. The next moment he had left the room.

We dashed out after him, first helping John Griffith to his feet in the corridor, Maloney having knocked him over in his haste.

The gate-keeper had seen him running towards the garage. We watched as a motorbike swerved wildly into the long avenue down the centre of the park.

"Bastard!" said Osborne. "Never again will I own such a brilliant bike."

"What next?" I asked.

"Let him be. The Earl doesn't intend taking any action against him."

We stood there for a while gazing after him, somewhat nonplussed.

"Are you tired, Doctor?" asked Osborne. "If it's not too much trouble, we might perhaps go up to the library. My uncle would very much like a word with you, in private."

I hurried up to the library, full of expectation.

The Earl was seated behind his enormous desk. He rose as I entered. Standing over me he seemed even taller than he actually was. It was as if some principle of monumentality were being deliberately stressed: his presence seemed to fill the entire library, immense as it was. Even the rows of books appeared to gaze down from their carefully ordered shelves with a different air—no longer items in a museum but living things responding to the benign gaze of their master. Everything now seemed exactly where it should be, in its intended place in the overall scheme of things: the unusually long reading tables, the globes of the world, the ascetically-robed statues of venerable ancients stooping over the bookcases.

We sat for some time, in a companionable silence.

"So he's gone," he said at last. "As a matter of fact I'm rather pleased it's turned out this way. Are you comfortable in that chair?"

I assured him I was, even though I was leaning forward, rather stiffly, watching every movement of his lips.

He stood up and rang a bell. Rogers brought in two finely-cut old glasses and a cobwebbed bottle on a tray.

"Try this port, Doctor. A unusual year, 1851. As a born collector you'll find it rather interesting. To our friendship."

The port was of a quality to make you weep. The Earl meanwhile was toying hesitantly with a large key.

"No doubt you already have the full picture of what has happened. It's your habit to order facts methodically, and you believe in causality. Nonetheless I believe I owe you an apology. I received you here the way the commander of a besieged castle would receive a good friend coming from the enemy camp."

"A very appropriate simile, My Lord. I don't see how you could have behaved otherwise. In your place I should have either thrown my visitors out, or left myself."

"Do you really think so?"

"Absolutely."

"Why?"

His method was worthy of royalty. He was aware of his own need to apologise, but he left the apologies to be made by the person to whom, in truth, he owed an explanation. But my respect for him was immense and I was happy to enter into the reversal of roles.

"They had twice tried to kill you before I arrived. You certainly had cause to think that one of your new guests might have come with bad intentions."

"I did have my reasons for suspecting Maloney."

"As for myself, I can see now that, thanks to his cunning, I arrived here fully equipped to arouse even greater suspicion that he did. I seemed to present the bomb on a silver salver."

The Earl smiled.

"Well, as you're so generously finding reasons to excuse my behaviour, I think I should do the same. Since I invited you, why should I have doubted you?"

"For a start, it must have been suspicious that I was Maloney's friend."

"May I just ask," he interposed, "had you known him long?"

"No. I'd met him just a few days earlier, at the British Museum."

"How's that? You met him after I'd invited you here?"

"Yes. It's obvious now that he attached himself to me in order to accompany me here, no doubt to divert suspicion onto me."

"Have you any idea how he, or those who sent him, knew of your intended visit?"

"Absolutely none."

"Then I fear there's a spy at Llanvygan. There's no other explanation. Who could it be? But please continue."

"Maloney told Osborne, and no doubt Osborne passed it on to you, that I'd only gone to Lady Malmsbury-Croft's to make your acquaintance and to get myself invited here. That is certainly not the truth. You must forgive me, but I am a foreigner, and until that day I had only a fleeting knowledge of Your Lordship's existence."

"I know. I've spoken since to Lady Malmsbury-Croft. She said you didn't particularly want to attend her soirée."

"Anyway, I arrived here in highly suspicious circumstances and at a particularly bad moment. You'd not even had time to rest after that attempt on your life in London. And all the circumstantial details were somehow linked by the ring I gave you on my arrival. Though I must say I don't fully understand the story behind the ring."

"I don't either. To be more precise, how did it come into your possession?"

This was difficult. I ought to have told him of my meeting with Eileen St Claire, but I don't like breaking my word. I gave a nervous cough, and said:

"I can't tell you that. I gave my word of honour not to reveal who I got it from, even though this was the first time I'd ever met that person and I've no real idea who he or she really is. All I know is that Maloney introduced us."

"Very good," said the Earl. "I know who it was. So shall we continue?"

"Given the situation, you were absolutely obliged to take some security measures against your guests."

"I'm really sorry, Doctor. I have to confess I gave Rogers only the most general instructions. I have no idea what he actually did."

"The first thing I noticed was that the cartridges had been removed from my revolver."

"How very embarrassing," he said, and reddened.

"Apropos of what happened, may I ask your Lordship to have them returned to me? I've no others in my possession, and I hope I never will have. But I don't sleep well if my revolver isn't loaded. I can't help it—it's become a habit."

"You shall have them back at once."

He got up and rang the bell.

"Do please continue."

"At the same time my suitcase was searched and a small packet removed from it."

"Do you know what was in the packet?"

"The fact is, I've no idea. Maloney gave it to me because he said it wouldn't fit into his rucksack."

"There was trinitrophenol in it. Again I'm terribly sorry, but one is sometimes nonplussed by the unexpected. I've never had a guest bring high explosives before. I'd already gathered, by the way, that it came from Maloney."

Rogers re-appeared. The Earl instructed him to have the park searched to see if anyone was hiding there, and to return my cartridges.

"Thank you for your confidence, My Lord. But may I now ask a few questions?"

"Please do, Doctor. I'll answer them if I can."

"I'd like to know how my innocence was established. Because I have to admit, appearances were all against me. I feel every bit as awkward as a rather nervous person would who was told someone had picked his neighbour's pocket and taken his gold watch. I'd like to believe I was free of suspicion."

"Well, it became more and more evident that Maloney was up to no good. The only way to shoot at me was through that window, and only a wonderfully gifted acrobat could have climbed the caryatids to the second floor."

"But that isn't proof that I wasn't an accessory."

"Gradually I got to know more about you through things Cynthia and Osborne said. I made inquiries in London, and I saw you flirting in the Library … "

"Excuse me?"

"With my books. Your way of life isn't compatible with premeditated murder. I don't think you'd even pick a flower, you have such a horror of any form of violence. I don't intend any praise by this. You are neither a good man or a bad man: the intellectual type cannot be forced into either category. You could be capable, out of selfishness or love of comfort, of omitting to do things which any decent man would do for his fellow creatures. But you would be incapable of doing anything which might deliberately hurt another. You're too passive for that."

"Thank you for the diagnosis. I'm afraid it's an accurate one, My Lord. But would such psychological inferences be enough to acquit me?"

"Absolutely. People rarely do things that are diametrically opposed to their own natures. Our friend Maloney will never take an interest in neo-scholastic theology. Cynthia will never become a professional singer. Osborne will never succeed in doing up his tie in the approved manner."

"From which it follows that Maloney, instead of engaging in neo-scholastic theology, will continue to make attempts on your life."

"Quite certainly. I have no doubt I'll meet him again. Or, if not him personally, then someone else. My enemies are as patient and resourceful as the Borgias. At times I feel almost proud of them. And there's so much money at stake I can understand why they spare no expense or effort."

"So you do know, My Lord, whom you're dealing with."

"Of course."

"William Roscoe's heirs?"

"Let's leave it there. It'll all come out in the inquiries after my death."

I could see that I'd reached an impasse. His natural reticence would allow him to say no more.

"And what do you propose doing to protect yourself?"

"Not a lot. I try to keep out of harm's way."

"By what means?"

"For the time being I've sentenced myself to house arrest in the castle. With Maloney gone there's little danger now in Llanvygan. I'll bide my time here. He who laughs last … And I would urge

116

you, Doctor, to stay with me, as long as you possibly can. I know how selfish it is of me to ask, when I simply want to keep you here to enliven the tedium of my imprisonment. But I'll do whatever I can to ensure that your time isn't wasted."

"My Lord … " I began, trying to devise some grand formula to express how glad I would be to stay after what had been said. It was the simple truth. But I always have trouble with these little speeches.

"So you will stay," he pronounced. "A wise decision. The books you've seen so far are certainly not the most interesting. I haven't yet given you access to the family archives that hold the truly rare material. Now it's all there for you. And, as far as I can with my limited knowledge, I'll give you whatever information you want, with pleasure."

He opened a mirrored cupboard that stood behind him—I hadn't even realised it was there—and a pile of ancient yellow pages was spread across the desk.

We sat there reading for ages, thoroughly absorbed and in raptures of delight. Every so often we would read out some specially interesting sentence to each other, and discuss it. Here was Fludd's correspondence with Asaph Pendragon, the text of Fludd's unpublished treatises and the minutes of the English Rosicrucians, all material of incalculable scholarly significance.

The following weeks and months, which I would devote to the thoroughgoing study of all these writings, rose up before my mind's eye—as a processional dance of learned bacchantes, their faces lit with divine ecstasy, each brandishing not a thyrsus but a manuscript in her hand.

I was waving one myself—a codex, in a very old calligraphic style, the so-called Friar's Gothic. I had no idea what it was, and couldn't place the curious lily-patterned binding, or the remarkable parchment on which it was written. But there was something strangely solemn about its appearance.

"What exactly is this?" I asked.

"You light upon treasures like the magic wand of the Venetians. That is quite possibly the most valuable work in the entire library. It's the T-book, the one the old alchemists and Rosicrucians wrote so much about."

"You mean, the book actually exists?"

"It's in your hand. It contains their ultimate wisdom."

"So this is the book!" I cried. "This is the work mentioned in the *Fama Fraternitatis*. This was in the tomb of Rosacrux himself. It's one of the secret holy books!"

The Earl smiled a strange little smile, and said nothing.

Rather as Faust did with the book of necromancy, I opened the codex and eagerly began to read. I was half expecting some instant miracle to occur: darkness would fall and, in a roll of thunder, the Spirit of the Earth would rise up before me in all its awesome grandeur.

The next moment I felt thoroughly ashamed of my naivety. The book was no different from all the others containing 'the ultimate wisdom of the Rosicrucians'. Its message was allegorical and so opaque I understood not a word of it.

The only bits of text that stuck in my brain were those written in the familiar Greek—the delightful but meaningless motto of the Persian sage Osthanes: *''E physis te physei terpetai. 'E physis te physei nika. 'E physis te physei kratei.* (Nature delights in Nature. Nature conquers Nature. Nature governs Nature.)'

"When was this written, and by whom?" I asked the Earl.

"No one can say. It's impossible to narrow it down by analysis of the contents. It may even be the Latin translation of an old Arabic text. The manuscript itself originates in the fourteenth century."

"And what is it about?"

"So far as anyone can understand it, it's about the way life can be prolonged for hundreds of years."

"And does it give specific instructions, or does it, like the other books, confine itself to allegorical generalities?"

The Earl pondered a moment, then answered quietly:

"You could say, it offers instruction to those who understand."

"Oh, My Lord ... one question. Do you think anyone has ever understood these mysteries?"

"Oh, yes. Fludd, for one. And Asaph Pendragon."

For a while he said nothing, but gazed at me searchingly.

"There is a fund of human wisdom, some primal revelation, of which all human knowledge is a mere dilution," he went on, in the same quiet tone. "But people forgot it in the very process by which they became able to think rationally."

"Yes," I agreed. "This has almost become a scientific truth. The myth-system of every nation begins with the wisdom of an ancient lawgiver: Hamurabbi in Babylon, Hermes Trismegistos in Egypt … "

"And all the great thinkers felt certain that truth had been given to man in some remote, primordial past. Think of Atlantis, in Plato's *Timaeus* … There was once a world, a great island, that sank beneath the sea. The drowned island could be just a symbol of the magical modes of understanding sunk deep in human consciousness, that surface only now and then, in the form of dreams …

"And there have always been individuals, or secret societies," he went on, "who insisted they were the guardians of some ancient knowledge. From the Egyptian priesthood it was passed down to the mystery cults of Alexandria; from the Alexandrians to the Hebrew Kabala and the Gnostics; from the Gnostics to the Knights Templar and from the Kabala to the late-medieval mystics, Pico della Mirandola, Pater Trimethius, Cardano, Raimundus Lullus, Paracelsus and finally the Rosicrucians. The Rosicrucians are the last link in the chain … "

"And then?"

"Then came the Age of Reason. People started to think methodically and scientifically. They invented the steam engine and democracy. So the ancient knowledge now exists as a paradox: our rational minds can't fathom it, just as we can't fathom the superstitions of the negroes. What followed—occult science— was nothing but fraud and parody: Rational Man's fancy dress frolic with the irrational. The eighteenth-century Freemasons, the spiritualists, the theosophists, St Germain and Cagliostro all claimed to be thousands of years old. Of course they were lying. On the other hand, lots of people falsely claim that they know the Prince of Wales, but does that make his existence a mere superstition? We just can't grasp these things with our modern patterns of thought. As we see it, the body is a machine which in time wears out and breaks down. But Asaph Pendragon and Fludd knew that human life could be prolonged at will. *Physis physei kratei.* Nature governs nature."

119

He stood up again and crossed the room with his long strides.

"My Lord ... so many people had the secret of making gold—even if none ever actually succeeded—so why is it that those who knew how to prolong life never tried to put that into practice?"

From somewhere in the depths of the enormous room his voice answered:

"Why are you so sure no one has?"

In that moment everything I knew about the Earl's experiments flashed across my mind. The huge axolotls whose lives he suspended for years on end and then revived ... and the rumour that he'd had himself buried and dug up again ...

Then other, even wilder connections, began to dawn on me.

"My Lord," I shouted, as I sprang to me feet. "This afternoon we went to the old castle."

"I know," he said.

"You know? Were you in the tower at the time?"

"No. It's not important where I was. I also know that you went down into the crypt. And I believe you solved the mystery of Rosacrux' identity."

"He and Asaph Pendragon were one and the same person, were they not?"

"Yes. Asaph was the Master. The others were mere disciples—including Fludd, who was by no means the outstanding pupil. He wasn't from a very good family, and he was desperate to publish everything he knew. That's why he wrote so much that now looks so ridiculous. Every explanation falsifies the original truth. Real scholars don't express their knowledge in words. Asaph hadn't the least desire to acquaint greengrocers with his discoveries."

I felt he was trying to evade the main question.

"Then where is Asaph's body? The tomb is empty ... "

For a long time he made no answer.

"He might have been removed to some other place. Possibly to the park here in Llanvygan. The tomb was opened by John Bonaventura, the thirteenth Earl."

John Bonaventura! I'd come across the name before, reading the family history in the British Museum. And even then I'd had the feeling I encountered it somewhere else before that. Suddenly I remembered where.

"That's right. He opened the tomb because the hundred and twenty years had passed."

"How do you know about that?" the Earl exclaimed.

"I read it in the memoirs of Lenglet du Fresnoy."

"Lenglet du Fresnoy? Who wrote that history of the alchemists, around 1760?"

"Exactly so."

"What else is in those memoirs?"

"I don't recall … but there was something rather strange. Something about Asaph Pendragon not having died at all … but the details have escaped me."

"How did you come by du Fresnoy's memoirs? Where are they?"

"The manuscript was a bequest of the Viscount of Braedhill. We catalogued it about a year ago. That's when I came across it. It's now in the British Museum."

"What are you saying? In the BM? That's horrible!"

He was pacing back and forth with his huge strides. I suddenly grasped that the dimensions of the room had been calculated for just those strides. The floor reverberated and the half-dressed old worthies on the shelves were trembling and nodding furiously.

"We must do something, Doctor; we must do something. I can't bear the thought that every Tom, Dick and Harry should have access to the most carefully guarded secrets of my ancestors. I feel as I would if a public promenade had been driven through the family crypt … And besides, I have to know what is in those memoirs. We must get hold of that manuscript … But right now I can't go to London … those gangsters … I have it! Doctor, you must go to London on my behalf."

"With pleasure, My Lord."

The Earl grew calmer, and returned to his seat, like the great wave that follows the storm.

"The BM is to some extent in my debt. When I succeeded to the title I presented them with a number of interesting volumes. You must call on the Director of the Reading Room and offer him an exchange. What do you think we might put his way?"

"One of the Persian codices, perhaps."

"A splendid idea. Tomorrow morning we'll draw up a list of everything we have in that line. You can tell him they are free to choose. Any one of them, I should think, is worth ten times the Fresnoy. If there are any problems, refer to my solicitor, Alexander Seton, of the Inner Temple. Call on him anyway, and talk the whole business through. I'll go and write the letters straight away—one to him, and the other to the Director."

"My Lord," I said, with real feeling. "I shall be very proud to mount the Museum steps as the emissary of Llanvygan."

There was a knock at the door, and Rogers entered. He handed my cartridges to me.

"I saw nothing suspicious in the park," he intoned.

"Take another close look at all the doors," the Earl replied. "And set a guard on the stairs going to Cynthia's and Osborne's rooms. Since that business with the trapdoor you can never be sure … "

I took my leave and went off to bed.

I was sitting in my room, smoking a cigarette and feeling generally agitated. On a night like this it was hard to imagine how a pipe of peace could bring philosophical serenity to the human countenance.

Tomorrow I would be on my way to London, on a commission for the Earl of Gwynedd. And how much had happened today! Rosacrux' tomb, the trapdoor, Maloney's sudden revelations and subsequent disappearance; the secrets buried in those books like so many winding subterranean passages. Who could sleep at such a time, between walls as changeable as theatrical backdrops?

There are times when everything seems to take on a deeper significance. Through the open window drifted a subtle blend of scents and aromas: the fragrance of flowers, the altogether more solemn exhalations of the trees, the rank odour of straw and stables, and something quite bitter that I could not identify. At times like this we feel the melancholy of the sixteen-year-old in despair at ever finding love, mingled with an anxious hopefulness about the days to come; we drink to great achievements we have yet to accomplish, and we register every tremor of noise within a radius of ten miles.

We become aware that there is a stir and bustle in the kitchen below, and that someone—a belated gardener?—is walking beneath the window. The light is still on in Cynthia's window: how I would love to go to her now. She is, no doubt, typing a letter. Every other day she writes a twenty-page epistle to her mysterious woman friend.

It is summer, yet I am intensely aware that it will again be winter—white-robed Christmas, when even tea has a somehow different taste. How I would love to be on a boat in the emerald lagoons of a coral island … How I should savour the experience, and surrender to all my desires.

People die on days like these.

Poor Joe, for example. I was feeling very much like this the night he took poison. Or again that morning just before I read in the paper that Jennifer Andrews and her party of holidaymakers had drowned at sea. We never know when our souls will meet their fate (my thoughts: the words are Madach's).

Sleep was out of the question, so I considered a walk in the park. But an indefinable fear smothered every impulse.

Eerie images attract one another. The less you want to think about them, the more they clamour for attention. My mind kept returning to the Earl's weird animals, the huge axolotls, and their deathly-white, gelatinous bodies cruising among the long-stemmed water plants. Some of them must have died ten times … if one escaped now, and got into my room …

I switched on the main light and paced up and down.

The eerie anxiety that filled me was some sort of reaction of nerves inflamed by a day in which too much had happened, more than enough to fill several months.

This rustling I can hear … must surely be an owl? Strange bird, able to see in the dark, like the Connemarans.

That call … must be the call of some bird, woken suddenly. If I knew anything at all about birds I might have been able to identify it …

That sharp crack—a stout branch in the wind?

Those velvet footsteps … no doubt one of the huge dogs. There are two of them, one called Maxim, the other a St Bernard called Emir. Strange that such large creatures should walk so very quietly.

And those muffled noises … as though someone were prodding my head with a pole wrapped in sponge … Someone is walking about in the Earl's room above my head. No doubt he can't sleep either.

The moon is like a … like a … but who nowadays could invent a new simile for the moon? The moon is the moon.

And now this noise, like someone scraping on the masonry. Perhaps the guardian angels of Llanvygan are polishing the walls to make them glow brighter in the morning sun?

But, Doctor, something really is scraping against the walls!

Then a horrible, utterly inhuman scream ripped the night to shreds; followed by a muffled thud, somewhere down below, in some unfathomable depth.

I rushed to the window. Below me, a dark body lay writhing. Above, out on the balcony, someone was standing. Or floating? I really can't say, the whole scene was so improbable. He was dressed in black—perhaps the millstone ruff was something my imagination added? Or was the entire figure a phantom of the mind, born of that strange night and its charge of secret significance?

The apparition remained there for a moment, then vanished.

Then reality returned in a triumphant explosion of noise: the slamming of doors, the pounding of feet, voices questioning loudly on all sides. Down in the garden people were running about with torches.

I dashed out into the corridor and down the steps to join them. I was again myself. The witching hour was over.

We stood around the body: the Earl in his dressing gown, looking dishevelled, Osborne in a raincoat; everyone looking altogether strange.

Someone raised the corpse's head and turned its face to the light. We recognised it at once. Maloney.

When someone dies everything becomes clear and simple. Alive, he was full of wiles and sinister intentions hidden behind his fantastical yarns. And here he lay. Having established a suitable alibi by escaping on the motorbike, he had returned, hoping to make his way up the wall and into the Earl's apartment. He had fallen—or been pushed by unknown hands. When they fall from a height of two storeys, even Connemarans die.

Once again the Earl was the great commander, soldierly and impersonal, giving orders for the disposal of the body.

But as it was lifted, I noticed how very oddly the poor chap had fallen. His neck was twisted round and his face turned backwards, the fate of sorcerers in the *Divine Comedy*.

As Osborne and I moved slowly away, I overheard the strange eulogy the Earl made over Maloney's corpse:

"He was the most amiable assassin I ever met."

That night I again heard the clatter of hooves. I never do sleep deeply, but as the hours ticked away the excitements of the previous day kept me in a constant state of tension. Every five minutes I awoke, then threw myself with a great groan back into the nightmare unfolding on the other side of the bed.

It was at around 3am that I heard the hooves. I ran instantly to the window and saw the rider, with the torch in his hand, galloping towards Pendragon—just as I had on my first night in the castle.

The Earl was present at breakfast the next morning. He had also invited the Rev Dafyd Jones. Everyone else bore signs of sleeplessness, especially Cynthia. The black rings around her eyes and her extreme paleness against the dark dress made her intensely attractive to me. She was again the legendary Lady of the Castle, hounded by the strange misfortune of her family.

The Earl told the vicar about the events leading up to Maloney's death: the deep suspicion he was under, his inability to produce any defence, his escape on the motorbike and secret return by night, his attempt to break into the Earl's rooms, his fall from the second storey and the horrible manner of his dying. Though no one knew what his religious affiliation was, the Earl ordered an Anglican burial, to take place that very day, and delegated the arrangements to Osborne. No one knew of any family or friends, as Maloney had never mentioned any, and Rogers advised that he had received no letters during his stay at Llanvygan.

The Earl also repeated his request to me to carry out what we had agreed the day before, and to do so without delay. It then occurred to us that we couldn't catalogue the Persian codices, as planned, since neither of us knew Persian. We could understand nothing beyond the pictures. He suggested that I should select the five that seemed from their illustrations to be the oldest and most valuable, and take them to London.

I did this, and packed my bags. We had lunch, and I took my leave of the Earl, promising him that I would return with the manuscript as soon as I could.

Next came the touching farewell to Cynthia. It was our first parting. Choking with emotion and British reserve, she stammered:

"I do hope you've enjoyed your stay with us … " And we were both overcome by an embarrassment that conveyed more than eloquence.

I arrived in London that evening, at my little hotel among the endless rows of similar establishments around the British Museum. Having unpacked, I went down to the dining room to face the compulsory roast beef and the gruesome vegetables that always accompanied it.

After the meal I sat gloomily stirring an orange liquid and debating whether the inability of the English to make a decent cup of coffee was the result of Puritanical Methodist inhibition, when a hand—the heavy hand of a stone statue—descended on my shoulder.

I looked up and discovered an old acquaintance standing over me. I felt mildly pleased to see her. It was Lene Kretzsch, who was studying history at Oxford on a Prussian state scholarship. Her vacations were usually spent in London, working in the British Museum, during which time she would stay at my hotel. As a fellow-researcher in the Reading Room I was a sort of colleague, and we were good friends.

However, I also went in some trepidation of her. If I felt low I would avoid going back to the hotel for supper in case she joined me for a beer afterwards. It wasn't that she was ugly. On the contrary, she was quite a handsome woman in her own substantial way, and she was always a hit with men. You might even say she was attractive, but she belonged to that class of girl whose stockings have just laddered, or who has just lost a button, or whose blouse has burst open, giving a chap the impression that she was in a state of non-stop physical development.

The awe she inspired in me was the result of her personality. Lene Kretzsch was *Gemütmensch*—thoroughly genial—and really just a large lump of kindness and generosity, but at the same time she was a totally modern woman, always two weeks ahead of the latest thinking. She hated sentimentality and romantic slush, and was a militant advocate of the *Neue Sachlichkeit*—the 'New Objectivity'.

This was how our friendship began: I set myself on fire and she put me out. I'd been sitting by the hearth with *The Times*. I've never been able to handle English newspapers—apparently one has to be born with the knack of folding these productions into the microscopic dimensions achieved by the natives—and, as I flicked a page over, the entire room filled with newsprint.

Just at that moment, it seems, the young bellboy topped up the fire, rather carelessly. *The Times* burst into flames, and I took on a resemblance to the Burning Bush. The details escape me. All I know is that in a trice Lene was towering over me, stamping on the blazing pages, sousing me with whatever cups of tea were on hand in the room and tugging at my hair in the belief it was being singed. Then she hauled me off to her room, washed me down, stripped me naked and dressed me in some extremely masculine woman's garment, which was far too big for me anyway—and all before I could murmur my undying gratitude. Then she gave me a thorough scolding for being so inept.

From that day on Lene could not be persuaded that I was anything other than helpless, hapless, and clumsy, and that I would rapidly come to grief unless someone took charge of me. Which she did.

Every day she would burst into my room without knocking (what's the point of knocking, anyway?) and hurl my clothes around the room in order to sew a few buttons back on. She warmed my milk for the night. She sharpened my safety razor. In the Reading Room she would descend on me as I was about to leave, bundle my notes together and tuck my briefcase under my arm. If I didn't hang on to it very firmly she would carry it back herself.

The situation got rather worrying until luckily, one specially warm summer's day, it occurred to her that the heat of London was bad for me, so she packed my bags, booked a ticket for the train and despatched me to Scotland.

This was not a bad idea. I had a fine time touring round the lochs and did not return until after the start of term, when she was safely back in Oxford. However we still met in the vacations and our friendship continued, though in a less tempestuous form. Fortunately for me, Lene liked to change her protégés on a regular basis.

This was the other thing about her that shocked me: her boundless and wide-ranging love life. Now I'm no Puritan, and I take the view that everyone's love life is their own affair. I also realise that Lene's willingness to give herself was simply part of her larger benevolence and generosity. It was her unprecedented versatility that terrified me.

For two days she might be seen with a Chinese engineer, then for a week with a Canadian farmer, who made way for a French gigolo, who would himself be replaced by an ageing German classical philologist on tour and a Polish ping-pong champion, simultaneously. And all these lovers, and myself, would be told about all the other lovers, in hair-raising detail and with a total absence of emotion, though she did make occasional reference to *das Moralische*, which *versteht sich von selbst* (I never quite discovered where the self-knowledge came in)—but it was all perfectly objective, quite terrifyingly objective.

And behold, no sooner was I back from Llanvygan than I was again firmly under her wing. After heaping relatively mild abuse on my appearance, she hauled me off for a beer. I never dared compete with the quantity of beer she drank, or the number of cigarettes she smoked. Through a haze of gentle melancholy I sat until closing time observing her epic consumption and listening to her tales: how she had pulled two Oxford athletes out of the river, how she saved a wealthy Scot from moral ruin after he had succumbed to an uncharacteristic fit of generosity, and how she seduced a Professor of Theology who had preserved his innocence until the age of forty-five.

At this stage I had no idea what impact her militant personality would have on my Welsh adventure. Had there been none, I should not have said so much about her, for I too am a qualified enthusiast of the 'New Objectivity' and am not in favour of purely incidental characters. But let's take things one at a time.

The next day I set out to execute my commission.

It was not a difficult one. When I called on the Director he had already received the Earl's letter. He explained to me, at great length, that it was quite unprecedented in the history of the Museum for an item in its possession to be given away. However, in view of the Earl's exceptional role as a contributor to the collection ... and he waxed lyrical about the treasures the Earl had presented when he had succeeded to the title.

He then looked over the codices and asked me to bear with him until the evening. By then he hoped to have obtained permission from his superiors to hand over the manuscript, and various oriental specialists would have decided which codex they would want in exchange. I took my leave of him and informed the Earl by telegram that I would return with the manuscript the following day.

I lunched in a little Italian restaurant in Soho. The only meal I ever took in the hotel was dinner. Two English meals a day would have done for me.

When I got in, after my short walk, there was a letter waiting for me.

Dear Doctor
I'm sure you must have got back by now. Kindly call on me at Grosvenor House.
Eileen St Claire

That was one thing I had no desire to do. Since the business of the ring I felt the deepest distrust of her. I was convinced that she was part of the conspiracy against the Earl, and I determined to avoid the whole area around that particular hotel.

That afternoon I called on one or two friends, then made my way back to the British Museum. Everything was in order, permission had been granted, and the experts had chosen their codex.

"The Museum is in fact making an excellent exchange," the Director told me. "Compared with others of its kind, the codex is worth five hundred pounds, while the manuscript is a lot of worthless nonsense, so far as I can judge. But the Earl certainly takes an interest in references to the family. There's some impossible story in it about one of his ancestors."

When I got back to the hotel with the various tomes, the porter gave me a meaningful look.

"There's a lady waiting for you in the foyer."

I went down and found Eileen St Claire. She was surrounded by elderly ladies from New Zealand, all sitting stiffly at their needlework. Not a word was uttered. They just stared at her with the profound contempt all women feel for a certain sort of beauty.

She greeted me with a smile, coolly and calmly, as if nothing could be more natural than for her to be waiting there for me. "You simply must have dinner with me," she said. "It's most important that I should speak with you."

With the awkward manner of a schoolboy I cobbled together a couple of lies. I'm not a good liar. My various appointments with supposed friends must have sounded pretty implausible, and I probably made too many excuses.

Not for a moment did she go through the motions of believing me. She didn't even dismiss my excuses as unimportant. She simply continued to insist that I dine with her.

My resistance gradually weakened. After all, it wasn't every day I had the chance to dine with such a beautiful woman. And dinner at Grosvenor House would surely be of a different order to the one that threatened me at the hotel. And what could possibly happen? I would tell her only what I thought fit. I might even learn some things I didn't know.

The reasons for my reluctance were not, in the first instance, particularly rational. No doubt I was clinging to the superstitious notion that nothing good could come from anything connected with Eileen St Claire because I found her so very beautiful. Such paradoxical taboos lurk at the heart of our desires.

In the end I gave my consent, by which time I would have been distraught had she changed her mind. I felt an inexpressible longing to see her doing such ordinary things as eating and drinking.

I took the books up to my room and locked them in the cupboard. As fast as was humanly possible, I changed for the evening, and went back down. She straightened my tie in the foyer.

One of her Hispanolas was waiting for us outside, and we glided off to Grosvenor House.

As soon as we were in the car she asked:

"So, how did it happen?"

"Exactly as you read in the papers. He fell from the second floor. Climbing was his passion, and it cost him his life."

"That's horrible. But I don't believe it. I was with him once in Switzerland. He went up the most impossible rock faces, with the very worst reputations. I can't imagine him falling from a simple balcony."

"It's happened to others. You climb a hundred rocks with no problem, and fall off the hundred-and-first, which is probably far less dangerous."

"It couldn't have happened to Maloney."

"So what do you think did happen?" I asked, somewhat alarmed.

"He was pushed."

"What do you mean? Who could have pushed him?"

"I don't know. I can't point to anyone in particular. But I've known the people at Llanvygan a lot longer than you have. You've no idea, Doctor, what you've got involved in."

I had no intention of letting her know that I did: that I was fully aware that she and Maloney were members of a very dark plot. All I wanted was to have dinner with the beautiful woman Eileen St Claire, and not to talk about anything beyond what one usually does talk about with a beautiful woman.

We arrived at Grosvenor House. I gathered, with a mixture of surprise, pleasure and anxiety, that we were to dine in her private suite.

The dinner-for-two began as if we had no secrets to exchange but simply wished to pass the evening pleasantly. But it was quite hard work keeping her amused. She gave minimal responses to my contributions and made very few herself. The same cannot be said of me: the fine meal and the wine were already loosening my tongue.

She ate and drank much as anyone else would; in fact she ate with good appetite and proved a serious drinker. The wine seemed to make her more human. Her voice became a shade more natural and casual, and she looked one in the eye in an almost friendly way—or at least very seductively. Every so often I would put a personal question to her, but she evaded it every time.

It was only when we were on the dessert that some promising mutual acquaintances finally emerged. Over coffee I ventured the remark that Lady Nichols always donned Russian costume for intimate meetings with her Russian chauffeur, to ease his homesickness … and that Edwin Ponsonby preferred boys because women reminded him of Queen Alexandra, for whom he had excessive respect … and that Mme de Martignan was so offended by certain habits of her countrymen that she put a notice on the palm trees outside her villa in St Juan les Pins saying, 'For dogs only' … and at last we began to make progress.

By degrees my imagination became bolder. Perhaps we might even get on more intimate terms. You never could tell with Eileen St Claire. My poet friend Cristofoli had little idea what would happen to him that memorable Fourteenth of July in Fontainebleau. It augured well that my chitter-chatter frankly amused her, and no mention was made of such uncomfortable topics as the ring.

The truth is, the dark secret I associated with her would have made her even more alluring, had she not already been alluring to an infinite degree.

And then, quite abruptly, I still don't understand why, it burst from me:

"I did give the Earl your ring."

"I thought so. And … no doubt he wasn't altogether pleased."

"Indeed. He made no comment; just turned his back on me."

"Did you tell him who gave it to you?"

"What do you think? I gave you my word."

"Poor Maloney wrote to me about some of the dreadful things that happened. Someone took a shot at the Earl. Who do they think was responsible?"

"They didn't tell me."

"If they did tell you, it wouldn't have been the truth. Some day, when I get to know you better, I'll tell you one or two facts about the Pendragons."

"And when will that be? I hope you'll give me the chance more often to become better acquainted. You find I'm the best fellow in the world."

"It's entirely up to you whether we become friends or not. So far I've only asked you one thing, and that you refused."

"But I gave him the ring!"

"The ring ... oh, that was such an age ago I'd already forgotten about it. I asked you to tell me the full story of Maloney's death."

I repeated what I knew about his nightly training sessions, that I'd actually heard him fall, and had stood over the body.

"Tell me ... just before it happened, had there been some sort of scene, between him and the Earl?"

"No. I know for certain that the Earl never spoke more than ten words to Maloney."

Which was true, in the literal sense. The message sent via Osborne was a different matter. But I didn't want to reveal that I knew about Maloney's machinations. I was taking care not to drink too much and lose control over what I should or should not be saying.

She changed her tactics. Her face and posture took on a softer expression and she embarked on a longer story.

"I've already told you, on the way to Chester, that the Earl was once my closest friend. No one knows him as well as I do, and perhaps no one will ever love him as much. And, just lately, I know things have been happening to him, horrible, dreadful things ... they want to kill him ... but of course you know that. The most awful thing about it is that the Earl won't do anything to protect himself. Only two people know who is trying to kill him: the Earl and myself. And he doesn't do anything, I feel it's my duty to save him. I would very much like you to help me. I gather you hold the Earl in high regard ... "

"Yes, I'd do anything to ensure his safety. Tell me more."

But I didn't trust her for a moment. Even if I hadn't known so much about her accomplice Maloney I would not have believed a word she said. One reason was that she was speaking like an automaton, in a cold, remote, inhuman voice. The other was that she was so very beautiful.

Nothing brings out my pessimism and distrust more than femi-
nine allure. Were I a dictator I'd have all such women locked up. It
would make the world a far more peaceful place.

"Now listen to me, Doctor," she went on. "You may think that
what I'm about to tell you is sheer fantasy. Or you may already
know about it. There must be, either in that house or its envi-
rons, someone … some being, totally mysterious and impossible
to name … or some person who knows how to make himself …
how to exploit all the powers of superstition … to make himself
unknowable and unapproachable. Maloney wrote to me about a
mad peasant who started prophesying, and about some strange
old man who was seen one night. The poor lad couldn't have
imagined at the time … Doctor, I am convinced he was the one
who killed Maloney."

I pushed back my chair and stared at her in astonishment. Yes,
I too had concluded that the mysterious night rider had been the
one who threw Maloney from the balcony. And I had actually
seen him, if only for a moment …

But I had never revealed this to anyone, apart from Cynthia.
How could Eileen St Claire know of it?

For just a moment, the temptation to trust her and tell her all I
knew was exceedingly strong. But I conquered it, and said nothing.

"Too late," she remarked. "It's no use putting that silly face on
now. You've just shown me that you do know about it. It's all I
needed."

"I can't deny I also saw the old man beside the lake. But I don't
see what he's got to do with the rest of it."

"Because it was him. He was the one who killed Maloney, and
who's trying to kill the Earl. And I happen to know who he is,
behind his disguise. If you help me, we can expose him."

"How, exactly?"

"Your evidence is necessary to neutralise him. Give it in writing,
before witnesses, that you saw someone in disguise on the balcony
Maloney fell from."

It was uncanny … How could she know I had seen him?

But I saw what she was up to. The trap had been set with con-
summate skill. Her request gave every impression of being made
in the Earl's best interest, and quite probably I might have been

taken in had Maloney not spoken out so rashly on that last night; if he hadn't betrayed the fact that he was one of those trying to stop the Earl getting possession of the Roscoe legacy; and if he hadn't invited me to join them.

"I'm sorry, I can't write anything of the sort without asking for the Earl's consent. Since it's his life at stake, he's the most competent person to decide, in the last analysis."

"Well, if you don't want us to save his life, or if you don't want to do it this way … "

"I must in any case discuss it with him first."

For a moment she was at a loss.

"But he won't give his consent. He won't let the police interfere in his affairs. He's too proud for that … but yet, we have to save him."

She stood up, and placed her hand on my shoulder. Her breasts were almost brushing against my cheek. I think the closeness of that body would have roused the passions of a mummy.

I held her round the waist and pulled her to me.

"Do believe me," she murmured. "You do trust me, don't you?" (stroking my hair).

At this point the mummy would most certainly have assured her of his undying trust. But inside me that quirky little devil which is stronger than all my other instincts, and which every so often makes me do the most surprising things, was beginning to stir.

"I don't trust you one little bit," I said, tenderly but with absolute firmness. "I know the whole story. I know that you too are interested in the Roscoe legacy."

She immediately pushed me away.

"What do you know about all that?" she asked, with a laugh.

I got up. For a while we stared at each other in silence. Anger did wonders for her looks.

"Go home," she said.

"I'm going," I replied. "All the same, wouldn't it be wiser for us to talk it over calmly?"

"I can't think what there is to talk about. Just go. Oh … you're so impudent. I've never been quite so disappointed in anyone. You looked such a meek and gentle soul … Who are you, really?" she asked suddenly, her eyes wide open.

"I'm not a detective, I do assure you, and this whole business is really nothing to do with me. I only got involved because of you, and your ring."

The fear in her voice made me master of the situation. All my timidity vanished, and I drew added strength from the fact that never in my life before had a beautiful woman been afraid of me.

The novelty of the situation made me almost cruel. I must have cut a rather comic figure, rather like Schlesinger the zoo garden hose, who discovered he was really a rattlesnake.

"It might interest you to know," I said, in my best rattle-snake hiss, "to what extent I am an initiate into these mysteries, and just how much I could harm you if I chose."

"Harm me?"

"If you're interested, sit with me here on the sofa and I'll tell you everything."

With a gesture of resignation she sat down.

No doubt a psychologist would describe what I did next as pure sadism—the strange ecstasy I felt as I stroked this peerless woman's body, always aware that her muscles were tense with a rage she could barely choke back, and that she longed to hurl herself at me in all her feline magnificence. But she had no choice other than to submit. She had no other way to find out what, by hook or by crook, she simply had to.

And I told her the little I knew. That Maloney was sent to Llanvygan by the Roscoe heirs, that it was he who took a shot at the Earl, who left the trapdoor open in Pendragon, and who tried to steal the documents by which the Earl could prove that William Roscoe's fatal illness had been artificially induced … I told her I was aware that she too was part of the conspiracy, and that she had given me the ring to put me under suspicion and divert attention away from Maloney.

There was in fact very little in my story that could have done her much damage in a court of law. It was all circumstantial, without the force of real evidence. When I finished I imagined my moment was over: that she would throw me out, with redoubled anger because I had frightened and terrorised her … and I would have gone quietly, my desires unquenched, but as a man who had outwitted Eileen St Claire.

But it wasn't like that. When my story was over and I had risen to my feet, she smiled a mocking little smile and purred:

"So, is Eileen not to be stroked any more?"

She held out her hand to me and before I knew what I was doing we were locked in a kiss that went on for eternity.

In the entire Llanvygan adventure, rich as it was in murky obscurity, this utterly contradictory kiss struck me as quite the most baffling development. Only later, when we had run out of breath and were again seated at the table—she having disengaged herself and sent for champagne—did it begin to dawn on me what it was all about. I am not vain, and I did not for a moment attribute my success to my manly sex appeal: not that she was the sort of woman who might be influenced by such ridiculous notions.

No. Idiosyncratically, but quite understandably, she had misconstrued my actions. A shocked Englishman, knowing what I did about her, would instantly have cried, 'Get thee behind me, Satan.' But I had joined her over an amicable dinner and forced her to flirt with me. It's an old truth that the wicked think everyone wicked. She had drawn the conclusion from my behaviour that it would be possible in the end to bargain with me, I just didn't intend to sell myself cheaply. The right moment had to be found, and the right price named. The price, or part of it, was to be herself.

But then, as we sipped the champagne and established ourselves on the very best of terms, the voice of the man who had taken all those half-yearly exams in Kantian ethics finally spoke up.

Since Eileen St Claire was not going to get what she hoped for—my testimony, or collusion, or whatever else was wanted— had I the right to accept her embraces? Wasn't my conduct every bit as reprehensible as that of the man who refuses to pay for the embrace he has already enjoyed?

But I soon quieted my conscience. In situations like this, one's conscience is very amenable to reassurance. I had promised her nothing. She was the one playing hazard.

"Now you really must go home," she declared, as we downed the last of the champagne. But her eyes said, 'Stay till morning'.

"You want me to end the meal with the *hors d'oeuvre*?"

"It was a very substantial *hors d'oeuvre*. And anyway, it's entirely up to you … "

"Well?"

"Just make yourself comfortable at the desk and write what you saw two nights ago at Llanvygan."

I stood up, Kant's ethics having surfaced again inside me.

"Eileen, to go home now would drive a man crazy … but I'd rather go. I'm not going to write anything, so don't count on me."

"Then go," she said, and the next moment she was already in the room next door, in bed, smiling at me expectantly.

To this day I can't figure out what sort of training she must have had to be able to undress at such speed. I cannot pretend my own progress was as rapid. Oh, how awkward is a man's apparel: on these special occasions I invariably get my shoelaces in a tangled knot.

Eileen St Claire's gift was a priceless one. I had never had such a night of love, with so rich and varied a programme. The body that writhed and rippled and trembled in my arms was mistress of a thousand strategies, and new with every new beginning—wondrous, astonishing, and mysterious as the sea.

I woke shortly before dawn, from a brief, utterly exhausted dream. The woman slept on, in her cruel, expressionless beauty, her head at rest on her right arm that curved with the sinuous grace of a Greek vase. I got up, went to the window and lit a cigarette. Below, bathed in the unearthly slate-grey tints of the hour before dawn, lay Hyde Park, with white patches of mist drifting, as if forgotten and abandoned, over the green, meadow-like lawns. Now everything seemed tainted with sin, with impropriety, with sheer wrong-doing. The bad conscience of the Piarist-educated schoolboy joined in lamentation with the neurotic's instinctive self-distrust: "How did I get here? Why am I not down there, on the dewy turf of Hyde Park, newly-risen, with fresh thoughts and an unclouded mind?"

"*Chéri?*" came Eileen's voice. The cigarette smoke had roused her. I went over and kissed her hand, absent-mindedly.

"*Chéri*," she asked wearily. "Have you given it any more thought?"

"What, *Chérie?*"

"You know, the written statement. *Chéri*, you know I have to have it … " she said, with gentle annoyance, as if I had simply had a moment's forgetfulness and she was quite sure I would write what she wanted.

I could have murdered her. And I felt utterly ashamed.

We had breakfast, then it was time to say goodbye.

Sitting on the bed, she smiled her charming smile and said:

"You've been so sweet, *Chéri*, I'd love to have you here again. But only if you bring that statement. Until then I won't even talk to you. But I know you'll bring it. Tomorrow, then? Now off you go!"

I took a taxi, feeling very self-conscious in my formal evening attire and cold for lack of sleep.

I did a lot of thinking in the taxi, and decided I had seen through her tactics. I remembered Cristofoli's little adventure and came to the conclusion that she relied entirely on the irresistibility of her erotic arts. She must have reckoned, no doubt on the basis of experience, that any man who had known her intimately would thereafter be unable to be without her, at least for any extended period. The memory of her body would haunt me like an obsession, a ruling passion, and would lead me back to her whatever the cost.

With these reflections, as I might put it, 'a bitter-sweet smile played on my lips', to no purpose, since no one could see it inside the taxi.

The fact was, she knew nothing of my real nature, or rather my unnaturalness. I wasn't like Cristofoli, who left her with the smug smile of the saved on his face, and went slightly mad because he would never see her again. All that remained with me was the unpleasant feeling of not having slept enough, and a gnawing sense of guilt.

Nor am I a connoisseur of the arts of love, to be ravished by the perfection of figure and the technical virtuosity she embodied. I am not an enthusiast by nature, except in matters of history or literature. What I look for in a woman is something rather different: not the transient harmony of lines and contours, not amorous expertise, nothing so cheap … Rather, through the woman I embrace something which is not in her, but which she represents.

With every woman I savour the thing she symbolises. There was one I loved because she was Sweden; another—whose beauty was as frail and delicate as Sèvres china—reminded me of the eighteenth century; one whom I dreamed of as Joan of Arc; one whom I imagined as the many-breasted Diana of Ephesus. Kissing Cynthia felt like dallying with the entire English tradition of sonnets and blank verse. In the docile, bovine amiability of yet another I revelled in Swiss and Alpine meadows. '*Die Weiber sind silberne Schalen, in die wir goldene Äpfel legen.*'—'Women are the silver bowls in which we place golden apples.'

Eileen St Claire I loved because she stood for Sin. But now I'd had the experience. I had known what it was to spend the night with falsehood and murder. It had been very pleasant, but my interest had waned, my sexual curiosity had been satisfied. And I felt quite sure I should never again yearn for the lips of that woman. If anyone had told me then that one day she would again become my mistress (and revealed in what circumstances) I should have thought him deranged.

I've no idea by what unconscious knack I manage it, but somehow every room I inhabit comes in no time at all to look hostile and abandoned. People say of rooms that you can tell immediately if a woman lives there: little knick-knacks, tablecloths, flowers, porcelain figurines appear, and personal toiletries suggest the warmth of the female body. My rooms undergo the opposite process. The knick-knacks vanish and the place becomes a cell. Piles of shabby books accumulate on every horizontal surface, their dusty monotony relieved here and there by a cheap pipe.

This time, as I entered, the room seemed particularly bleak. This might have been due to the still-made bed in which I had not slept, or to the fact that I was half-asleep and feeling cold. But the room seemed to be positively creaking with hostility. I was filled with an deeply unpleasant feeling.

And then, like a flash of lightning, I knew what it was, and rushed to the wardrobe. The lock had been forced open. I counted the Persian codices. They were all there. But the manuscript, the memoirs of Lenglet du Fresnoy for which the Earl had sent me to London, had gone. Someone had stolen it.

My first impulse was to jump out of the window. Then, at my wits' end, I raced down to the ground floor to the manager's office.

I explained what had happened and showed him the lock. He was distraught, but had nothing to add. So many people had come and gone. In particular, the previous night a horde of Scotsmen had pitched up, travelling half-price to the England-Scotland rugby match; in fact the whole town was swarming with bare-kneed Scots in their Tam o' Shanters. But in any case the police should be informed.

"Yes, I'll nip round to Scotland Yard," I replied. With soaring hope, my petty bourgeois soul took refuge under the motherly wing of the Metropolitan Police. But then my innate pessimism took hold of me again. The manuscript was almost certainly no longer in the hotel, and it seemed most unlikely that such a thing might be found in a London of eight million people in an area the size of an entire county back home. Possibly it was no longer even in London. It could just as easily be on its way to the Southern Seas, via the mail plane to India.

But I'd go to the police station anyway. I went back up to my room, had a bath, shaved and put on my daytime clothes. I had a sudden sense of wellbeing: the fresh clothes, the sudden strangeness of everything, my various loves … perhaps the evil spell of the theft would be broken by a clean, soft collar? Perhaps everything would return to rational order again.

Down in the foyer there was a message for me. According to the porter, a boy had brought it fifteen minutes earlier. In typed lettering I read as follows:

Don't do anything rash. If you want it back, be at the Café Royal at nine this evening. If you inform the police before then, you will never see it again.

The writer was probably correct in suggesting the police would never be able to trace the manuscript. And it would certainly not be the Earl's way to have them called in. For a start, it would be in the papers the very next morning, which he would have hated above everything else. After much thought I asked the young bell-boy to send him the following telegram:

MANUSCRIPT STOLEN BUT AM ON TRACK AND HOPEFUL LETTER FOLLOWS

Then I set everything down in a letter and despatched it by express delivery.

After that, I had lunch, took a sleeping pill and lay down to sleep. The world might be falling apart but I wasn't going to give up my afternoon nap.

The Café Royal is effectively London's only real café. It aims at Frenchness in every detail. As if the place had been built by Napoleon himself, the grand entrance, the doorman's cap, and even the cups and spoons are adorned with a capital *N* crowned with laurel. Coffee is served in glasses; the air is so foul and the chairs so very uncomfortable it's as if you really were in Paris. It was once the meeting place of the British intelligentsia, and the clientele has remained interesting to this day, consisting mainly of aspiring actresses and clever foreigners.

I sat beside the wall and waited, nervously. At nine fifteen a stranger approached me.

"Doctor Bátky?"

"Yes."

He took a seat. I recognised him immediately. It isn't every day that you see such an unpleasant, grey-green, corpse-like, degenerate face, with such deep rings around the eyes. It was the man I had seen with Eileen St Claire at Fontainebleau. The man who was said to be her doctor, who had caused Cristofoli such heartache.

"So, can we talk here undisturbed?" he asked, glancing around.

There was a vacant table next to us, but as he spoke a bearded Indian wearing a turban and his unusually tall lady companion seated themselves at it.

"If you've no objection, we'll talk in German," he muttered, in a thick English accent. "I don't think our neighbours will make too much of that."

"As you wish," I replied.

"Intelligent people don't need to say very much anyway," he added.

I have to concede that his face, for all its repulsiveness, did look decidedly intelligent.

"The manuscript you came to London for is in my possession. We have precise information about everything. We knew even before you got here that you were coming for a document of particular interest to the Earl."

"My congratulations," I said. "But there is something I would like to mention, for the sake of brevity. Your next sentence will be: 'Dr Bátky, you are a famous physician.' Allow me to verify, by means of my passport, that I am not a medical doctor."

"I am aware of that. We've got past that stage. But let's take things in their turn. There's no reason not to tell you candidly that the manuscript was a disappointment. I notice that it contains some references to the family, and to some of the bees in his Lordship's bonnet, but nothing of interest to us."

"And who are 'us'?"

"I'll come to that in a moment. What I came to say is that I don't really need it at all. I would be happy to return it, on certain conditions."

"So, you wish to blackmail me. I am not a rich man, sir, and none of this is my business anyway. I suggest you apply to the Earl of Gwynedd himself."

"What an idea! Compared with us, the Earl is a penniless wretch. We don't need his money. This is about you."

"I don't follow you."

"I'm asking you for the same thing as Eileen St Claire. Give us, in writing, what you recall of Maloney's death, with particular regard to the person standing on the balcony when Maloney fell."

"I have already said, sir, that I cannot do that. Especially as I did not see anyone on the balcony."

"But I know, for absolute certain, that you did."

"How could you know that?"

"Read this."

"I had a clear view of Maloney as he stepped from his room in the castle on to the balcony just outside it and climbed up to the balcony immediately above. An extremely tall man dressed in a black costume came out and seized him. They struggled for a short while, then Maloney plunged from the balcony. He was dead before anyone got to him. No one mentioned the fact that his neck had been wrung. Only one person apart from myself saw the man on the balcony, the Hungarian doctor. He came out on to his own balcony just as Maloney uttered his death cry … "

So, I hadn't been the only one to see that terrifying apparition. I could no longer assume it was an hallucination caused by my jangled nerves. Someone did push Maloney over the side, or at the very least wrestled with him before he fell. That was what saved the Earl's life, at the cost of Maloney's. And now his enemies intended to use the fact against the Earl.

The conclusion was also unavoidable that there was indeed an informer in the house, someone who knew everything down to the finest detail. But who could it be?

"I see from the letter that someone else witnessed Maloney's accident. In fact they seem to have seen rather more than I did. Why don't you use their evidence?"

"You're too nosy. I'm the only one here in a position to ask questions. But to the business in hand. If I get the witness statement from you, then you get the manuscript from me."

"Excellent. But would you explain what this manuscript is to me, János Bátky? It's not my fault that it was stolen. If I don't get it back, I'll return to Llanvygan tomorrow and leave the rest to the police. After this little interview I can at least give them a detailed description of you."

"Fine. But don't you think their first action might be to arrest you?"

"Me? Whatever for? The Earl knows me, and knows how innocent I am."

"Are you so sure?" the loathsome stranger asked. And he laughed quietly to himself, very unpleasantly.

"I'm absolutely sure," I replied heatedly. "The Earl told me so himself. Otherwise he would never have sent me for the manuscript."

"That was the day before yesterday. Since then, things have changed. You might well be innocent, but appearances are now against you."

"How?"

"Thanks to your wonderful naivety. I find it delightful that there are still such innocent souls in the world. Look, before you'd even arrived in London the Earl wrote to his solicitor, Alexander Seton, to inform him of your business. I've had dealings with Seton. He's the canniest Scot who ever left the Highlands. You can be quite sure he's had you tailed ever since you arrived. His man is probably here in the room as we speak. You began your series of blunders by not calling on him. But actually, you did well not to. If you'd gone in a taxi, the taxi would have had a very nasty accident … But you didn't call on him. Instead you did everything you could to bring suspicion on yourself."

"For example?"

"The moment you got hold of the manuscript, the first thing you did was to contact Mrs Roscoe. Moreover, you were her guest for the night."

"Mrs Roscoe? … But I've never had the pleasure of meeting the lady."

"Of course, you could claim that you didn't know Eileen St Claire was Roscoe's widow. But who would believe you, when every shoeblack in Mayfair knows it?"

I grabbed at the table, and succeeded in tipping my coffee cup over. Luckily it was empty.

My friend with the green face ordered two brandies from a passing waiter. I certainly needed a lift after this thunderbolt. So Eileen St Claire was the mysterious Roscoe heiress on whose person all these threads converged. And I … well, well, well …

"Better now?" he asked. "Anyway, if for nothing else than Mrs Roscoe's … er … hospitality, the noble lord will hate you for the rest of his life. For sentimental reasons. I don't know whether he is still in love with his former fiancée, but in any case this is his Achilles' heel. He's destroyed the career of a great many men who got too friendly with her. My own among them."

Lines of unexpected bitterness appeared on his coldly evil face. This must have been his Achilles' heel too …

"But it occurs to me that I've forgotten to introduce myself. James Morvin, physician, family doctor to the Roscoes. The same Morvin the Earl believes killed William Roscoe with an artificially induced tropical disease. You see the connection."

"Yes," I agreed. I felt sick. How had I come to the point where a murderer bought me brandies? Anyway, I ordered another two, if only to get on level terms.

"Now," he continued. "If Seton is having you watched, he'll supply evidence that you spent this evening in my company. I reckon it would take divine forbearance not to find that suspicious. Since you arrived in town, the only people you've spoken to are the Earl's enemies."

"The truth has triumphed over worse appearances," I proclaimed grandly, without conviction.

"But it's not all over yet. The manuscript has of course disappeared, and you can give no explanation where it might be. However, one fine day, the Earl will get it back, together with a nice friendly letter from me. In the letter I shall specify the sum for which you sold it to me."

"I don't think he'd believe you."

"Sir, even the most palpably false libel will leave a stain on a person's character. But that's not all. Prior to that, the Earl will learn, from someone in whom he has total confidence, that you put it about the length and breadth of London that Maloney was murdered."

I had a sudden idea.

"Don't forget that I've written proof in my hands. The letter I got this morning. In that letter you clearly state that the manuscript is in your possession."

For some minutes he was unable to speak for laughing.

"What could you prove with that? With an anonymous letter, typewritten and produced on your own Royal portable. People will say you wrote it yourself."

By now I was so distressed I could hardly stay in my seat.

"Sir, if you propose a campaign of lies and slanders against me, you could say even more fantastic things about me. That, for example, at the age of three I impaled my grandmother. Or that I've sworn to cut off the King's beard. But tell me, for God's sake, what good it will do you to start persecuting me? What have I, János Bátky of Budapest, got to do with this? I think I'll leave the country tomorrow."

"Relax. Pull yourself together. It's all very simple. All I wanted was to show you that your standing with the Earl has been destroyed, once and for all. There'll be no red carpet rolled out for you at Llanvygan. I really don't know what you were after. Did you expect the Earl to pay money for your services?—though I'm aware you don't specially need it. Did you plan to run off with the little blue-stocking Cynthia, or do you fancy young Osborne … ? But it's all one. Whatever your plan was, you must say goodbye to it. On the other hand, things could open up very nicely for you, if you're clever, and listen to what I have to say."

"What do you mean?"

"I don't know whether you've any idea of Mrs Roscoe's wealth and influence. The mind of gentleman scholars such as yourself isn't usually capable of imagining it. I don't want to list the companies, the mines, the real estate … but, to give you a rough idea, her wealth accumulates at the rate of fifty pounds a minute, even when she's sleeping."

"That's obscene!"

"Now it depends entirely on you whether you connect yourself with this vast fortune, in whatever way you prefer. If you were of an active, outgoing nature, you might become the managing director of a major company … "

"I'd rather not."

"No, I didn't think that would fit in with your inclinations. But give it some thought, and tell me what you'd like. If you have academic ambitions, let me know at which British university you'd like to be a reader. If it's literature you fancy, we can create a journal from which you can demolish every other literary periodical in the country. Or, you might like to become a great landowner in Hungary, on the Great Plain. If you like travelling, you could have a yacht and all expenses paid for a year … two years … three? Well?"

" … "

"But if you're a total book maniac, I'll get you appointed chief librarian in Mrs Roscoe's castle at Rainbow Head. This library doesn't exist at the moment, but you could buy whatever you wanted.

"And on top of all this," he added with a leer, "you can be sure of Eileen St Claire's friendship for life, if you put any value on that."

"And what must I do in return?"

"Nothing wicked, nothing inhuman, nothing to upset your delicate sensibilities. You would only have to testify that Maloney was murdered. In short, you would have to do nothing but tell the truth."

I felt as if an ocean-going yacht had smashed into my head. How simple and plausible was the disguise in which evil presented itself. It was quite true: Maloney had been deliberately killed. Perhaps the Roscoe heirs were right? But the temptation quickly passed.

"I don't know what you're after," I said, "but it's quite clear you want to harm the Earl. But this won't get you anywhere. If Maloney was killed, it was done in self-defence. You know the facts. He intended to force his way into the Earl's suite of rooms … not, I think, to bid him a tearful farewell. If it so happened that someone tried to stop him breaking in, and Maloney had an accident, no one's to blame for that."

"Put like that, no one is. But it all depends on you—on what you say, and how you phrase it. Can't you see? Who knows about these accusations against Maloney, and about his departure? You, the Earl, the two younger Pendragons, perhaps a servant or two. You are the chief witness, because of what you saw. If you chose, it could be established that the gigantic figure was none other than the Earl in disguise. You could swear under oath, in all good faith, that you had seen him in that disguise more than once before."

I clutched my brows. Myself as chief prosecution witness. No occupation could be more hateful. I'd rather lead a revolution in South America. It was a nightmare.

"And I'll tell you something else, to ease your loyal and kindly conscience. It's actually my strongest argument. The only way for you to save the Earl's life is to consent to do this."

"Don't try to be funny."

"Oh, but it really is. If you do as I ask, what will happen next? We have the proof in our hands that the Earl murdered Maloney.

The Earl has proof that we got rid of William Roscoe. You say Maloney was killed in self-defence … it's all one. The Earl will sacrifice anything to avoid having to appear in court or in public, and have his name in the papers."

"So?"

"An honest barter will follow. We shall exchange proofs, and after that neither will be in a position to harm the other. A blessed peace. However if none of this happens, then no one can vouch for the Earl's safety. Naturally that's nothing to do with me, or with Eileen St Claire. But sadly, as time goes on, desperadoes like Maloney get themselves involved. People who will stop at nothing to prevent the Earl putting his evidence to good use.

"I must also warn you, most emphatically," he continued, "that after what has happened your own life isn't particularly safe. You've become too significant a person. You can't just go on reading quietly in the British Museum. One of the greatest fortunes in Britain is at stake. You'll be watched night and day. From now on, the danger that hangs over the Earl, and Osborne Pendragon as his heir, will be lying in wait for you too. I'm just giving you a friendly warning."

"And you can sit here, telling me all these dreadful things," I shouted, "in the heart of London, in a brightly lit room … I thought that this sort of skulduggery was uttered only in cellars lit by kerosene. Aren't you worried someone might hear you?"

"Do speak a little more softly," he said with a smile. "Wherever we talk I run the risk of Seton's men boring a hole in the wall and listening in. That's why I chose the one place in London where everyone can see us. And where I can keep an eye on them. No one could have overheard our conversation, with the slight possible exception of these two brown people at the next table. But they've been chatting away excitedly the whole time. Secret plans to liberate India, I should guess. But you haven't yet given me a reply to my offer."

"I won't either. Tell me on what terms you will return the manuscript. I'm not interested in anything else."

"Good Lord! When we've settled everything else, of course you'll get the manuscript back. It's a ridiculous point of detail."

"Do you have it on you?"

"I do."

"Show me. How do I know you aren't trying to trick me?"

With a sardonic grin, Morvin reached into his pocket and pulled out the manuscript. He held it at a cautious distance.

If only I had a bit more aggression in me … like a tiger, I'd … But I didn't.

Again he laughed silently.

"I know that violence isn't in your nature."

Suddenly an idea hit me. It seemed like a stroke of genius.

"You would do better to just hand me the manuscript and clear out," I uttered, with blood-curdling calmness. "You've fallen into a trap, Dr Morvin. I arranged this morning for two detectives to be here. They are in the room. The moment you step through that door they'll nab you and whisk you off to the police station. But I can spare you that, if you'll just hand over the manuscript."

His silent laugh went on for two whole minutes. Eventually he regained speech:

"Do you really think I'm an imbecile? That's wonderful. You can be quite sure that we've been watching every movement you've made since you got back to your hotel. I know that you didn't go out until this evening. And you didn't telephone anyone. You sent a wire, and an express letter, both to Llanvygan. By the way, they suffered little mishaps and won't get through. Your little bellboy isn't quite as unapproachable as you are. You don't really think I'd be here to negotiate with you if I wasn't quite certain of my ground? It's you that Seton's men are watching, not me."

I gave a deep sigh.

"This is nothing to do with me," I said. "Have you anything else to tell me, or may I go?"

"What's the hurry? You're the one who has to consent—like a beautiful woman. Not immediately, of course. Though I can't myself see what there is to dither about."

"I have to have that manuscript," I pleaded wildly.

"Look here, dear Doctor; I think you must be a little slow on the uptake. That's nothing to be ashamed of, it's not uncommon among even the best scholars. You often find a surprising distance between abstract thought and practical common sense. Go back to your hotel and have a good sleep. I think you must also be rather tired. I'll find another time for us to continue our exchange of ideas. I'm quite sure that sooner or later you'll see things the way I do ... Until then, think about it."

And he made for the exit. In a trice he had paid at the cash desk and disappeared.

I remained sitting at the table, in a dull stupor. Yes, there certainly can be a distance between abstract thought and practical common sense. It almost hurt to think how stupid I had been, how helpless and utterly, utterly stupid.

Gradually the place emptied. The two Indians were no longer at the next table. In the middle of the room a group of some twenty Americans, perpetually young old ladies and men with their neckties askew, were creating a steady din like the roaring of metal.

I collected my coat and shuffled out, completely crestfallen.

As I reached the door someone called my name. I raised my head, to find the Indian couple arm in arm with Morvin.

"Doctor Bátky, step this way," the woman said, in German.

As I approached I noticed that the two well-built Indians were holding Morvin by force. He was a rather small man, and was struggling desperately to free himself.

"*Ruhe, ruhe,*" the lady urged him, with the solemnity of a grenadier of Frederick the Great. "Don't make a scene in the street, it'll ruin your reputation. Dr Bátky will now call a policeman from Piccadilly Circus. We three will testify that you have stolen the manuscript that you have on your person. If necessary, we shall summon the Director of the British Museum by telephone. We shall ask him to testify that the Doctor received the manuscript from him. On the other hand, you may spare yourself all this trouble, and also the poor innocent Director of the British Museum, if you just hand it over."

"How can I do that when you're holding both my arms?"

"Tell us which pocket it's in, and Dr Bátky will take it out."

"The right one," he squealed.

With mounting joy, I extracted it from his pocket and placed it in my own.

"So that's the business side dealt with," the Indian gentleman stated. "Dr Morvin, sir, I must draw your attention to the fact that

I have a revolver in my right pocket. Don't try anything funny. Just clear off as fast as you can."

They let him go. The next moment he was in a taxi and had vanished out of sight.

"János Bátky," I said, in a trance.

"Pleased to meet you. I'm Lene Kretzsch."

"And I Bannerjee Sadh Mukerjee Osborne Pendragon am," said the Indian, removing his beard and his turban.

"Let's drink to this," I said, as soon as I had begun to recover myself.

But to get a drink in London after eleven isn't easy. We had no choice but to visit a Lyons Corner House, where you can have alcohol late at night provided you also eat.

We took a table on the first floor of the four-storey tea palace where, among the fake, gaudily-decorated marble columns and blaring orchestra, the less well-off Londoner briefly pursues the illusion that he too is an inhabitant of the glittering party world of the cinema screen.

Osborne adjusted his hair and tie with a fastidious grace. Lene gazed at him with undisguised admiration, and moved forward to put her arm around his neck. Visibly embarrassed, he drew his chair away. I was hardly surprised.

"So, what are we drinking?" I asked.

"Beer," Lene proclaimed confidently. "Lager for a celebration."

Beneath his mask of brown, Osborne went pale.

"That's one drink I have never had in my life. Something else perhaps, just now?"

And to our dismay he ordered champagne: Veuve Clicquot.

"I must seem to you an angel from Heaven," he began. "One of those you see hovering over the right shoulder of the martyr in Renaissance paintings."

"Something like that," I replied. "Could you explain a little more about the workings of Providence?"

"Oddly enough, it's all quite simple. I can tell you in very few words. Just after you left, the day before yesterday, my uncle sent for me. We had a long chat, something we don't often do, to our sincere mutual regret. Since I was coming to London anyway, he asked me to call on Seton and tell him what had gone on in the last few days. I suspect he wanted to save himself the trouble of writing a letter: it's something he hates with a passion. He prefers to send an envoy—that's another of his princely characteristics.

"But as an historian you will also be interested in the mental and psychological springs of great events. When you finally come to write the history of our family, I'd like you to recall the following passage:

> *In the last days of July 1933, the youngest scion of the House of Pendragon underwent a strange transformation. In his soul there had long burned an unquenchable craving for adventure which, with nothing to feed on, was consuming his very bosom. During those fateful summer days he came to understand his historical mission. He felt that the grave, possibly fatal, but overriding and exalted duty lay before him to explore the impenetrable web of mystery and vice which, in the first decade of the second quarter of the twentieth century, had enveloped the ancestral seat of his family."*

"It's like listening to a great … " declared Lene, with yearning in her voice.

"My starting point was the following observation, a somewhat Sherlockian, or more properly Holmesian, one: Maloney never received any letters at Llanvygan, and always took his own to the post office at Corwen. I was there with him on two of these occasions, but on both I stayed outside. It didn't seem totally improbable that when he called he also collected his mail. So in the morning I went straight there. His death was still a secret. I asked if there was anything for my friend. The girl knew who I was and immediately handed me an envelope addressed to him.

"As one determined to do whatever was necessary—like a pirate of the Southern Seas—and had renounced all conventional morality—like an ambitious waitress in search of a career—without a moment's internal struggle, I opened the letter. It was typed, unsigned, and pretty unsympathetic in tone. It threatened our poor friend—who must by now inhabit one of the lower circles of Hell—that unless something decisive happened fairly soon, not only would his future funding be cut off, but he would be handed over to the police, obviously for some earlier misdemeanour. I had the impression it wasn't the first hint of this kind he'd received. It certainly explains his desperate attempt that last night."

"This much I knew," I said.

"As soon as I arrived I went to see Seton. In some way I don't fully understand I must have made an impression on him, made him think I was now old enough to know my own mind, because for the first time in my life he spoke to me seriously. The conversation certainly opened my eyes. I learnt from him that my uncle had only to stretch out his hand and strike, and with a single blow he could become the master of a mind-numbing fortune.

"For a month or two now," Osborne went on, "he has been in possession of evidence which points quite unmistakably to the fact that William Roscoe was murdered by his doctor. Or rather, not so much proof as a biological discovery which I don't actually understand, nor I think does Seton, but on the basis of which it is quite clear that it was murder. Roscoe's rather romantic will stipulated that if he fell victim to murder the estate should pass to the Earl of Gwynedd."

"I know this too."

"But my uncle, to Seton's perfectly understandable despair, is unwilling to instruct him to take the necessary steps. He carried out the experiments with a Dr McGregor, who died in a car accident."

"I believe this accident was also Morvin's doing."

"What makes you think that?"

"Because before I came to Llanvygan someone threatened me over the phone, and told me the same would happen to me. I now understand the whole thing. At that time Morvin and Co thought I was a doctor on my way there to continue what poor McGregor had begun … But why doesn't the Earl want any of this made public?"

"The reason for his reluctance, so far as I could wheedle it out of Seton, is emotional or sentimental. This may sound unlikely, but my uncle was in love with the lady who is now William Roscoe's widow and sole heiress. It seems he still has a soft spot for her because he's convinced that she had no part in Roscoe's death, and if the full terms of the will were enforced it would punish an innocent person. Morvin's gang are aware of the Earl's discovery," he went on, "because my uncle somehow let Mrs Roscoe know about it, hoping to persuade her to sever her connection with Morvin, whom my uncle considers the only one guilty.

"Seton however is quite certain that Roscoe's widow knew her husband was murdered. He thinks the only way to get the Earl to take action would be to convince him that she's been party to the attempts made on his life since the biological evidence came to light, and that she was fully aware of Maloney's mission. It's my job now to provide that proof. But where does one start? Even Seton, who is as canny as any man alive, hadn't the faintest idea. I had nothing to go on but the name Morvin. That much Seton did know. He even gave me Morvin's address, and that's what I set out with.

"By the time I got going it was already lunchtime, so I went to a small restaurant in an old corner of the City, a place people from my college use when they're in town. There I met Lene. I'd known her at Oxford as one of the outstanding women athletes.

"Well, I don't want to flatter her, but I've always thought of her as a clever, active, thoroughly decent sort—in a word, a real man. I decided to ask her to be my assistant. Luckily she had the time."

"When would I not have time to be with such a lovely man?" she interposed.

Again he quickly turned away, and continued.

"We put our heads together to see what could be done. For inspiration, we tried to dredge up memories of our reading and films we had seen, but unfortunately neither of us had ever been a devotee, not realising how useful it might turn out to be in later life. We thought of reading through the entire works of Edgar Wallace, but there wasn't time. The only memory we did share was of the German film *Emil and the Detectives*. "Drawing on what we could recall, we went through it trying to establish the method by which little Gustav-with-the-Horn and the other children caught the man in the bowler hat. We discovered that it was every bit as simple as great truths usually are. They just followed in his footsteps until all was revealed."

"Never let him out of your sight," Lene intoned, as if it were a moral axiom.

"But it occurred to me that Morvin might recognise me. Events have proved that someone has been providing him with precise information about everything to do with Pendragon House—just the sort of thing you would expect from a systematic murderer. We decided to disguise ourselves, myself so as not to be recognised, and Lene to fit in with me."

"Indian costume was best," Lene interjected, " because in London it doesn't stand out, it really does change your appearance—and it's nice and colourful. I've a lot of Indian friends, male and female, so it wasn't difficult to borrow what we needed."

"Anyway, we put on our stunning disguises, took up position outside Morvin's house, and when a man came out looking like what we expected from Seton's description, we followed him by taxi and on foot. First he went to Grosvenor House, then on to your hotel. He hung around there for quite some time, and spoke to a man in Highland costume—obviously the one who took the manuscript—and then went to a chemical works in Southwark. After that he had lunch at the Elephant and Castle, as we did. From there he went all over the place, but nothing of interest happened. In the afternoon he went back for tea in the lounge of Grosvenor House, with a rather good-looking lady."

"She was nothing special, just very expensively dressed," Lene remarked, rather warmly.

"I hope you had a good look at her," I said. "It was probably Mrs Roscoe."

"So that's my uncle's taste … " said Osborne, and paused for thought. His face gave no indication whether he shared it.

"A really repulsive woman," said Lene. "How could anyone have her hair that vulgar reddish-blond colour?"

"So that's how we got to the Café Royal. You can imagine my surprise when I saw Morvin approach you. He was right about one thing. If we hadn't overheard that conversation, appearances would certainly have been against you. But we caught every word."

"And that was enough to complete your mission," I retorted. "Now you and I both know that Mrs Roscoe was a party to Maloney's expedition. I also know it from when we drove together to Chester. Did you hear what Morvin promised me? Where would he get the money for all that if he didn't have access to the Roscoe millions? Besides, as you will have gathered from our conversation, I spent some time in her company. Like Morvin, she tried repeatedly to persuade me to give evidence. I've no doubt that if we tell all this to the Earl he'll see that she certainly isn't innocent, but a real threat to his life."

"Do you know, I'm not so sure of that. My uncle is much cleverer than we are, and a clever man always manages to find reasons for what his instincts dictate. You might tell him all this and he'd still give you 'proof'—as broad as daylight to him—that she's innocent. Besides … I don't know … if I were you I certainly wouldn't mention the intimate relations you had with Mrs Roscoe. Given his past—and possibly still current—feelings, it wouldn't be very tactful."

"That's very true. But what should we do next? There's no time to lose. After today's setback Morvin will almost certainly resort to desperate measures. I think we are in some danger, all three of us."

"Well, I'm not scared. We'll use another disguise tomorrow. But you should get straight back to Llanvygan and wait there for developments. Don't tell the Earl any more than the simple facts, the theft and recovery of the manuscript, not forgetting my manifold merits. We'll prowl around London for a day or two, this time after Mrs Roscoe. Perhaps we'll have the same fantastic luck as we did today."

"Never let her out of your sight," Lene chanted again.

Cows were grazing in the meadows, and the English ladies in my compartment were being served tea on trays as we trundled by. I leant back and once again perused du Fresnoy's *Memoirs*, the recovery of which had been such an adventure.

Lenglet du Fresnoy led a busy life. A defrocked clergyman, he was one of those unsatisfactory types who later came to be known as 'seekers'. In his day, however, 'seekers' did not grow beards and question the existence of God. Fresnoy's quest was for the secret of making gold and he was the author of a book on the history of alchemy which is still in use today.

His memoirs reveal the intellectual life of the second half of the eighteenth century in all its (for me) charming confusion. These were the years when people tried to create gold and produced the iron of the industrial revolution: a mental climate woven from the threads of Freemason quackery and theatrical philanthropy, the world familiar to us from *The Magic Flute* and Dumas' biography of Cagliostro. The manuscript advanced deeply religious, ethical and humanitarian ideas side by side with anecdotes that even today would be considered bawdy, in which Casanova himself, the truest son of the century, makes a fleeting appearance.

Then one day du Fresnoy came suddenly face to face with the unbelievable in which he had always nominally believed, the terrifying way in which 'nature conquers nature'; and at this point his simple, straightforward narrative turns into the fragmentary jottings of a man shaken to the core of his being. Awestruck with terror, he saw everything larger than life, and his account would have lost all credibility had I not been forced to consider that he would not have been so shaken without good cause, and if his wildest assertions hadn't so closely reflected my own recent experiences, about which doubt was no longer possible.

But I must let him speak for himself. Some time later, after returning to Llanvygan, I prepared a rough translation of a key passage, describing the period from his initiation into the Hope Masonic Lodge to the moment of revelation. I reproduce it here, with minor omissions:

After much pleading from me, Monsieur Ch——, the Great Inquisitor of our Lodge, finally promised that as soon as the next stage of the work was completed he would begin the necessary preparations for my initiation to the higher level.

When I next presented myself at the door of the Hotel V——and gave the secret sign, my heart was beating wildly. 'So, today is the day,' I told myself. 'Today you will, at long, long last, place your first foot on the royal path you have yearned for since your youth.' In the same moment I made an undertaking that whatever treasures I might glean through the noble art would be devoted to the wellbeing of mankind as a whole.

That night the work of the brotherhood was even more solemn and inspiring than before. Once the introductory ceremony was over, the curtains, which enclosed the raised section of the hall to make it like a theatre, were parted. In the centre of the stage, under a canopy of garlands and Japanese lanterns, a woman sat in mourning beside a broken column. She represented Mankind. A lame warrior entered. He gazed in sorrow at the woman and she, seeing him, burst into violent sobbing.

The man sitting next to me explained that the limping veteran was a certain Thibaud, who had been wounded at Rossbach, was now on the verge of starvation, and had turned to the Lodge for help. We were all deeply moved by the terrible plight of this well-deserving hero.

Then a dragon entered, followed by a Knight Templar in full armour. To the distant strains of heavenly music the Knight transfixed the dragon with his spear and drew out a purse from his side. It was filled with donations previously collected from the brotherhood. He gave it to the old warrior, who shed tears of pure gratitude. The woman representing Mankind wept likewise, and embraced the Knight Templar as representative of the Great Lodge. Little angels appeared and performed a charming ballet to yet more music. Next, the Grand Master spoke movingly about the penury the old man had suffered and urged us to continue our work for humanity. With tears in their eyes the brothers saluted one another, and went in to dinner.

I did not go with them myself, but instead approached the Grand Inquisitor and gently reminded him of his promise. He questioned me closely about my own preparations, and I assured him that for three whole weeks I had partaken of neither meat nor liquor, and had withheld myself, to the great distress of poor Thérèse, from the joys of Venus.

(Scribbled in the margin: *'I later discovered that her distress was feigned: throughout this time she had been deceiving me with a young butcher from the Rue St Denis.'*)

'Then come with me,' the Grand Inquisitor pronounced.

We made our way to a hall where three or four masked gentlemen stood round a mystic pentagram. The Grand Inquisitor donned his own mask, depicting the symbols of the Sun and the Moon. I was made to stand in the centre, whereupon they drew their swords and pointed them at me. I commended my soul to God and betrayed no sign of fear, especially as I knew this ritual was routine: no one had ever actually been cut down in the process.

The Grand Inquisitor commended my courage, murmured some magical formula in an oriental tongue and presented me with my mask. Then he and another masked gentleman took me by the hand and led me through several corridors, all draped with funereal hangings, to a room at the centre of which stood an enormous coffin. There was a door cut in its side, through which we entered.

We stood there for some time, in the pitch darkness. I became aware, from the sounds of breathing all round me, that there were a number of others with us. Then suddenly the space was filled with light. I found myself before a low table on which a garter and a crystal ball had been placed between two pistols.

Behind it stood a man. He was a remarkable figure, with a face of profound solemnity. From his insignia he could only have been the Great Chosen One, the highest rank in our lodge. A second man stood at his side, bearing the insignia of the Knight of the Orient.

'Do you know the Estuary of the East and West?' the Great Chosen One demanded.

In my confusion I was on the point of explaining that I had never actually been there, but he nudged me in the ribs to indicate I should answer in the affirmative, which I did.

'Do you know the Six-sided Columns, the Spheres of the Universe, and the little animals with basalt heads in the foyer?'

Again I affirmed, and the Knight of the Orient smiled his satisfaction with my reply. I suddenly recognised him from his enormous girth. He was none other than the Englishman, Lord Bonaventura Pendragon.

'Can you rotate an axis from left to right, and sharpen a vine-stem from right to left?'

I said I could, and the Great Chosen One discharged one of the pistols. The coffin around us rose slowly into the air and came to rest against the ceiling. We were left standing on the floor of the room. The Grand Inquisitor was present, as were the others, but no longer masked.

'I find that Brother Malakius (this was my esoteric name) knows the Mysteries of the Lower Orders,' the Great Chosen One proclaimed. 'I shall now question the Archangel Uriel, manifest in the crystal ball, to determine whether our Brother is worthy of admittance to the Higher Orders. Bring forth the innocent maid.'

Two gentlemen led in by the hand a winsome maiden, perhaps thirteen years of age. The Great Chosen One fixed her with a penetrating gaze.

'Are you truly immaculate?' he intoned.

She hotly protested her innocence.

He raised his arms over her head and murmured a prayer in an unknown language. Then he conducted her to the table and invited her to gaze into the crystal ball. She obeyed.

'Do you see the Archangel Uriel, bearing in his right hand the Spheres, and the Double-headed Whale?'

'I do not.'

'Then you cannot be truly innocent,' the Great Chosen One retorted, with an air of exasperation.

'Oh, I really am. There it is!'

'Do you see the Archangel Uriel?'

'I do.'

'What is he doing?'

For a while she was silent. Then:

'He is giving a present to a tiny little man, who is jumping up and down.'

'Good,' said the Great Chosen One. 'The diminutive figure is Brother Malakius, upon whom the Archangel Uriel is to bestow Mercur Philosophicus, *the Philosopher's Stone, the possession of which is our collective aim.'*

Then he embraced me to his bosom, and the gentlemen all congratulated me warmly, with the exception of Lord Bonaventura, who was deep in conversation with the Innocent Maiden.

With this, the night's work was over. Lord Bonaventura took my arm and invited me to dinner.

No sooner were we seated in his coach than he asked me whether I had taken a fancy to the Innocent Maiden. The question was so out of keeping with the solemn occasion I was extremely surprised by it. But Bonaventura was a true Epicurean. His sole purpose in pursuing the Philosopher's Stone was to acquire limitless amounts of gold in order to ensure an endless flow of pleasures. It was the very reason he had failed to discover it.

And as I sat there, waiting in vain for the Knight of the Orient to expound uplifting and edifying secrets, he chatted away unceasingly about the Maiden, weaving plans to insinuate his way into her presence and that of her mother, and demanding to know how much gold I thought should be offered to secure her. I was cruelly disappointed. However, to keep on good terms with him, I promised to call on the Maiden's mother and attempt to suborn her.

Bonaventura had rented a little palace on the Île St Louis for the duration of his stay in Paris, and it was here that we dined.

When we had eaten, and he seemed in thoroughly good humour, I skilfully worked the conversation round to the ceremonies that had taken place that evening. I spoke admiringly about The Great Chosen One, and his solemn and dignified manner.

My host laughed, and told me the man was called, or rather gave his name as, the Comte de St Germain. He was altogether rather mysterious; nothing was known of his origins. Some claimed he was the son, by a Jewish banker, of the widowed Queen of Spain. But one thing was sure: he was held in high regard at the court of Louis XIV. He would be closeted for hours with the King, deep in alchemical studies. Bonaventura had little faith in their efficacy, or the French public finances would not have been in their current dire straits.

But what was certain, was that he was in possession of some secret whereby he could make diamonds soft. In that state they grew very much larger before he hardened them again, and they retained their enlarged size. The fact was beyond question. Bonaventura had personally seen such diamonds.

It was also clear that he commanded great wealth, because he readily showed his friends caskets of jewels which he always took about with him.

So, even if he was something of a fraud, my host went on, it was merely for his own amusement. There was no financial motive.

Astonished, I asked how he could possibly suggest that the Great Chosen One of the August Mother Lodge of Scotland might be a fraud. I was terrified that at any moment the walls would part and the gentlemanly swordsmen burst in and cut us to shreds.

But, smiling his habitual broad smile, Bonaventura explained that he was a man of advancing years who had sought the Mercur Philosophus *since his tender youth, and had met so many infamous cheats who had trimmed his purse that if the Archangel Uriel himself were now to appear, with the written testimony of God himself, he would have difficulty crediting him. I listened to these blasphemous words in a state of shock.*

Then, turning again to the subject of the Comte de St Germain, he told me the man never ate but survived on some beverage he had concocted. On the other hand, he was extremely fond of women. The strangest assertion of all was that he was over a thousand years old. A number of people had stated—most notably an elderly countess whose name escapes me at the moment—that they had known St Germain some fifty years earlier and that he still looked exactly the same. It seemed he really did possess an elixir that could restore and prolong youth.

There was also a story that he once gave a lady a vial whose contents would make her twenty-five years younger. But it was drunk instead by her greedy maid, a woman of thirty. When her mistress summoned her, a little girl of five appeared, in an adult-sized dress that dragged on the floor, sobbing bitterly. The poor creature was now a pupil of the Sisters of St Ursula.

The following day I paid a visit to the noble lady whose address Bonaventura had given me. I explained, very politely, what a profound conquest her daughter had made of his Lordship's heart. At first she would hear none of it: she had the royal blood of Valois in her veins, and anyway the girl was too young.

(In du Fresnoy's day a maiden was considered marriageable at thirteen, as is apparent in Casanova's predilection for young 'women' of this age.)

However when I added that His Lordship was prepared to offer two thousand livres in gold, and moreover, that after a possible cessation of their friendship he would make a further present to the same value in precious stones, the warm heart of the mother could stand no longer in the way of the daughter's happiness. We agreed that she and the girl would walk the following day in the courtyard of the Palais Royal, where the gentleman would begin his courtship with all the forms and graces of true decorum.

His Lordship thanked me for my trouble and presented me with an extremely valuable snuff-box bearing the enamelled representation of the Temple of Friendship. It was later stolen from me, along with a great many other jewels, by highwaymen near Lichfield.

But who could find words to express our astonishment the following day when we arrived at the courtyard of the Palais Royal to see the young lady offering her arm to the Comte de St Germain, stepping into his carriage and setting off with her mother, without even deigning to greet us?

Bonaventura cursed like an Englishman, and spoke scornfully of the inability of the French to keep their word. He determined to drive to the ladies' residence to convey his opinion.

Outside the house we found St Germain's carriage. His notorious man-servant was standing guard, grave and motionless.

'Now listen here,' His Lordship began. 'Your master is a fraud and a cheat. For a start, he claims he is several thousand years old.'

'Don't take his word for that, my good sir,' replied the man. 'My master is full of wiles. I've been in his service for a hundred years, and he was no more than three hundred when I joined him.'

Bonaventura began to hammer furiously on the door. It did not open. Instead, the mother appeared at the window above our heads and emptied the contents of a chamber pot over us, abusing us in the coarsest terms all the while. With more than justified indignation, His Lordship departed.

I was dining with him the following day when the butler announced the arrival of St Germain. He had come to apologise. He had not known, he said, that the young person had kindled the flames of passion in His Lordship, and he offered to vacate the field; he did this all the more readily as his attachment to the fair sex was purely Platonic, having had his fill of carnal pleasures in the first five hundred years of his life.

Bonaventura thanked him for his courtesy, but declared that after the insult he had endured he had no further wish to enter into an alliance with the said lady. Besides, his three current mistresses were making excessive demands on his rapidly failing masculinity. But he would ask St Germain to oblige him with one of his secret panaceas, lest he be put to shame before one of them in particular. The promise of assistance was given, and so began their friendship, which resulted in such remarkable adventures.

The Count presented His Lordship with an elixir which increased his manly potency to such a miraculous extent that when he left his mistress the next morning his amorous propensities were still unquenched, and he gathered up three drowsy ladies of the night, whisked them away and paid a generous tribute of love to each in turn.

From that point onwards, Bonaventura's faith in St Germain was absolute. He confided to both him and me—I had by now become his permanent guest and companion—that, his huge estates across the Channel notwithstanding, his financial affairs were in such a dire state that his only hope lay in the alchemists' secret, and he implored St Germain to tell him whether he actually knew it.

In the course of a lengthy evening's discussion St Germain admitted that, while he knew a great many things that were hidden from ordinary mortals, the Magnum Mysterium, the secret of turning base metals into gold, was not among them. His view was that no one presently alive knew it; nor did the great artisans of earlier times; but the Rosicrucians of the previous century must have been very close to it. The finest scholars of that era, notably the renowned Theophrastus Bombastus Paracelsus of Hohenheim *and his pupil Robert Fludd, were simply waiting for a moment, a moment of mystical revelation, which they described as the coming of Elias Artista, the great Artist-Prophet, for the mystery to be fully revealed. But the Prophet Elias had not come.*

Hearing this, Bonaventura observed that St Germain might possess a great many secrets, but he too had one that was unknown to anyone else, one that was passed down through his family with the title, and that, if they put their information together, they might perhaps be able to solve the central mystery. It would involve travelling to Britain, as the secret was closely bound up with a specific location.

After some thought, St Germain expressed his willingness to visit a country where he had many dear friends. I too was happy to accept His Lordship's invitation, as I had no particular business to detain me in France.

(Here Lenglet du Fresnoy relates at some length how he broke off with Thérèse, whose charms had in any case begun to pall. Breaking with her was not easy. I have, I am sorry to say, a strong suspicion that he owed this worthy woman a significant sum of money, and he simply fled Paris, leaving his belongings behind, to join Bonaventura at Arras. The reason he gave for this clandestine departure was that he had not wished to cause her undue distress.)

My heart was beating wildly when, for the first time in my life, I put out to sea. At my first glimpse of the crested waves I knew how Moses felt when he put his faith in God and waited for the waters to open rather than surrender himself to their mercy. I grew more and more violently seasick and spent the entire voyage in penitence and contrition, wracked by dark forebodings as to the outcome of our adventure.

But at last the white shores of Albion rose out of the sea. At the sight of their beauty I began to trust again in Divine Providence.

We spent just a single day in London. St Germain took the occasion to visit the Grand Master of Freemasons in England, and I accompanied His Lordship round the coffee houses and taverns.

Towards evening we were strolling around the Vauxhall pleasure garden, and generally observing the ladies, when we were accosted by a man of striking and unusual appearance, dressed in the splendidly exuberant colours favoured by Italian grandees on their travels. Every finger was encrusted with rings, gold chains swung from every conceivable part of his person, and during the time we were together he produced no fewer than four watches and three snuff boxes. Though his face was not generally handsome, the eyes and play of features were more lively and expressive than those of any man I ever met.

He greeted His Lordship as an old acquaintance. The conversation quickly turned to the Comte St Germain, whereupon the Italian warned my companion to be wary of that gentleman. Bonaventura changed the subject with a well-timed joke, and began to question him about his various conquests.

'I am no longer the man Your Lordship knew in Paris,' he confided. 'I feel as if I am starting to die. A man doesn't die all at once. It's a gradual process. The senses grow old and fail. And when I look back on my past life, I no longer know whether I was the greatest fool, or the wisest man alive.'

At this, Bonaventura jested that anyone as famously omniscient as he should surely know St Germain's prescription for restoring youth. The Italian turned a bright red, observed that His Lordship was no doubt alluding to the story that St Germain had promised eternal youth to Mme d'Urfé, and then cried out:

'Stay where you belong, in the clutches of that man. Those who make sport of others deserve to be made sport of themselves.'

And, without any sort of farewell, he left us.

In answer to my question as to the name of this strange gentleman, His Lordship told me he did not know whether he was more renowned for his impostures or his countless love affairs. He called himself the Chevalier de Seingalt, but his real name was Giacomo Casanova.

The next morning the three of us set off for the province of Wales, where His Lordship's estates were situated, and on arrival were entertained in princely style in his castle, known as Pendragon. The following day was spent receiving the ladies and gentlemen of the neighbourhood, and it was not until late that night, when we were left finally to ourselves and sitting by the fire, that we again broached the topic of the occult.

In a voice quavering with excitement, His Lordship told us of an ancient castle that stood close by. Its name meant Dragon's Head, and beneath its ruins was buried his ancestor Asaph Pendragon who in his day was none other than Rosacrux, the founder of the Brotherhood of Rosicrucians.

'If this is so,' St Germain exclaimed, 'then his body will be lying uncorrupted in his tomb!'

'The truth exceeds even that,' whispered His Lordship, leaning closer towards us. 'Rosacrux is alive, just as, even now, the wizard Merlin and

the Welsh hero Bloody-Handed Owen still live. He lies there, in his tomb, waiting for the moment to rise again.'

Family tradition, handed down from father to son, confidently claims that Rosacrux, feeling the hand of old age upon him, summoned his closest friend Robert Fludd, the physician and fellow member of the Brotherhood. It was to Fludd that he entrusted the great secret he had brought back from the Orient, the secret of preserving the life of the body. The body thus rendered immortal lies unmoving in the grave, but lives, contemplating the mysteries of Heaven and Earth.

Rosacrux then lay down in the tomb he had prepared for himself in the image of the universe, and Fludd, having carried out the relevant magical procedures, closed it and left. Then, like a man who has fulfilled his calling, he died in the same year.

St Germain and I listened to his tale in a paroxysm of horror and fear. We asked—in some alarm as to how he might reply—what he desired of us, and what he proposed doing. He answered that Rosacrux was still there, alive in his tomb: he knew more than any living person; he had known more when he was mortal, and had since spent a hundred and twenty years in mystical contemplation of the secrets of Heaven and Earth. If it were possible to rouse him and seek his advice, we could surely come closer to the Magnum Mysterium than anyone ever had. If St Germain, with his power of restoring lost youth, could employ the full force of his knowledge, we might manage to persuade the living dead to break silence.

For what seemed ages, St Germain made no reply. Then, rising from his chair, he announced that he would have first to think it over, and consult his family oracle; and up he went to bed. I remained alone with Lord Bonaventura who, from that moment onwards, filled me with mounting terror. His extraordinary girth, which until then had seemed to me merely an amusing consequence of his unbounded Epicureanism, now lent him, in the glowing light of the fire, a perfectly diabolical aspect, as though he were Mammon himself, clothed in human form and calmly preparing to exhume his ancestors from their graves.

He asked me whether I had been fully ordained before I renounced the cloth, and was delighted when I told him I had. He remarked that, if nothing else served, the black arts would be resorted to, but they would require an ordained priest and a consecrated wafer. If St Germain's nostrums failed, he said, it would fall to me to celebrate the Satanic Mass over the tomb, on the body of a naked woman, pronouncing the sacred words of the service in reverse order.

Such was the oppressive weight of the terror that again passed over me, I dared offer no protest against this diabolical plan.

At that moment St Germain reappeared. He had now donned the robes of a Freemason and the insignia of the Great Chosen One. His hands held a wand and a cut-glass bowl.

'We must be quick,' he said. 'If we are to achieve anything, it must be done tonight. There is a new moon, and Venus lies in Capricorn. Such nights are auspicious for acts of magic.'

I fell to my knees and implored them to abandon this terrifying plan, which might jeopardise their eternal salvation. But Bonaventura replied with an evil laugh that he wouldn't give a groat for the salvation of any of us. I begged them to allow me at least to stay behind, or to go away, because I felt something unspeakable was about to take place. At this, His Lordship drew his sword and threatened to transfix me if I left them, now that I was party to their secrets. Thus he compelled me to accompany them.

In the courtyard three horses had been prepared for us, saddled in black. His Lordship led the way as we galloped at lightning speed through the dark night. Our path led to a high mountain, on whose peak loomed the ruin of an awe-inspiring castle, the haunt of owls, ghosts and witches. We tethered our steeds to the gatepost of a dilapidated wall, His Lordship lit the torches we had brought, and we stepped into the ruin.

Lord Bonaventura performed some sort of secret action, and a blackly-gaping spiral staircase opened at our feet. I stumbled down it, my knees shaking uncontrollably. Words cannot express my horror when I suddenly felt the step I was standing on begin to sink under me. I grasped wildly at a wooden rafter, but it soared upwards with a Satanic laugh. I screamed in terror at His Lordship, but he remained where he was, describing strange circles in the air with his flaming torch, then dashed on ahead of us, like a madman.

We arrived in a vast hall, whose furthest corners seemed to disappear into the far distance. From them, it seemed to me, I could make out the dull roar of the sea, or some other sound very like it.

The hall was full of coffins, whose lids slowly rose and then descended again, like so many mouths, gaping and shutting, ready to bite, warning us to go no further.

Half-crazed with terror I stumbled into the next room, where a horror awaited us that would prove even more dreadful than anything that had gone before.

At its centre stood an altar, which His Lordship pushed to one side.

*Beneath it we found the stone slab of a tomb, which, with miraculous inge-
nuity, St Germain managed to move from its position.*

*Inside the vault stood a catafalque, and on it lay an ancient figure of
gigantic height. He was gorgeously apparelled in the robes of an earlier
period, and the rings on his fingers bore jewels the like of which I had never
seen. He lay with his eyes open, as do the blind; he neither saw nor did he
move. Bonaventura and I hid in fear behind the altar that had been pushed
aside. St Germain was deathly pale. He too would doubtless have drawn
back had he not been ashamed to show his fear.*

*With his wand he drew a line above the figure lying in the tomb, then
slowly sprinkled the contents of the vial on its forehead.*

*The sleeper shook himself, and turned his head towards us. The face was
that of a man who sees. Very slowly, he raised his head, leant over on one
arm, and uttered the most terrible cry.*

*At that moment the subterranean sun that lit the room began to darken, and
bells, which we suddenly noticed around the sides of the room, began to toll.*

*Petrified with terror, we saw that the figure was slowly rising and prepar-
ing to leave his tomb.*

*At that point St Germain uttered a loud shriek and fled, with His Lordship
and myself hard on his heels. Clambering up the spiral stairs was almost
impossible, as he could barely move his limbs for fear and needed my constant support, which, given his enormous weight, was no mean imposition.
By the time we had returned to the castle he was delirious with fever.*

*St Germain's elixirs were of no avail. We remained constantly at his
bedside. He must have suffered for about a week, then passed away, having
remembered us both in his will …*

At Rhyl I changed to a smaller train, which slowly wound its way
through a landscape that became steadily more sombre and mysterious as it neared the heart of the North Welsh Mountains. The
names of the stations became increasingly outlandish, barbaric
and ancient-sounding. We were now in the Celtic Forest, the
land of myth and legend, the birthplace of fairies and of Merlin
the magician, the unfathered child conceived from the ashes of
the dead. Today the Welsh are a sober, sardonic people, but the
trees, the rocky outcrops and the lakes remain, as does the old

atmosphere. Once it teemed with marvels, and even now it silently fosters the seeds of fresh mystery.

At Corwen the Earl himself was waiting for me, with a car. I gave him the manuscript, and was about to tell him why I had tarried a day in London.

"You must be tired and hungry," he said. "First we'll have dinner."

But he looked tired himself, and worried. We spoke little before reaching the hotel, where he was received with all the deference due to a feudal lord. We dined in a private room, but again there was little conversation. Only after coffee and cognac did he finally ask about my adventures.

I told him everything that was directly relevant to the matter. I did not mention where I had spent the night after the manuscript was stolen, only that I had not slept in the hotel.

What shocked him most was that the letter written to Morvin described how Maloney had wrestled with a giant before falling to his death.

"Now I am certain! There is a spy at Llanvygan!" he exclaimed. "Someone is writing to Morvin. That's how he knew you were going to London to fetch a manuscript. But who could it be? No one, apart from Osborne and Cynthia, knew of your trip … Could someone have been eavesdropping?"

Then, after a pause for deep thought:

"So you actually saw someone on the balcony?"

"Oh, yes."

He averted his gaze.

For a long time nothing more was said.

Eileen St Claire, too, had spoken of a mysterious, indefinable presence. And Lenglet du Fresnoy's memoirs had provided a key which, however horrifying and capable of inducing insanity, could explain everything—the rider with the flaming torch, the old man beside the Castle Lake, the voice deep in the bowels of Pendragon that made Osborne stop before the open trapdoor, and Maloney's quasi-ritual death by wringing of the neck …

What terrifying secret did the Earl's silence conceal? Or rather, what did it betray?

"Perhaps you should continue," he suddenly remarked. The spell was broken.

I went on with my tale. Osborne's miraculous appearance amused him greatly.

"What is the lady's name?"

"Lene Kretzsch."

"Would you mind spelling that?"

I spelled it.

"Magnificent! T-z-s-c-h! Five consonants for a single sound. That's really grand.

"I'm glad you found Osborne with a girl," he continued. "His horror of women has caused me some concern. One of us has to get married, and I'd rather it were he. What is she like? I'd like to know his taste."

"I think the only taste that could be inferred would be hers. I have the impression that Osborne plays an extremely passive role in the friendship. But Lene Kretzsch is a robust, fine-looking creature. Her figure is quite perfect, in the classical sense … "

"Do you mean she has large feet and hands, like a Greek statue?"

"Exactly."

"Hm. And her character?"

"Very modern."

"That is to say, of easy virtue?"

"Not exactly. She is *sachlich. Neue Sachlichkeit. Bauhaus. Nacktkultur.* The chauffeur type. Love is a psycho-physical fact. Nothing romantic or complicated about love."

"And this is what you call 'modern'?"

"Well, according to the international conventions drawn up by journalists and women-novelists, this objectivity is what characterises modern love."

"On the other hand, one should remember that even in our grandmothers' time women did not limit their concerns to embroidery and fainting. They were much more active and controlling than they are today; they just did it more gracefully. Mme de Pompadour and Queen Victoria may not have smoked pipes, but they ruled the roost. It really makes me angry when I hear this myth of the modern woman. There is no modern woman. Or modern love. There have always been people so emotionally impoverished they were incapable of investing love with anything higher than 'objectivity', to use your term. It's just that, in the old days, you couldn't get away with propagating this debased form of love. There was too much intellectual rigour. Anyway, it was something a well-bred author just didn't write about.

"The true artists and champions of love," he went on, "have never been 'objective'. For Casanova, every woman he encountered in the street was a goddess, and every one more beautiful than all her predecessors. That was his secret. 'Objectivity' … it's man's ability to see more in things than meets the eye that distinguishes him from the animals. 'Objectivity' … is there any such thing? Every one of us constructs a private universe out of his personal obsessions, and then tries to communicate with other people with hopeless little flashes of light. But enough of this … So, like St Anthony in the desert, you underwent temptation. Satan appeared at the Café Royal and promised you a journal. I just wonder what Morvin would have done if you'd taken up his offers. Where would he have got the money?"

"Well, from Mrs Roscoe's fortune … "

It had slipped from my tongue. I was furious with myself. I'm sure that for years no one had dared mention her name in his presence. He must have felt like a man who had been stabbed. He clutched his collar and went deathly pale.

"What's that? … Where do you get that from?"

And now I saw that he had turned pale with anger; it was fury that was choking him. But it was too late to turn back.

"It's what Morvin said. He used the royal 'we'. 'We'll buy you a yacht … we'll be much obliged to you' … "

The Earl stared at me. The expression on his face was horrifying. Then he lowered his head, rang for the waiter and ordered whisky.

After a long, long silence, he said, very calmly:

"St Anthony, you were tempted by the Devil. But never forget that the Devil is the father of lies. Every word Morvin utters is a lie. That's his real crime, not the murder. To protect himself … to protect himself from me, he manages to make it all look as if Eileen St Claire is his partner in crime. He's taken everyone in. Even Seton, the canniest Scot on the planet. But not me. I … I know her too well."

I thought of what he had said earlier: "Each of us constructs a private universe out of his personal obsessions ... " The Earl had erected a myth about Eileen St Claire and remained attached to that myth, even though estranged from the woman herself. But I did not say this.

After another pause, he continued:

"Eileen St Claire ... Mrs Roscoe ... has an unfortunate nature, in several respects. There is something in her of the automaton, something not quite human, something ... as if she were permanently locked in some sort of hypnotic trance. To say she is susceptible to influence doesn't go far enough. She has never done what, according to her own standards, she should: she's always surrendered to the will of others. And if anyone ever tried to snap her out of her somnambulism, she immediately hated them. I don't know why I'm telling you all this ... I never speak about these things ... Perhaps because you're a foreigner, here today, gone tomorrow ... Like writing in sand ... Anyway, it's an easy game for Morvin to turn appearances against her."

"My Lord, those appearances could have a strong basis in fact."

"In what way?" he demanded, somewhat irritably.

"In what way? You, My Lord, are not a great friend of Morvin. Surely, with the evidence you have against him, you would have handed him over to the police, unless you felt that perhaps Mrs Roscoe herself ... "

"That isn't true!" he yelled, finally losing control. "How dare you speak of things you know nothing about? How can you possibly think you understand the motives behind what I do ... ?"

At that moment, in that spontaneous outburst of unguarded arrogance, I suddenly understood him. Just minutes before, he had said that what distinguished man from the animals was the capacity to see beyond appearances. The animal sees his mate as simply another animal, but man views his as more than human.

And for a proud man no error can be more painful than to admit that in this regard he has blundered: that the woman he has chosen is not what he thought her. For a truly proud man the worst horror of disappointment in love is not the slight he has received: far, far worse is the failure of judgement that led him to construct a myth with no basis in reality. And a man as supremely proud as the Earl of Gwynedd has thereafter to maintain the illusion, in the face of every contradictory circumstance, lest he be forced to admit to himself that he has blundered.

That was why, for all his self-control, he gave way to superhuman rage when anyone attacked the Eileen myth. Had I revealed at that moment that she had been my mistress he would either have refused to believe me, or he would have found some proof that she had been unable to help it: that she had been hypnotised, that it was all Morvin's fault …

"I beg your pardon, My Lord," I said. "It was quite wrong of me to raise the subject."

"No, it is I who must apologise for my loss of self-control," he replied, his old calm self again. "You must bear with me; I'm not fully in command of myself these days. While you were away there were more 'happenings'."

"What? Another attempt … ?"

"No, something quite different. Something altogether more horrible … "

"For God's sake, My Lord … ?"

"Doctor, Goethe's *Zauberlehrling* … *Die ich rief, die Geister* … 'I had a jewel in my hand/I dropped it on a snowy slope/It rolled and rolled and grew and grew/And soon became an avalanche'. But it's quite another story, and not one you could possibly understand. Do please forgive my little outburst. You aren't offended, I hope. So many people attack Eileen St Claire—it isn't just you—and appearances certainly are against her. I can't bear to hear them glibly passing judgement on an innocent person. It isn't actions that speak, Bátky, not actions. Actions fall away from us like shorn hair. You have to see human beings independently of their actions, as God sees us … But perhaps we should be on our way?"

It was dark by the time we reached the car and got in. The wind searched impatiently among the trees in the woods beside the road, and every so often the bloodshot face of the full moon lit up the clouds, as they chased each other eastwards in a wild, silent ecstasy.

The Earl bore his tragic inner conflict like a rock. His silence was that of a man who intended to say nothing for months on end. The road twisted and swayed before us like a living thing.

Approaching a bend, the Earl suddenly slowed.

"Do you hear anything?" he asked.

"Only the roaring of the wind."

We continued. But a few hundred yards further on he stopped the car and, without saying a word, got out. To my astonishment he lay down on the ground. It took me a while to work what he was doing. He had his ear to the earth and was listening intently. At last, with an inexpressibly care-worn face, he got back in the car.

We drove on, but only for a few yards. Then he turned off the road, first into a field, and then slowly back, bucking and bouncing, the way we had come. Finally we stopped again.

"I'm sorry about this little delay," he said, and got out again.

The part of the field in which we had parked was separated from the main road by a hedge. The Earl stood behind it, very tense, watching the carriageway.

In the damp west wind, the place was bleak and uninviting. Here or there, in the dark, a clump of trees or the fantastic outline of a bush could be made out. It was the sort of field you find yourself in in a nightmare, with snakes coming at you from every direction.

What can a man do at such a time? Light a cigarette.

But I had hardly taken a puff before the Earl came dashing over to ask me not to smoke for a minute or two. With a pang, I threw the cigarette down.

Gradually I began to hear what he was listening for. It was a dull, rhythmic thudding. Of course: horses' hooves.

At the same time something was approaching, very rapidly. I say something, because it wasn't horsemen, it was some sort of thick fog, bowling along at terrifying speed down the middle of the road, as if driven by a gale or the chariot of Satan himself, and billowing out on either side like the smoke from a runaway train.

Moments later the fog reached and engulfed us. It was only then that I realised it wasn't fog but a suffocating smoke that made me feel dizzy, and whose odour reminded me of incense.

From inside the car I could no longer see as far as the hedge, where the Earl had been standing. In that strange obscurity I wasn't even sure if he was still there—or whether he was anywhere at all.

I jumped down and made my way as quickly as I could through the dense blackness to where I supposed he might be. Eventually my outstretched hands came up against the low, thorny branches.

I froze in my tracks.

The sound of galloping hooves was now almost upon me, and then, with astonished eyes, I seemed to see a horseman flying past, at breakneck speed, down the highway.

Then the fog was gone.

The moon came out, revealing the last billows disappearing rapidly down the road.

"So," I said to myself, "the Rosicrucians' claim to invisibility was only half true."

The Earl was back at the wheel, sitting with his head in his hands. I dared not accost him. I climbed in, and he set off for Llanvygan.

At breakfast next morning I gave Cynthia a brief outline of what had happened. Naturally I avoided any mention of Eileen St Claire; nor did I tell her about Lenglet du Fresnoy's vision (or whatever it might be termed). I also did not tell her I had encountered the midnight rider.

There are some things that are true only at night. There was no way I could have discussed them. I would have been ashamed to. One is ashamed of the incomprehensible, the irrational, as though it were a form of mental illness. I tried to avoid thinking about it.

Besides, it was such a perfect summer's day. There was nothing but Cynthia in the world—Cynthia, and her little favourites, the farmstead piglets. We ambled up to the top of a hill, sat ourselves down and basked in the sun.

When silent, she was a vision of beauty. Sitting there on the brow of the hill overlooking the farm, in the clear Welsh sunlight with the towers of Llanvygan in the background, she was the fulfilment of everything I saw in imagination, and loved: the Lady of the Castle, innocent and remote from the cares of man. Only piglets, chickens and mighty oak trees can understand the touching, faintly comical yet utterly sublime mystery of young womanhood—when the young woman is well-to-do. A girl who is poor is never young in quite the same way: the seriousness of her daily cares makes her more like a man.

With her fair hair glistening in the sun, Cynthia had the silent beauty of a line of Theocritus. It was that special, brief moment of summer when you could believe time stood still and all was well with the world.

It seemed she had given herself up to the pleasure of sunshine on skin and the well-being of the body, and that there was nothing going on in her head. I felt supremely at ease myself.

She sat up, rather anxiously, and announced:

"You mustn't get the idea I'm not thinking about anything. I can't abide girls who just live for the moment."

"And what are you thinking about, Cynthia?"

"I read in the morning paper that the number of unemployed in South Wales has risen by another five per cent. It's dreadful to think that here we are, sitting on this hill, and all the time … "

"That'll do," I cried, rather rudely.

It was as if she'd poured a bucket of cold water over my head. I can tolerate any form of sentimentality better than the bogus sympathy of the rich for the poor. It's every bit as unnatural and offensive as a manual worker denying that he envies the boss's wealth. Let the classes carry on with their mutual hatred—it's the proper order of things—and leave me at peace in the sunshine: it happens so rarely in these islands.

"Oh, Cynthia! … "

But there were two Cynthias. The words she had just uttered were not at all in harmony with the person I saw in her.

The Cynthia of my imagination was the sort of girl who, on the one hand, would swoon if she caught her beloved devouring a hot dog, but, if the need arose, would be capable of giving her maid a thrashing. She was the Lady of the Castle, proudly enthroned in her fairytale tower, blissfully ignorant of entire nations dying of hunger.

I had not yet abandoned the hope that Cynthia really was the person I believed her to be, it was just that she hadn't been brought up properly. No doubt her mother was to blame. Under the influence of who knows what disappointments of her own, her mother must have dunned into her the great middle class myth that intellect mattered, and that every one was equally human.

"Cynthia, let the poor feel sorry for the poor. You should be proud and pitiless. If I were in your place … my whole life would be an unending parade of low-level sadism. It would be a byword for nonchalance and aloofness. I would never once take up a book, not even by accident. I'd fill my days with golf, or, if there is some sport even more exclusive and boring, I'd go in for that. I'd travel. I'd visit galleries and decide that Leonardo painted rather well considering he was so common. I would say very little: pride is so much more easily expressed through noble gestures. I don't suggest it would be very amusing, but to do one's duty never is."

"Would you really change places with me?"

"Would I? This minute."

"I really don't understand you. I'd so much rather be in your position. To devote one's life to scholarship … to truth, and the service of mankind … "

"You may rest assured that my personal scholarship has never served mankind. Because there is no such thing as justice, no universal humanity. There are only versions of justice and different sorts of people. And it has always given me particular pleasure that my own scholarly efforts, let's say, in the field of old English ironworking, have never been of the slightest use to anyone."

"You speak like someone who has no ideals."

"True. I am a neo-frivolist."

"And how does that differ from old-fashioned frivolity?"

"Mostly in the 'neo' prefix. It makes it more interesting."

She was making a childish wreath from some yellow flowers called dandelions in English, and staring despondently into the distance. Our intimacy had come to a critical moment. I now bitterly regretted having said so much. What is the point of talking to the woman you love? It can only cause unpleasantness.

"I'm afraid we don't really understand each other," she said, in the sort of far-away voice she might have heard in a theatre. She should have added a 'sir'.

Then she started to chatter with great animation about her lady friend, who did understand her.

We set off back to the castle. I found it impossible to speak, as always happens to me when I have done something really stupid. And I felt rather sorry for myself. Only now did I realise how much she mattered to me, the little Lady of the Castle, who had lost her way.

When we arrived there was a telegram waiting for me.

OSBORNE CAPTURED STOP IMPORTANT TELL NOBODY STOP COME IMMEDIATELY—KRETZSCH

I was back at the very heart of the battle.

Morvin's gang must have recognised Osborne as he followed Eileen St Claire in one of his ridiculous disguises. Assuming nothing worse had happened to him, they had now rendered him harmless. But of course, they were after his life too …

I packed my bags at once. Though I had no idea what I might achieve, I could hardly wait to get to London.

I did not tell the Earl or Cynthia the reason for my departure: I didn't want to alarm them prematurely. I comforted myself that everything might still turn out well.

I managed to get away on the afternoon train. London had never before seemed so far from North Wales, nor with so many superfluous cities in between.

Arriving, I dashed to the hotel and enquired after Lene.

"Miss Kretzsch … ? Miss Kretzsch?"

A somewhat casual search for her began. She hadn't been seen at lunch. No one had noticed her at breakfast. Finally, the cleaner reported that she hadn't spent the night in her room either.

Dinner time came, but no trace of Lene. By nine o'clock I could wait no longer. I left a note with the porter to say I'd be back by eleven. Then, like a tenderly grieving lover returning to scenes frequented with his dear departed, I went round every pub where at one time or another I had drunk with her. I knew she couldn't possibly go to bed without her nightcap. If she were to be found anywhere accessible to reason, it would be in a pub.

In my distress, and because my thoughts were entirely focused on her, I knocked back a couple of pints wherever I went. I did not succeed in finding her, but by the time I returned, some time after eleven, I was in a thoroughly pleasant beer-haze and looking forward to a good night's sleep.

"Has anyone called for me?" I asked the porter, with less than perfect articulation.

"Yes, sir. A gentleman."

"You didn't recognise him? It was Miss Kretzsch, in disguise."

"That is indeed possible, sir," he replied gravely. "He said he'd come from a Mr Seton, with an important message."

"What wonderful notions she has!" I said to myself. "She must be up in her room." And I dashed merrily up the stairs.

I knocked, but there was no answer. I hammered on the door and began shouting, in German:

"Lene! Lene! Open up. It's me, Bátky! Come on, open up, will you!"

Roused by these barbaric syllables, the proprietress appeared, in her nightgown.

The proprietress was a woman of strict moral principles. The hotel rejoiced in its reputation for the highest respectability, a virtue that in England calls for rigorous policing. Seeing me battering on a lady's door she paled and gave me a look which, had I been sober, would doubtless have turned me to stone.

"Mr Bátky! … "

With what bleakly chilling tones she could prolong that unfortunate first syllable!

But I was drunk, my sight and hearing blurred the harsh edges of reality, and I was in an optimistic frame of mind.

"Hello, Mrs Stewart! How are you?" I exclaimed happily. "Do you know, you're putting on weight."

"In my establishment ladies do not receive male visitors in their rooms, especially at this time of night. Mr Bátky, you astonish me. Go downstairs at once. I must ask you to kindly remove yourself from this hotel at your earliest … "

Cowering under the weight of her authority, I crept back to my room and was soon fast asleep.

I woke early the next morning, stone cold sober. I dressed rapidly and hastened down to the porter. My head was buzzing with all the steps I had failed to take the night before.

"Is Miss Kretzsch back yet?" I asked.

"No, sir."

I had a vague notion that someone might have enquired after me the previous day.

"Who came asking for me?"

"A gentleman. From a Mr Seton."

"And what did he say?"

"He said he'd call again this morning. He asked if you would wait for him without fail."

This reassured me to a certain extent. My gravest omission of the night before had been not to let Seton know what was happening. But apparently he was already fully informed. Lene must have been in touch with him. My visitor would make all this clear.

I finished my breakfast and passed the time restlessly perusing the papers. I simply glanced at the headlines, rather cursorily. But one suddenly hit me:

CHILD ABDUCTED
MYSTERY HORSEMAN IN ABERSYCH

Strange occurrences have been reported over the past twenty-four hours in Abersych, Merioneth. Sian Prichards, thirty-six, a local farmer, was woken some time after midnight by someone at the door calling his name. Not recognising the voice, and filled with a sense of foreboding, he debated for some time whether to go out, but eventually decided to do so. Outside he found a man on horseback. He appeared to be very old, and was dressed in black. His enormous size, his striking costume and pale face struck terror into the witness. The man then uttered something in a strange tongue, after which Prichards remembers nothing more. When he recovered consciousness he was standing where he had been, outside his front door, but the stranger had disappeared, and with him Prichard's ten-year-old son. The Police are understandably treating his report with caution. Initially they were concerned that the informant might be mentally disturbed, but his reputation in the village is that of a sober, respectable citizen who has never been known to do anything unusual or eccentric. The boy's mysterious disappearance lends a degree of credibility to his story. The police are baffled. No trace of the horseman has been found, and no one other than Pritchards has seen him.

Abersych was perhaps six miles from Pendragon …

I was in no doubt as to the identity of the abductor. But what possible motive … ?

However I gave it no further thought. The whole thing was beyond rational understanding. The mere fact of its happening was a slap in the face for logical analysis. If indeed it had happened …

But then from the depths of my mind, used as it was to making historical associations, rose an alarming image: that of Bluebeard. It seemed to me to explain everything.

I wasn't thinking of the legendary Bluebeard, who killed his wives, but the historical one.

His real name was Giles de Rais, Marshall of France in the fifteenth century, at the time of the Maid of Orleans and the Hundred Years' War. He spent his entire, very considerable, fortune on alchemical experiments, without result. In the end, he decided to turn to the dark powers for help.

To win favour with Satan he hunted down and murdered small children by the hundred. The entire province became depopulated as if smitten by plague.

And, as the notes of the subsequent inquiry reveal, these murders became increasingly cruel and satanic. At first he merely tortured the children and chopped them into pieces; then he came up with the idea of roasting them over a slow fire. The next refinement was to use them for various obscene acts while torturing them to death. As he later confessed, the greatest pleasure of all involved squatting on the butchered bodies of his victims. In the final phase, they were sexually violated.

None of this had any effect. The Devil did manifest himself on a number of occasions, but was unremittingly hostile. At one point he flogged one of de Rais' friends, an Italian alchemist, almost to death. The Devil is not a kindly master.

Eventually the Inquisition caught up with him. They excommunicated him as a follower of Satan and handed him over to a secular court, which sentenced him to death.

He repented his sins and begged the people, on his knees, to forgive him his crimes. And the wonderful people of that time pardoned their children's murderer. Sobbing and wailing, they accompanied him to the scaffold and implored God to have mercy on his soul …

"The gentleman is here," said the porter. "The one who was looking for you."

I made my way quickly into the foyer.

A sharp-eyed man, looking like a detective, was waiting for me.

"Are you János Bátky?" he asked.

"I am."

"Excuse me, but I must ask for some proof of identity. The matter is sufficiently serious to oblige caution. Mr Seton specifically asked … "

"As you wish," I replied, and showed him the photograph in my passport. All foreigners have to carry one in Britain.

"Thank you. You are aware that the Hon Osborne Pendragon has been abducted by James Morvin and his accomplices. Miss Kretzsch gave you this information."

"She did."

"We've been looking for him since yesterday afternoon, on Mr Seton's instructions. Events have played into our hands, and since last night we've had a pretty good idea where he might be. Morvin owns a chemical works in Southwark. From remarks let slip by one of his workmen we think they're hiding him there. We can force an entry without attracting attention this morning, as it's closed on Sundays. Mr Seton would very much like you to accompany us. This is obviously going to end up in court, and he will need witnesses. He and Miss Kretzsch are already in Southwark, waiting for you. Are you prepared to join us?"

"Of course."

"Then perhaps we should be on our way."

We climbed into a taxi and were driven to the south bank, then raced through the squalor of Southwark between endless factory buildings. The streets were deserted. It was a Sunday, in England.

We stopped in a little backstreet. We stepped out and four men came up to us. A tall gentleman with a silver moustache and a bowler hat held out his hand.

"Seton."

"I'm Bátky."

"Do you have a revolver? Then we're ready."

"Yes. Excuse me … Where is Miss Kretzsch?"

"She'll be here in a moment. But I think we should start."

We came to a wooden fence surrounding one of the smaller factories. The gate was unlocked, and we entered the yard.

The first building was an office. The man I had come with, the one who looked like a detective, opened the door with a master key. The office area consisted of three rooms. None of them yielded anything of interest.

"He must be in one of the warehouses," said Seton.

One of these had a particularly grim exterior, massive and windowless. From the very first glance it aroused my suspicion. I said as much to Seton.

"Right. We'll do this one first. Sheridan, go and stand guard by the gate."

There was a padlock on the door. The detective-type picked up a stout plank and, with an impressive swing, smashed it off. Then he opened the door with a master key.

"After you," I gestured politely to Seton.

"You first," he replied.

Then, dispensing with any further courtesy, they grabbed me and pushed me inside.

I rolled down some steps. The big door banged shut behind me.

Had I broken any bones?

But there wasn't time to investigate. From out of a corner two huge negroes came rushing at me. They seized me and began to throttle me.

"Mr Seton! Mr Seton!" I yelled.

The negroes let go and stared at me, their white teeth gleaming.

"You too?" they shouted, and they started to laugh.

It was Osborne and Lene.

"What do you mean, 'me too'?"

"They got you as well."

I still hadn't grasped it.

"But … but … I came here with Seton."

"Seton? What did he look like?"

"Nice-looking chap, getting on a bit. Silver moustache."

"Splendid. Seton never had a moustache in his life," said Osborne.

"But how did you get here? Why did you leave Llanvygan?"

"Why? Because Lene wired to say you'd been abducted and that I should come immediately."

"I what?" she choked. "I've been sitting in this dump since yesterday afternoon discussing the finer points of sociology with Osborne. But it's impossible to get through to him. And all this time I'm fainting with hunger."

"Do you think … they intend starving us to death?"

"Looks like it. All they've done is throw in a few ham and cheese sandwiches, and a couple of apples—as if we were circus bears or something. What do they think I am?"

"But how did you get here?" I asked.

"Very simple," said Osborne. "As per our programme, the day after you left we disguised ourselves like this and followed Mrs Roscoe. We didn't have much luck at the start. Mrs Roscoe spent the whole day doing whatever she does with her life. But yesterday, first thing in the morning, she came here. We'd seen Morvin here once before. When she went inside Lene had the bright idea of following her in. We'd pretend we were looking for work and take the opportunity to have a look around."

"It was a brilliant idea," Lene chipped in. "The instant we stepped through the gate, ten guys rushed at us and threw us in this cellar. I didn't even have time to say *Heil Hitler*. We've been sitting here ever since."

"And that's it," said Osborne. "The profession of detective is not without its hazards."

"And now you're here as well," Lene added. "These people seem to be very thorough."

"What do they want?"

"It's a little matter of death by starvation. My God, when I think of all the sauerkraut in Schmidt's … "

"Or perhaps they intend blackmailing my uncle," said Osborne.

We sat in thoughtful silence.

"In all the books I've read," I remarked, "when it gets to this point the captives try to think of ways of escape."

"So let's try to think."

"The classic formulae never quite apply," Osborne sighed. "We can't tunnel out through the wall with our bare fingernails. We're underground."

"Perhaps we could force the door?" suggested Lene.

"Doesn't seem likely."

For a long time we talked and talked. My companions were very lethargic. For all their resolute cheerfulness, the confinement seemed to have sapped their energy. It was already the lunch hour. By the time night fell, I thought, even the hotel fare would be something to rejoice over. And above all, how would I cope without my cup of tea?

"We should try the lock," I insisted. "I may not know much about the triumph of modern technology, but I've read a lot about old English ironwork. Maybe I'll think of something."

I stood up and tentatively pushed the handle down.

The door opened. It hadn't been locked.

This was not the solution I had expected. For some minutes I stood in the open doorway gasping with surprise.

Then we drew our revolvers and dashed out into the yard.

We looked to the right, then to the left. Not a soul anywhere. We raced over to the fence, pulled the gate open and were in the street. At this point we noticed a large sign hanging on the gate:

TO LET

But there was no time to ponder this new mystery. At the first telephone box we summoned a taxi and drove to the Pendragon mansion in Eaton Square. Lene and Osborne washed their colourful disguises off, and we went out to dinner.

Lene resisted Osborne's invitation to the Ritz.

"Impossible. You'll see why."

We went instead to a little place in Soho. No sooner had we finished the dessert than she ordered another bowl of soup, and followed it with a meat dish. In all, she disposed of two complete meals, swiftly and in total silence. Then she leant back in her chair.

"Now, let's do some thinking."

We started thinking.

"The real puzzle isn't that they abducted us," Osborne began systematically, "but that they let us go. Why did they do that? Or, why did they let us go so soon after they'd caught us?"

"Obviously, because the reason for keeping us no longer applied," I suggested. "So what follows from that? That something occurred while we were in there."

A new kind of unease flooded over me. Who knows what might have happened to the Earl, or perhaps Cynthia … ?

"I think we should phone Llanvygan at once."

We paid the bill and left.

As we stood waiting in the Post Office for a long-distance connection, Lene suddenly smacked her forehead.

"It's so simple. They captured us because they didn't want us following them. They kept us out of the way so that we'd lose the trail."

It rang true. Meanwhile Llanvygan had come on line, and Osborne was speaking. We waited in mounting anxiety for him to emerge from the booth.

"I spoke to Rogers. My uncle is fine. He's in his laboratory and didn't want to come to the phone. However … "

"Well?"

"Cynthia left yesterday afternoon. She went by car, taking a suitcase. She hasn't come back. Rogers has no idea where she went. There was a telegram."

My heart sank. A telegram. She too … Yes, she too must have been ensnared with a piece of fictitious news. And here was I, her sworn champion, with her favour in my shield, helpless.

Lene stroked my head.

"Poor little Doctor. But don't fall apart just yet. Look … assuming that like us she was lured away by Morvin's lot, it's unlikely she's come to any harm either. She's got the least reason for anything to happen to her."

"Well," said Osborne. "Of the many possibilities inherent in the universe, only one is relevant right now. We must go to Grosvenor House and see what Mrs Roscoe is up to."

This made sense, and we went straight there. The Delage, emblazoned with the Pendragon coat of arms, worked its usual effect. We were received with the greatest deference.

Osborne went up to the reception counter and called out to one of the distinguished-looking gentlemen gathered behind it:

"Mrs Roscoe?"

"Mrs Roscoe left yesterday."

"Oh, dear. Where was she going?"

"Just a moment, please."

And he began thumbing through a book.

But at that point an even more imposing dignitary pushed him roughly aside and snarled:

"Mrs Roscoe did not say where she was going."

She had obviously left her instructions.

We went out, and carried on walking down Park Lane, full of nervous excitement. A procession of limousines glided past us, carrying fairytale princesses. Oh, London … (But I'm writing this 'Oh London' bit now: I didn't have time for it then.)

Suddenly Lene stopped in her tracks and whooped: "Hoi-hoi!"

"What is it?"

"I've got it. Listen. We've worked out why Osborne and I were held—so that we couldn't follow them. But that doesn't explain why the Doctor and Cynthia were lured away from Llanvygan, assuming of course it was Morvin who wired her. The connection is this: we were detained to stop us realising that they were going, and you were called away to stop you seeing them arrive. They must have been preparing to leave for Llanvygan, and they wanted to find the Earl there without you present."

"That's awful!"

"It isn't awful yet. Half an hour ago the Earl was alive and well and working in his laboratory. I like people who work in laboratories … but never mind that. If we leave now we can get there before midnight."

It seemed an excellent idea. We jumped in the Delage and set out for the west. We were there by eleven thirty.

The staff were all fast asleep. After a great deal of knocking we were finally let in. We asked Rogers to let the Earl know of our arrival.

"I'm very sorry, but that's impossible," he replied. "His Lordship took a sedative before going to bed and gave strict instructions that he was not to be disturbed under any circumstances. I really am very sorry, but you must please understand, I would be risking my position here … "

We knew his stubbornness well, and resigned ourselves to the fact that we would not see the Earl before the morning.

A sudden thought occurred to Osborne, and he turned to Rogers:

"I say … did anyone call on His Lordship while I was away?"

"Only the Reverend Dafyd Jones."

"No one else?"

"No, sir."

I was back in my historic bed (Queen Anne, I believe). With time, this room had come to seem like home. A not entirely restful home. Somewhere above my head the giant axolotls swam. A few yards from my window stood the balcony Maloney had fallen from. And there was the vivid memory of the night rider circling the house with his flaming torch. It was home to me, as a trench would be to a soldier. I pulled my head down under the blanket.

There was a knock at the door and Osborne entered.

"Forgive me. Rogers was lying. I saw it at once, the way his whiskers kept twitching."

"What do you mean?"

"I woke Griffith and gave him a grilling. It isn't true that no one's been to visit. A woman came, twice, in a car. From the description it's obviously Mrs Roscoe. She first appeared in the morning, but he was out. He hadn't slept here that night. And he was out the whole day. She left a message to say she'd be back in the evening. And—can you imagine?—she did come back, and he refused to see her."

"He refused to see her? But that's marvellous. So the danger's over. Or rather … "

"Or rather, you can't be so sure. They're very resourceful, and it won't be easy to talk them out of their little schemes. You could even call them stubborn. But at least we're here now. We'll take care of him. Lene has a gift for looking after people."

We wished each other a restful night.

My night wasn't particularly peaceful. I kept seeing Cynthia, exposed to a thousand dangers, now in the clutches of Morvin's gang, now among the axolotls.

The next morning the Earl joined us at breakfast. Lene was late. While we waited for her we brought the Earl up to date on what had been happening. He listened without interest: something else seemed to be preying on his mind. I thought of the stolen child, and an oppressive sadness, mingled with a paralysing sense of fear, descended on me.

"Uncle," Osborne asked, "where did Cynthia go?"

"Cynthia?" he replied, distractedly. "She went to London. Your aunt, the Duchess of Warwick, wired to say she was unwell and would like Cynthia to nurse her. Her gout, I should imagine … "

Osborne leapt to his feet.

"I'll ring Aunt Doris. I'm afraid it's another of these fictions … "
And off he went.

A this point Lene entered. Her apparel was in interestingly bad taste, the sort of thing that would go down well in Berlin.

The Earls' greeting was a mixture of obliging kindness and extreme detachment. She didn't like it.

"You remind me so much of my poor uncle Otto," she remarked.

"I do?"

"Absolutely. He also studied the flies on the wall when speaking to you. I can't stand it if someone doesn't look me in the eye when he addresses me."

The Earl stared at her in astonishment.

"That's better. You know, you have a really intelligent face. Your family all seem to be fairly bright. I always thought old families were full of idiots."

"Osborne will show you round the park," he replied. "It's rather pretty." And he buried himself in his tea.

Osborne returned, ashen-faced.

"Trouble," he announced. "Aunt Doris is in perfect health."

"God bless her," Lene added.

"Hang on a second. Aunt Doris says the telegram must be in

error. Cynthia got there the night before last, slept there, and left, quite early the next morning, saying she'd be back. That was yesterday. She hasn't been seen since."

I glanced at the Earl. He was stroking his forehead.

"Where could she be?" he asked in a completely neutral voice. He seemed overwhelmed by a grief so profound that nothing new could touch him.

We all felt desperate and helpless. Even Lene was unable to drum up her usual reassuring indelicacy.

Osborne took her out to show her the park. I was pacing up and down the terrace, when the Rev. Dafyd Jones appeared.

"Oh, Doctor, I am so happy to find you. You lead such a spiritual life. I must speak to you whatever the cost."

In silence, his face anxious as ever, he dragged me off to a remote section of the park.

"What do you make of it all?" he whispered, when we were out of sight of the castle. "Is it not unspeakably dreadful?"

"It is dreadful," I replied. "We haven't the slightest idea where she might be."

"But there was no other way, sir. It was inevitable. I told you, did I not, that no good would come of it. All these experiments."

"But what are the experiments to do with Miss Cynthia?"

The vicar wasn't listening.

"Because that's the way it is. First with animals. Axolotls," he shuddered. "Then people."

"What exactly are you talking about?"

"Why, about the child he abducted in Abersych."

"Oh yes, the child … Who do you say abducted him?"

"The Earl," he said, in a fierce whisper.

"Never. Why would the Earl do a thing like that?"

"To experiment, sir. To experiment. To kill him, and then revive him. He's grown tired of mere animals."

"But the little boy was taken away by an old man in black. The midnight rider."

"The midnight rider is the Earl of Gwynedd. As I told you. I know it. Or if not the Earl himself, his double."

"Or a different Earl of Gwynedd," I said.

"Since that day the Earl has never been at home. He prowls

about. Sick. With a guilty conscience. The boy isn't hidden here. Somewhere in the mountains."

"Nothing of the sort. I have seen, with my own eyes, that the Earl and the midnight rider are two different people."

"Do not trust what your eyes tell you, Doctor. Try to put yourself in my shoes … I know I must say the words of exorcism over him. But in such a way that he is not aware of it. He'd be very offended, and, after all, the Llanvygan living is in his power and I am totally dependent on him."

Just then my hypersensitive ears picked up the sound of a motor horn. I abandoned the mad vicar and ran towards the castle.

There, outside the front door, stood the little Rover.

I dashed inside, to find Cynthia eating her breakfast. She was in radiant spirits and greeted me loudly.

"Cynthia, where were you?"

She looked at me in surprise.

"Excuse me … when did you become so very inquisitive?"

"Forgive me, my dear, do forgive me, my only … We've been almost dead with worry. Osborne phoned your aunt, and she said she hadn't sent for you, and that you'd left her yesterday morning. We thought … we really thought, you'd walked into Morvin's trap."

She laughed.

"Not in the least. What should Morvin want from me? I'm in excellent health, and I've had a marvellous time. But, since you are so curious, I might as well tell you. After I left Aunt Doris I went to see my lady friend. It turned out that it was she who sent the telegram, because she was missing me so much and she wanted to entice me down to London whatever way she could. I found her at home, as beautiful as ever. And she was just about to go and spend her Sunday at Llandudno. So we went there together, and I had the day with her. And now I'm here … So, are you happy now?"

And then something quite appalling happened. I am normally as circumspect as an engineer with particularly short sight, but I threw inhibition to the winds, hurled myself at her and covered her in kisses. It was such a relief to know she was all right.

She disentangled herself, thoroughly discomposed. Before her mouth had even recovered the usual shape for speech, she informed me she had been reading a study of Ivan the Terrible.

Soon it was time for lunch.

It is something I truly cannot help, but I adore women who eat heartily and with real pleasure. One of Cynthia's major shortcomings was that she considered it undignified, as a spiritual being, to surrender to the pleasures of food. She ate with a faraway expression on her face, like a woman at her needlework. The fork appeared to find its way to her mouth by pure accident. It might just as easily have fluttered away, like a little butterfly.

Lene was precisely the reverse. She didn't eat: she fed herself. In a fever of excitement she refuelled the large and ever-developing organism, glowing with vitality, that was her body. I could see that the Earl, despite his best efforts, couldn't bear to watch her. And how much wine she drank! (These were the dangerously full-bodied reds of southern France.) She grew steadily louder, holding forth about her university experiences, and I waited in fear and trembling for her to get round to the more erotic of these, and the self-evident nature of *Moralische*.

Osborne and I sat there, like orphans huddled in a storm. But the Earl seemed to take a sort of masochistic pleasure in her brashness, and he questioned her constantly, encouraging her to talk.

"You haven't said how you like the castle," he remarked.

"In short, I can only say I don't. First of all, those columns at the entrance. Why so many? The place isn't going to fall down. Each storey is in a different style. And all this furniture. Queen Anne in one room, Chippendale in another: it's a mess. There's no single *motif*, no metaphysic holding it together. And tell me, why such a huge building? Sixty rooms … it's utterly irrational."

"I think you could say the same about the wives of oriental kings. They had three hundred and sixty five, not because they needed them, but because they were kings."

After lunch we younger ones went for a walk down the long avenue leading from the castle to the village.

Coming towards us, very slowly, was a strange figure. He was walking with a stick, and was followed by several others, all rather small. With my short-sightedness I could not make out who they were, and only started to pay real attention when my companions, whose eyes were sharper, stopped to discuss the situation.

"What sort of procession is it?" asked Osborne. "Perhaps you can tell us, Cynthia. Is there some sort of Welsh festival today?"

"It's the Pied Piper of Hamlyn and his retinue of children," Lene suggested.

"No," exclaimed Osborne. "Look, it's Pierce Gwyn Mawr, the old prophet Habakkuk. My, he does look in a bad way."

We quickened our pace to meet him, and now I too could make him out quite clearly. The poor man was even more prophet-like than before. His appearance was exactly what you would have expected of John the Baptist, clad in the traditional attire of one crying out in the wilderness. Except for a rag around his loins he was stark naked—not something you expect to see in broad daylight in these islands. The stout branch in his hand served as a walking stick; the grey shock of his beard and hair flew in every direction. It was a disturbing, fantastic, strangely threatening sight, complete with the obligatory wisps of straw in the hair that every self-respecting lunatic in Britain has sported since the days of King Lear.

He was followed by a procession of village children. But this was not mockery: they were really frightened, ready to take to their heels at the first hostile gesture from the prophet.

Osborne called out to him:

"Hey there, Pierce Gwyn Mawr. What's new in the world?"

The prophet gave no reply. Though he looked towards us, I don't think he saw us. His eyes were flickering and ecstatic; they also seemed, to me, to be filled with a supernatural fear, the universal fear felt by children and madmen of a world possessed by demons. I can't say this for certain of course, being no expert in the reading of eyes.

Then, when Cynthia said something to him in Welsh, he stopped, appeared to recognise her, and a very specific terror seemed to engulf him. But he still made no reply.

She repeated her question. He spun round and, with astonishing nimbleness, sprinted towards the village with the children at his heels.

"For Heaven's sake, Cynthia," I asked, "what did you say to frighten him so badly?"

"Nothing," she said, clearly shaken. "I only asked if he was hungry."

"Interesting," said Lene. "It sounded as if you were asking what it was like in Hell."

"The Welsh language has a wonderful sound," said Osborne. "It's quite different. From another world. For example, can you imagine a language in which the word for beer is 'cwrw'?"

By now my mind was making rapid connections, and it left me feeling uneasy again. So far as I knew, Pierce Gwyn Mawr was the only person apart from the Earl who had spoken with the midnight rider. The Castle Lake ...

We joined the urgent migration to the village. Halfway there, the Earl overtook us in his open-topped tourer.

"Have you seen Pierce Gwyn Mawr?" he asked .

"Yes. He went down to the village."

We climbed on board.

In the main street we found a large throng. Everyone was talking; everyone was excited and nervous. As the Earl approached a respectful silence fell and they made way for him.

We climbed out.

"Which of you has seen old Pierce Gwyn Mawr?"

"We all have," said a farmer. "He jumped over the churchyard wall and vanished."

We set off at speed in that direction, and the Rev Dafyd Jones came into view.

"He's disappeared," he said. "Vanished. As if swallowed by the graves."

We carried on towards the burial ground. As we passed the front of the church we spotted John Griffith, leaning with his back against the door and waving triumphantly.

"I've got him," he shouted. "I've got him. I'm not letting him out."

"Of course," the vicar cried. "The side door opens on to the graveyard. I didn't realise it was open."

The old man was sitting in a pew, exhausted. His head was slumped forwards, his body motionless. The vicar addressed him in Welsh; he slowly raised his head and stared around vaguely. At first he seemed not to see anything, then he noticed the Earl and his face twisted into a mask.

With an astonishing, ape-like agility he jumped up, leapt over several pews and made for the exit. But Lene was waiting by the door. She grabbed him round the neck and held him firmly until the others arrived and surrounded him.

"Get a good grip on him," the Earl said to Griffith and another guard from the house whose presence I hadn't noticed before.

The two men seized the old prophet, bundled him out of the church and lifted him into the car. The Earl climbed in, waved us goodbye, and drove off back to the castle.

We were left standing outside the church gazing after them. The prophet's arrest had all the strangeness of a medieval pre-rogative being exercised. The others were completely flummoxed by it. By now however I had a theory. I'm never at a loss for these little explanations, and the intensive training of recent weeks had further developed my deductive propensities.

The prophet was the last man to see the midnight rider. He would have been acting as his servant while he was in residence up at Pendragon. Something dreadful must have happened to cause him to leave, his mind utterly deranged: the abducted child, Giles de Rais ... And his feelings of horrified revulsion now extended to all the Pendragons, including Cynthia.

When we arrived back at the castle we were told that the Earl was preparing to set out on a journey.

"Miss Lene, I really am most sorry to leave while you are here as our guest. I have to go to Caerbryn. Osborne, would you have my mail forwarded there? I'm staying with old Mansfield, at Oaklea Farm."

"My dear Earl," Lene retorted. "I am distraught that my femi-nine charms seem to have so little power over you. But quite apart from that, I must caution you, in your own interests, not to leave Llanvygan just now. Consider, there are sixty rooms here, and thirty unemployed persons with halberds. And I'm here too. Here, we can look after you. But on a farm ... Who is going with you?"

"No one. Old Mansfield will take excellent care of me. I've stayed with him many times."

"These Puritan tendencies. But aren't you worried about your enemies making use of the opportunity? I can't tell if this is sheer indifference or just stupidity. You're amazingly casual about it."

He smiled.

"It's where I'll be best hidden from those enemies. So, unless you write and tell Morvin, he'll never know where I am. What's more, I'm being so careful I'm not even telling Rogers where I'm going. Now, do I have your permission?"

"Go then, and God go with you. But I must warn you, I shall call on you there."

"I'd be delighted."

I believed I knew the reason for the Earl's rapid departure. He must have learnt from the prophet where the midnight rider had based himself since leaving Pendragon. He was going to find him; no doubt with the intention of saving the little boy. For that, he was prepared to face whatever irrational, unknowable, immortal danger lay ahead.

We young people stayed on in the castle. We certainly enjoyed our time. Morvin seemed to have been forgotten, and the other, more mysterious, threat was so irrational it was hard to focus on, and I didn't take it very seriously.

The next morning Osborne came up to me.

"Doctor, would you like to go for a little spin in the car? We should be out looking round the countryside. Let's put our trust in the luck of idiots: we might even hit upon Morvin's traces somewhere. If his people are in any of the villages round here we're sure to find out. If of course they really are in Wales. We haven't heard of them for some days now."

"With pleasure," I replied. "But shouldn't we take Lene with us?"

"Er … Miss Kretzsch said she was going to lie in this morning. Perhaps just the two of us."

We drove round all the local places of note. We went to Corwen, to the railway station, and even to Abersych, where the child was abducted. We found a large number of policemen there, and were told that they were following a definite lead.

What would happen if they actually caught him? Such a mountain of absurdities would come spilling down into this complacent world of ours that everyone would be talking about it … The Earl

would be required to give evidence, as would Osborne, and perhaps even myself. Maloney's death would come into question …
The Earl would never survive the scandal. The thought of such things bandied about in the London papers to entertain the man on the Clapham omnibus … We went back for lunch, without having discovered anything of the slightest interest.

Waking from my post-prandial nap, I went for a stroll in the park, where I bumped into Lene. She was in high spirits, and devouring enormous peaches from a basket she had found on one of the garden tables. Briefly suspending the refuelling process, she took me by the arm and led me further into the park.

We sat down beside a little stream. The spot was enchanting.

"It's so lovely," she said. "It really fits my mood today. I'm so happy here."

"I haven't heard you say that very often. You mean, you actually like it here?"

"Very much. Such nice, uncomplicated people. The Earl is quite batty, but he has a beautiful head. The girl is very pretty, and very sweet, though she's horribly conventional. I'm surprised she doesn't bore you. But that's not the point—you know I never poke my nose into your affairs. But I feel really good about myself. It finally happened."

"What did?"

"Why do you think I came to Llanvygan?"

"To save the Earl's life?"

"That too. But only by the way. I mean, why should I bother about the Earl of Gwynedd or any other old aristocrat? They aren't my sort."

"You're telling me you came because of Osborne."

"You see, you aren't so dumb after all. And I can tell you, as my old friend and ally, that my trip here has not been in vain. Last night … "

"Oh, Lene, congratulations. Compared with Osborne, an innocent theologian of forty-five is a sex-crazed Italian from the deep South."

"Not bad, hey?"

"Fantastic! But confess: Osborne only surrendered under extreme duress. You must have threatened him with a revolver."

"I didn't go that far, but it certainly wasn't easy. If you're inter-ested in the details, I'll tell you. You know how reserved Osborne was with me, until yesterday. Or, not exactly reserved: he just treated me in the same very polite way he did his male friends. If I were as easily offended as my mother's generation were, I'd have been cut to the quick. But thank God I'm not one of your super-sensitive females. In fact I was rather glad he treated me as a man. I knew that the mere fact that he didn't find me repulsive was no small achievement.

"All the same, when I took his hand he blushed scarlet and started to lecture me on the dramatic works of Shakespeare's con-temporaries. I thought: just you wait, I'll get you in the end. I'd worked out over time that women's wiles cut no ice with him. In his innocence he just didn't notice. That time in London, when we were dressing up in funny costume, it was a waste of time parading myself before him in my flimsy underwear. Whenever I started to undress he was desperate to get away. But when I told him it didn't bother me, he just lit a cigarette and stayed put. After that, he found it quite natural to see me naked. But I could see from his face that there was nothing in the way of manly desire stirring in him. As far as I was concerned, his innocence was all the more provocative.

"It went against the grain, but I even tried sentimentality. I said all the usual things: how lonely I was, how sad my evenings, how no one had truly loved me, and oh, how heavy my heart was. He listened, very sympathetically, and promised me that when we got back to Oxford he'd introduce me to some really top people—he thinks everyone else is as great a snob as he is—but until then I should make a study of the contemporary English novel, since a good book was the best friend one could have.

"And that's how I came to Llanvygan. I was really ashamed of myself. In the time it had taken I could have become the mistress of a French king and enjoyed limitless power, or seduced a couple of ambassadors. Last night, when I managed to get him out here in the park, my hopes were really high. You know how the English love nature …

"I suggested we sit on the grass, but he was afraid it might be damp, so we found a bench. I leant my head on his shoulder and started kissing his ear. He sat there in total silence, very polite. When I got bored with that, he told me with a smile that it was no doubt a German custom, and probably very ancient. I said I didn't know about that, but anyway it was a nice one. 'Interesting,' he said, in a contemplative sort of way. I asked him if he'd like to kiss me. 'Oh, yes, he would,' he said, again very politely, and gave me a peck on the forehead. 'If I were a man,' I told him, 'I'd rather kiss someone on the lips.' He thought that would be unhygienic. Then he asked me if I'd rather be a man. 'What about you?' I retorted.

"That rather shook him, but I could see this wasn't getting us anywhere. Then I had a stroke of genius. I said I wanted to climb a tree, and would he help me? I clambered up on to a branch, with his support. Then I swung out, gave a loud scream, and fell on top of him. Now if I fall on anyone, with my build …

"We both ended up on the ground. So that was how I got to the point where kissing was possible—at the cost of a few bruises. My ribs were aching, but the goal was in sight.

"Needless to say, even in that position Osborne remained the perfect gentleman. There was no point in leaving him to take the initiative. Half an hour later we untangled ourselves and I asked him if he'd enjoyed it; he said he had, quite definitely, and he sounded reasonably sincere. He said he was pleased to have had one of life's richer practical experiences. And—would you believe this?—that he'd had his first lover.

"That made me really angry and I told him the English were a bunch of well-bred idiots if they thought that after a bit of nonsense like that they could call you their lover. So he lapsed into day-dream again and said he was sorry. Then he started to get up. I grabbed hold of his jacket, following biblical precedent, and told him he needn't worry: if he asked me very nicely he really could be my lover, and he'd get even more hands-on experience. He knew what I meant. But he just sat there, and went on thinking.

"Finally I snapped at him and asked what he was waiting for. He said he was trying to remember what one was supposed to say on such occasions. I assured him that actions spoke louder than words. 'That's good,' he said, 'because I couldn't think of any words.' And still he just sat there. 'So let's see some action,' I said.

'Try to be a bit more passionate.' So he grabbed me and shook me. I won't go into any more detail, because I can see from the expression on your face that you would have done rather better in his position, and I don't really fancy you just now. I'm having a monogamous day today, for the first time in my life. I shall be true to Osborne."

"Well," I said, "am I free to imagine the rest?"

"As you wish. The scene of what followed wasn't the park but my room. It went on the whole night. Because you see ... Osborne wasn't a disappointment. And he got his satisfaction too. He said he hadn't enjoyed himself so much in ages. Oh, and he hoped we'd tie the marriage knot soon."

I was horrified. Such a misalliance! My snobbish heart wept blood. The poor Earl ... This was all the Pendragon destiny needed. It would be the end of everything.

"My congratulations," I muttered, with tears in my voice.

"Come off it, you idiot. You don't think I'd really marry him?"

"Why not? It's not a bad match."

"No, my dear boy, I'm not that stupid. Marry into such a degenerate aristocratic family? What would my friends in Berlin say? Anyway, I'm still young. I've hardly known anything of life. So many experiences are waiting for me. I've never had an affair with a tenor. Or a Hohenzollern. And only once with a negro. I really can't get married just yet."

"You're absolutely right," I said, heaving a deep sigh of relief. "You've got the whole of your life ahead of you."

"I'd just love to know," she went on, "whether this little 'life experience' will change Osborne in any way. Will he now be more like a man?"

"In his dealings with you, yes," I said—"just as long as you expect him to, and not a minute longer. The moment you're gone, everything will be just as it was before. That's my experience of young Englishmen. Very occasionally, when he's out one evening with a few close friends, and the conversation turns to women, he'll tell them—without mentioning your name—that he did once have a girl, and it was all rather wonderful. He'll live on the memory for the next ten years, until another Lene comes along and seduces him."

"Oh my God," she said. "How stupid, how utterly immoral, how thoroughly screwed-up. On the other hand—don't you find?—there's something rather sweet in all this purity of soul."

I didn't answer. Something had just occurred to me, something that had happened during our outing that morning, which I hadn't thought anything of at the time. We were driving through a wood, beside a clear little mountain stream. Osborne stopped the car, stripped off and had a swim, though there was quite a chilling breeze. As he was getting dressed again, shivering with cold, he said to me:

"Oh, Doctor, if only I could live on an uninhabited island ... a coral island in Polynesia ... where there was no one to talk to, only birds and fish ... and not a soul to be seen, especially not women ... then a chap would be able to keep his human dignity."

I remembered the look on his face. It bore all the misery of a dog that feels thoroughly ashamed of itself.

I had another tense and restless night. I dreamed of Eileen St Claire as a whore in a sea port, somewhere at the back of beyond. All sorts of obscene, and at the same time deeply horrible, things were going on. The next morning I woke, still rather tense, with the strange feeling that I had briefly understood, but had then forgotten, why the Earl still loved her.

Cynthia was in happy mood and looking her loveliest, seated golden-blonde at the breakfast table in a sleeveless dress that showed off her girlish, sunburnt arms. She made quizzical faces over her tea to ask why I was looking so dull when we happened to be alone—Lene and Osborne had gone out to bathe—and she came over to me, kittenish and intimate, to ask why I was so sad.

"I had a very strange dream," I told her.

"Tell me."

"You shouldn't ask me such an improper thing."

"Oh," she cried. "So, it was about a woman?"

"Certainly."

She looked downcast for several minutes, then steeled herself to ask:

"Was it me?"

"I'm sorry, but it wasn't."

"Recreant, traitor! So who was it then?"

"You don't know her."

"What does she look like, then?"

"She's taller than you, has reddish-blond hair and a stunning figure. She has the face, sometimes, of an Etruscan statue."

"Tell me what her name is."

"You don't know her, but you've certainly heard of her … " and something suddenly struck me. "I was dreaming of Eileen St Claire."

"Eileen St Claire? But she's my best friend! I was with her that day in Llandudno!" she exclaimed, blushing prettily. "So you know her? Isn't she wonderful, a real angel?"

I put my pipe down and stammered:

"What are you saying? Your best friend?"

"Yes. She's the one I've been telling you all about, the person whose name I didn't want to say. My great friend, my only true love."

Oh the silly, tragic little goose! God knows what she had done in the innocence of her heart.

"How did you come to know her?"

"Two years ago I was having my summer holiday in Brittany and she was staying in the villa next door. I was still very upset— it was just after my mother's death. She gave me back my *joie de vivre*. She's so beautiful. And she was so good to me. But not just to me. She knows my uncle very well. They used to be very good friends. She's the only one who knows what a truly wonderful man he is. Why are you looking at me like that … like a police superintendent?"

"Nothing, nothing. Please carry on."

"What else can I say? I've told you how much I like her. How much she means in my life."

I was gradually piecing it all together. Of course Cynthia had no idea who Eileen St Claire was. No one dared utter her name in the Earl's presence, and this taboo extended to all the other Pendragons. No one had told Cynthia that Eileen St Claire and Mrs Roscoe were one and the same person.

I had only ever spoken of her as Mrs Roscoe. I had told her nothing of what the woman was like, or how I knew her. I had had no wish to discuss the night I spent with her, so I had said no more than was strictly necessary.

And Cynthia was as dreamy and romantic as all the other Pendragons. She too had projected her most cherished fantasies on to the beauty of Eileen St Claire.

"Oh, Cynthia … and have you kept in touch with her ever since? Have you been writing to her?" My alarm was growing by the second. "Do you mention the Earl in your letters?"

"Oh yes, I didn't tell you—I promised to report everything that happened to my uncle, and I have done, all this time. And now you must tell me how you came to know her."

So here was the 'spy' who had kept Morvin's gang informed of everything.

I leapt up and walked round the room twice, at great speed.

"I've written to her about everything," she continued dreamily, and quite untroubled. "I've told her a lot about you too. Even before you got here I told her you were coming. I felt your coming here would be a major event. And when you went back to London I explained exactly why you'd gone. I've written lots of bad things about you. You'll hear all about them the next time you see her. But what's wrong with you? What is it? You mustn't tease me."

By then I think I must have been tugging at her arm.

"Cynthia, did you also tell her where the Earl is right now?"

"Of course. I gave her the precise details. She's taught me that whatever I do I must be thorough."

"When did you write to tell her the Earl was going?"

"But why? What's the matter with you? I wrote yesterday afternoon."

"Where to?"

"Llandudno. The Palace Hotel."

I made a rapid calculation. The letter could well have got there by the evening. So they could already have set off to find him. There was no time to lose—if indeed there still was anything left to lose.

"Cynthia my dear, you must telephone your friend this minute. We absolutely have to know if she's still in Llandudno."

"But why?"

"I will explain everything. But you must phone her now. Tell her whatever you like, but go."

And I dragged her to the phone.

A few minutes later she was put through to the Palace Hotel. Mrs St Claire (as she had registered herself) was out. She had left the night before. She hadn't left word when she would be back.

No doubt, the moment she got Cynthia's letter …

"Pack your suitcase, and have it put in the tourer. Now. Immediately!"

With bewilderment on her face, she hurried out. I rang for one of the page boys and sent him dashing off to the stream where Osborne and Lene were bathing. They were told to come at once. Then I went up to my room to pack.

I was filled with energy, and hard as steel. I could barely recognise myself. I knew we were going into the last great battle. Unless it was already too late … The Earl was caught between two opposing catastrophes, and I wondered which was the more dangerous—the increasingly sinister spirit or the coldly-calculating twentieth-century assassin. The Knight, Death and the Devil …

Thirty minutes later we were all together in the reception area. I told the others how things stood. Cynthia went deathly pale and burst into tears. Her world was in ruins.

But every detail tallied. She recalled that during the day she had spent at Llandudno her friend had gone out twice in the car alone, once in the morning and once in the late afternoon, leaving her with some acquaintances. They were precisely the times when Eileen had tried to gain admittance to Llanvygan.

We piled into the car, excited and confused, four children left on their own by the grownups to wrestle with Death and the Devil.

"I just need to know where this Caerbryn is," Osborne announced from behind the steering wheel. "It's some godforsaken little place up in the mountains."

Close study of the map ensued. At long last we found both it and the shortest way to get there. Thereafter we drove in silence, awed equally by fear and the magic of speed.

Half an hour later we were in the mountains. Soon we had to slow down. The main road had come to an end and we found ourselves on tracks that had never been intended for cars. We had to consult the map every few minutes.

Meanwhile the morning that had been so friendly had turned dark and threatening.

I would never have believed that in Wales, in Great Britain, there could be such ancient, truly Nordic places, without trace of people or human dwelling. The road was either lined with bald rocks of the most fantastical shapes and sizes, or it led through forests of gigantic trees bearded with moss. But as the view closed in around us we grew steadily more impatient: at last we seemed to be getting somewhere.

Somewhere, at the end of the world, the road came to a halt. The car stopped beside a lake whose waters, in the gloom beneath the mountains, were black as ink. The reeds sighed endlessly, and the trees stretching out their branches were inexpressibly sad.

At the edge of the water sat an old woman. She seemed to have been there since the days of the first Earl. She didn't even look at us, she just carried on mending her ancient and endless net. Every so often she would toss a pebble into the water.

"Excuse me, but which is the way to Caerbryn?" Osborne asked her.

She looked up but gave no answer. Cynthia put a question to her in Welsh, but again there was no reply. She seemed quite unaware of our presence. Somehow, though we never admitted this to one another, she filled us all with deep foreboding.

"This lake isn't on the map," Osborne remarked. "Perhaps it didn't exist in 1928, when they made it."

"Or else you're looking in the wrong place," Lene said. "We aren't where you said we were. You've lost the way."

"Then this must be Llyn-Coled. We'll have to turn back."

"Oh, Llyn-Coled!" cried Cynthia.

I knew something had struck her, some dark, superstitious thing she didn't want to name. The same wild superstition raced through me too, adding to my worst apprehensions.

With much difficulty, we turned the car around.

"We've lost three quarters of an hour," Osborne muttered. "But if we turn right here we'll find a short cut."

We were driving between two steep cliffs, in almost total darkness, pitching and jolting violently. Suddenly we bounced up out of our seats, almost thrown from the car. An enormous rock had fallen on the road, blocking our way. Turning here was impossible. The passengers had to get out and walk alongside as the car reversed slowly out of the canyon.

It had now started to rain. As a pleasure outing, this would not have been a success.

Then Cynthia's nerves gave way. She came to a halt in the driving rain, trembling and shaking with the violence of her sobbing.

"You press ahead," she wept. "Just leave me here. I'll go back to Llyn-Coled. Leave me, leave me!" And she stamped her feet hysterically.

Osborne and I looked on helplessly, but Lene was an angel of God. With a couple of affectionately crude remarks she got Cynthia back on her emotional feet, and we continued on our way.

At long last we were out of the canyon and back on a proper road. Soon we found ourselves on a relatively friendly plateau, from which we might have found our bearings had the rain not obliterated the view.

Eventually a village appeared in the distance, clinging to the side of a hill.

"That can only be Caerbryn," said Osborne.

We were again up to full speed, so far as the road would allow, softened as it was by the rain. Then the car decided to follow Cynthia's example and have a nervous breakdown. It gave an almighty groan and stopped dead in its tracks. Osborne crawled underneath it, and after a while Lene joined him. Snatches of a fierce argument could be heard from beneath the chassis. After fifteen minutes they slithered out again, unrecognisable under their coating of mud.

"I just can't imagine what could be wrong with it," said the person who had once been Osborne.

"It doesn't matter," the other one stated. "That's Caerbryn over there. It looks less than two miles. Let's just walk it. We can leave the car here. It'll take a genius to steal it."

We set off on foot. Slowly the details of Caerbryn came into focus. It was a strangely picturesque mountain village. Every cottage was flattened against the precipice; on the summit stood the ruins of a timeless castle, soaking in the rain.

It was three in the afternoon and not one of us had given a thought to lunch. We reached the village by four, drenched to the skin and almost dead with fatigue. But we were finally on inhabited ground. The people could even speak English, and showed us the pretty little cottage where John Mansfield lived.

We knocked for some time before the door opened. The man was very old, but with a fine, handsome face.

"Mr Mansfield?" Osborne enquired.

"Yes, sir," he replied, eyeing Osborne and Lene with evident surprise.

"Mr Mansfield, you must ignore our alarming appearance. I am Osborne Pendragon, this lady is my sister Cynthia, and these are my friends."

"Come in, come in," the old man replied, his face brightening. "I'm sorry there's no fire for you to dry yourself against, but I'll make one up. Meanwhile, you must have something to eat. A bit of cheese?"

"That would be excellent," said Osborne. "But first, where is my uncle?"

"His Lordship isn't here. He went out, perhaps an hour ago. He didn't say when he'd be back."

"Did he say where he was going?"

"No, I'm sorry, he didn't. A lady came for him in a car, and he went off with her."

"A lady? What did she look like?"

"Quite tall, reddish-blond hair: very handsome. The sort you must be familiar with in London."

"Eileen St Claire!" Cynthia exclaimed.

"She didn't give her name."

"Mr Mansfield," I asked, "do you know whether he was expecting her?"

"No, sir, he wasn't. He was extremely surprised to see her. In fact, he seemed rather shaken. But I couldn't say … "

"Where did they go?" Lene asked.

"I don't know. I've really no idea."

We went outside and held a council of war.

"We're too late," said Osborne. "We've been pre-empted. He's been lured into a trap. It's all up with him."

Cynthia uttered a loud scream. Lene comforted her.

"We don't know anything yet," she growled. "We can't afford to think the worst. Perhaps she's only invited him for a friendly chat. Perhaps even as we speak they're coming to an amicable agreement about the legacy. She chose her moment, when she could get him completely alone, so she could raise the question without any distractions. Up here, the Earl couldn't refuse to see her."

I didn't want to say it, but Lene's theory sounded rather improbable. If it was a question of a friendly chat, why not stay and have it here? No, they'd caught him in a snare. There could be no doubt about it.

We went back inside and flopped down around the old oak table. Mr Mansfield brought us cheese and some cider, and Lene made a show of eating and drinking voraciously to cheer us up. We all had a bit of the cider.

"What do we do now?" asked Osborne. "We can't go home. Who could repair the car?"

"We'll just have to wait," said Lene. "Wait patiently and calmly. The Earl will be back soon, and we'll know everything."

And we waited. Not because we had much hope; we just couldn't find anything better to do. Osborne had slumped into an ancient armchair and gone silent. Cynthia quietly sobbed, and Lene comforted her. I felt like a man whose insides had become paralysed. I couldn't think of anything constructive, and had nothing to say. I just kept telling myself it was too late: too late for everything.

The rain drove down steadily. Giant mushrooms were growing in the woods; slowly the flora of decay was covering everything. Evil had been unleashed, and the last bastion had fallen. The Satanic kidnapper would continue to haunt the mountains, and the one person who might have stood up to him was dead …

"They threw them into Llyn-Coled," Cynthia suddenly burst out. "The English Lords of the Marsh, took them there, the five hundred Welshmen. It was in the days of Llewellyn ap Griffith … Ever since then, the Lake has been grieving in Welsh."

In the end it was Lene who could bear to wait no longer.

"No. We must do something. After all, we're in a civilised country. This isn't Maeterlinck's Castle. The police … Where's the nearest police station?"

"In Bala," Osborne replied. "We could get there in an hour by car."

"Yes, we must go there. To warn the police and the military. We can't just sit here like this. We should have gone ages ago."

"But how do we get there?" I asked. "Mr Mansfield, does anyone in the village have a car?"

"No one, sir. It's rather old-fashioned around here."

"Or a carriage?"

"There could be. Apple wagons, the sort farmers use."

"How far is the nearest place where we might find a mechanic to repair the car?"

"Well, it depends, sir. There are many sorts of place in the world, and Merioneth is very large."

"True. But which is the nearest?"

"As I say, that depends, sir. By cart, the nearest is Abersych. On foot, Betws-y-teg."

"Why is that?"

"The road to Betws-y-teg goes all the way round the mountain, but the footpath cuts straight across it. You can walk it in an hour and a half."

"And in which of the two would there be a car?"

"In both. Merioneth is a rich county."

"Then to be on the safe side, we'd better go to both, and meet at the police station in Bala. Mr Mansfield will kindly get us a cart to take us to Abersych, and one of us will go on foot over the mountain to Betws-y-teg."

My suggestion was accepted, and Mr Mansfield hurried out to look for one. Now we had to decide who would ride in it, and who would walk. By this stage we realised that poor Cynthia was in such a state she would have to remain where she was. She had taken no part in the discussion; she had just sat shivering and trembling in a corner. Since we couldn't leave her on her own, Lene would have to stay too, as the only one who could do anything to calm her. However Lene also undertook to arrange for the broken-down car to be transported home, should we not return.

That left Osborne and myself. The more practical thing would have been for him to do the walking. As an athlete and a native he would more easily find his way about. He then confessed, rather ashamedly, that on the last part of the journey he had sprained his foot and didn't think he could use it for another hour and a half.

We ate some of the cheese to give us strength.

Meanwhile Mr Mansfield had returned with the cart, and Osborne set off for Abersych. I took my leave of Cynthia, who sat staring straight ahead, apathetically, said goodbye to Lene, and went out with our host.

The old man accompanied me to the far end of the village, pointed out the path and explained the route I was to take. I was unhappy from the start. The explanation took the form that I was at various times to pass through a beech wood, then one of birch; and an oak wood would also play a major role. But I, alas, had been city bred from a child, and had studied only the liberal arts. I had never been able to tell one tree from another.

However I dared admit none of this to Mr Mansfield. I took my leave of him and set off on my journey. In the final analysis, I thought, all I had to do was go over the mountain.

At first it was plain sailing. The importance of my mission and the sense of being on a real adventure filled me with childish pride. Whistling cheerfully, I progressed up the slope with rapid strides. I thought there would be some sort of view from the top to show me the way. By the time I got there I was thoroughly exhausted. Only then did I realise that there was not just a single peak, but several, one after the other: it was only from lower down that they appeared to be a single feature. And it was growing steadily darker.

I went over to a tree and tried to determine what sort it was. I couldn't. It was a tree, a generalised tree.

Never mind, I thought, just keep straight on ahead. I lit a cigarette and started downhill, in the direction that seemed to me to be a continuation of the way I had come. But I had some misgivings. I knew that as a rule my intuitions of this sort were seldom reliable.

Nonetheless, I pressed on regardless. It was only when I had come down from the ridge into a valley and found that the peak facing me was altogether too craggy and precipitous for me even to think of climbing it, and there was no sign of a path leading upwards, that I started to worry. The old man had said a regular, and easily visible, path went all the way to Betws-y-teg. I was obviously lost.

The best thing of course would be to go back and look for the track at the top. But a Roman does not retreat. And to climb a steep hill one had only just finished coming down presented certain psychological difficulties.

In the little valley where I stood, a path wound away to the left. Perhaps if I followed that I'd be able to work my way round the mountain and get off it somewhere. So I set out again.

Meanwhile darkness had descended. Not pitch darkness: the clouds had dissipated, and a crescent moon and some stars had appeared. I made my way 'by the uncertain light of the moon', as Virgil puts it, and I felt the full force of that magnificent epithet 'uncertain'.

It was all utterly confusing. At the back of my conscious mind lurked the anxieties of the actual world: what might be happening to the Earl, and what would be the outcome of this adventure. But in reality I could think of nothing but the complete uncertainty of my route, and what direction I should take. And the only thought I had on that subject was to follow my instincts, however unhappy and uncertain they might be.

I am not exaggerating their demerits. For the first fortnight after arriving in London I lost my way back to the hotel every single day, though it was a mere ten minutes' stroll. What hope had I now of finding my way in the great Celtic Forest, where I had never been before? My situation was as comically painful as it had been at school when the maths master got carried away, deriving one formula after another and covering the entire blackboard in scribbles, while we grinned and sniggered at one another in despair, having lost him at the second step he had taken.

My spirits steadily sank. The forest was becoming more and more hostile as my weariness grew and the darkness deepened. I was forced to sit and rest briefly on a tree stump. I lit a match and looked at my watch. It was eight o'clock. I had been walking for a whole hour.

When I looked at my watch again it was eight-thirty; the next time it was nine. I sat down, then stood up again. I pushed on stubbornly and miserably, and always it seemed to be through the same bit of forest.

At last I caught a glimmer of light, and hastened towards it. Ahead of me lay a sort of luminous clearing. As I drew closer I realised it was a lake reflecting the moonlight. The trees dipping their branches in the water conveyed an inexpressible grief, and the little reeds endlessly sighed.

It was Llyn-Coled—or its twin.

I recalled what Cynthia had said: the five hundred Welsh soldiers thrown into the lake in the days of Llewellyn ap Griffith; the waters grieving all night in Welsh. And yes, the reeds were whining, whimpering, sighing in the wind, so human-like …

The old woman was still sitting by the shore, spinning, spinning her net, as if she were Fate itself; from time to time she threw a pebble in the water. It did not occur to me to ask her the way. In fact, the very thought that she might see me filled me with horror. I turned and retreated back into the woods.

Weariness and hunger infused my thoughts with a mild delirium, tinged with nausea. I was no longer walking: I was fleeing.

I was in the Celtic Forest, where every improbability becomes possible. Every ten minutes held a new terror. A bush would take on the precise appearance of an old hag, a rock became a crouching giant: worst of all were the ink-black brooks, the hollow trees and the sudden, loud flurry of owls taking flight.

It was now eleven o'clock, and I was wandering over a plateau. Here at least there were no woods: no trees, no owls, only moonlight. There was no Birnam Wood to come to Dunsinane, but little piles of stone scattered about as though the very bones of the earth were thrusting up beneath its skin. Ahead, to one side, stood a much larger pile, perhaps a Celtic burial site, I guessed, from pictures I had seen.

Approaching nearer I realised, with a sort of half-pleasure, that it was a building. The pleasure was qualified because, on a remote upland like this, I could imagine that the old peasant couple dwelling there might not be very friendly. I did my best not to think of any of the many phantom possibilities, and resolved to be brave.

I had now reached it. It couldn't really be termed a house; it was rather an immense cube. I could see neither windows nor a door. I found none on the next side, or indeed on the third. When I had gone all the way round and ascertained that there were none at all, I was filled with an unspeakable terror. Nothing is more frightening than the completely inexplicable.

I was desperate to get away. Even the trees were better than this man-made enigma. But—I can't say whether through sheer fatigue or my overexcited imagination—I stood rooted to the spot, as paralysed as a man in a dream. I just stared, hypnotised, at the whitewashed wall.

Then the wall moved. With infinite slowness, it slid to one side. Behind it was utter darkness. Out of this darkness stepped a man, very tall, dressed in black from head to foot, with only his hair and ruff-collar glinting white. I uttered a terrible scream.

Tiny circles were spinning before my eyes, like little flashes of lightning; they grew in size, turning lilac-coloured and carmine; then one small spot became larger, larger, and unbearably bright.

I was enclosed by four walls. It was pitch-black, and only by groping about could I establish that I was incarcerated. The silence was so deep it was almost tangible.

I wondered: how could I be sure I wasn't dead? I lay down on the stone floor and sank into an exhausted, dreamless sleep.

My memories of what followed are extremely confused. Even in normal circumstances my dreams tend to be vivid, and I sometimes mistake them for things that have actually happened. Already during this strange adventure I had totally lost my sense of reality. As I don't wish to distort or exaggerate I shall need to exercise extreme caution when narrating what occurred next.

My exhaustion and unbearable mental stress were intensified by the fact that, as I always do, I had caught a cold in the endless rain and was slightly feverish. My inner censor was working only fitfully, and every fevered vision took on the solidity of fact.

For instance, it seemed to be entirely real that from time to time I would eat and drink, though I do not ever remember feeling hunger or thirst. What I ate, and how I came by it, have quite escaped my memory.

Quite understandably, I have no sense of how long my ghostly imprisonment lasted. My watch had stopped. The place in which I was incarcerated had no windows, so I was unaware of changing night and day. My periodic recurrences of sleep were no guide either. I dozed in patches, lay in a half-dream or felt superhumanly alert. There must have been hours which I experienced as minutes, and minutes which felt like hours. It is of course well known that fever alters our sense of the passing of time.

When I think of that episode, my most lasting memory is also the first, that of a certain smell: the smell of some kind of smoke that pervaded the entire building. It was not unlike incense, but more bitter, and prone to induce giddiness. I know that all sorts of herbs are burnt in magic rituals, and this particular blend must have been one used for liturgical censing. I believe it was one of those I had read about in occult tomes—verbena, myrrh, carib grass or ambergris, perhaps—but I really don't know: I had only read about them and could in no way identify any by name. However it was the same smell that had enveloped me when the midnight rider galloped past, on the road from Corwen.

… A strange, greenish light filled the room and a tiny figure swayed and tottered before me. It is difficult to describe what it was like—rather as I always imagined gnomes to be. It wore a kind of miner's outfit, with something like a pilot's cap on its head, which only intensified the clever, malevolent, thoroughly unpleasant look on its face. The most real thing about it—or him—was the screeching voice.

But even then I realised my visitor was not flesh and blood, because—this was really grotesque—his size changed constantly, flaring up and dying down, like a flame. Occasionally he flapped his wings and crowed, and sometimes he had no wings at all.

"Greetings, Benjamin Avravanel. I shall bring your robes at once."

"There must be some mistake," I said. "I've never been called Avravanel. And I don't recall ordering any robes."

"It's no matter," the gnome retorted, and crowed shrilly, which by now seemed entirely natural.

He was sitting on a high stool, which hadn't been there before, and he was flickering—steadily and continuously flickering.

"Honour and glory to the Great Adept," he declared.

"As you say," I answered, not wishing to offend. "Honour and glory."

"The Great Adept is preparing to complete the Great Work. It is the Will of the Stars, the Stars, the Stars … "

Strangely enough, I could see everything as he described it. One moment the stars were revolving in the sky, and the next they had suddenly, and significantly, stopped.

"The Great Adept requires an assistant," the gnome continued. "He has chosen you for this task, Benjamin Avravanel, Scholar."

"But excuse me, I know nothing of these mysteries," I remonstrated.

"You know rather more than most, and much more than the people of Merioneth."

I took this as a great compliment.

"But, damn, damn, damn," he exclaimed.

He fluttered and sizzled, like damp wood when you try to light it.

"The Great Work has been arrested at some point. We cannot proceed!"

Again I was able to see what he meant: a vast apparatus had appeared, glowing with its own light. It consisted of alembics, glass tubes, moving pistons, spirit lamps and bowls assembled in a wild Heath Robinson manner, though the overall effect was rather pleasing, like the body of a fine animal. Along the tubes, and down into the basins and alembics, flowed a golden liquid.

"This is where the Great Work has been arrested," the gnome said, indicating part of the mechanism. "Here. It has stopped moving. Do you observe how golden is its colour? But it is not yet gold. Not yet gold."

Then the gnome and the apparatus both vanished, leaving me with an intensely painful headache.

After some time the gnome and the apparatus appeared again. He was now dressed in black, and immensely solemn.

"Lean closer to me, Benjamin Avravanel. I have a terrible secret to whisper in your ear. The Great Adept has been compelled to turn to Black Magic for the Great Work to proceed. The Highest declined to help, so he has called upon the Deepest. You, oh wise master, are the assistant. You must participate in the ceremony. Rise, and prepare the sacred site. The hour has come, the hour has come."

An hourglass shimmered before my eyes, its last few grains running out. I rose and followed the gnome.

We were in a pentagonal room, lit from above by a luminous body identical to the one I had seen in the depths of Pendragon.

I was wearing a black, sleeveless robe and immensely heavy shoes, made, I should think, of lead, with astrological symbols embossed on them.

I immediately began preparing the room. There was a wand, the end of which I dipped in some blood-coloured liquid in a bowl and used to draw two large concentric circles on the floor. Inside these I drew a triangle, and inside that three further circles, not concentric.

I placed an incense burner in one of these last, and a black, crescent-shaped candlestick in each of the others. I then nailed a dead bat to a point along the line of the outermost circle, and that was the North; and to another point a skull, and that was the West. To the South went the head of a goat, and to the East the corpse of a black cat.

Meanwhile the smell wafting up from the burner was growing steadily heavier, and I staggered back to my room. The whole building was humming and vibrating like an organ. In my room stood a large, comfortable couch, covered in black, and I lay down on it.

How shall I account for this strange episode? I did not do so at the time: I lived it. It all took place as naturally and self-evidently as furnishing a new flat. Since then I have thought about it constantly, and have come up with two possible explanations.

The first, and simpler, is that I dreamed it. The business of preparing the site, the drawing of circles and the ancillary items are all minutely described in a book by Eliphas Levy, or to give him his proper name, the Abbé Alphonse-Louis Constant, with the addition of the fantastical circumstance that the candles were made of human sweat, the black cat had been fed for five days on human blood, the bat had been drowned in blood, and the goat was one *cum quo puella concubuerit*, as Levy rather delicately puts it: 'with whom a maiden had conjoined'. And the skull would have been that of an executed patricide. I had read this particular work of Eliphas Levy a year or two prior to the events in Wales, though I had of course forgotten the details. It may well be that the strange surroundings and fantastic events I had been experiencing had stirred up all these images and made them part of my dream. In dreams we sometimes remember whole poems read decades before and long since forgotten.

The second explanation is that I might have been in a state of hypnotic suggestion. What I identified as a gnome was my own subconscious mind, which, in trance, became detached from my ego and took on a life of its own. Such a divided ego has often been described by psychologists as part of the condition experienced by spirit mediums.

… Beyond the walls of my room the whole house was awake, filled with some hideous, teeming life, like an anthill. Footsteps could be heard, heavy objects being dragged about; something was sizzling, something else was whistling, and every so often the deep voice of a gong made the whole place tremble with its black renunciation.

The wall opened and a woman in a black cloak entered. As soon as she saw me she put her hand to her face and began to scream, "Who are you? Who are you? Who are you?"

I recognised the voice. It was Eileen St Claire. I rushed over to her and seized her.

She screamed again, wrested herself from my grip, and fled to the far corner of the room.

"Don't be afraid, " I said. "You know me. Look at me. I'm János Bátky, the Hungarian who took your ring to the Earl of Gwynedd."

She stopped screaming, and for some time gazed at me intently. Her every gesture betrayed a mind unhinged.

"Of course, you're the little scholar with the manuscript," she exclaimed, and burst into hysterical laughter.

"How did you get here?" I asked, and repeated the question. "And what are you doing here?"

She darted towards me, clung tightly to me and whispered in a voice of terror:

"Tell me, who is that man? Who is he? Whose house is this? Is it the old man's?"

"The midni— I don't know. I've no idea."

"Are you quite sure it … it isn't the Earl of Gwynedd, fifty years older?"

"Eileen," I cried, "What has happened to the Earl? You were the last to see him … he went off in your car … what has happened to him?"

"I don't know. I don't know what happened to him. I brought him here … where everything had been prepared. But then … I've no idea what happened to him after that. Are you quite sure that man isn't the Earl of Gwynedd? … Oh, I'm so cold … Give me your hand. Is your blood warm? Yes, yes, it is. Please, sit beside me here, nice and close, and make me warm. I'm so cold, so very cold … "

She certainly was shivering, though the room was rather warm.

"When I was a girl, at home in Connaught," she jabbered, "it was as cold as this once … the rivers were frozen solid … sit closer, please … we had very little money at the time. There were ten of us siblings … what could a poor little girl do?" Her patter had become steadily more mechanical.

" … so I went to Father Considine to confess, and told him why I had needed the money … please, please, don't pull away … I'm so cold … I didn't steal the five pounds from the old man just because I wanted the money, but because it was so very cold … I can't bear the cold … Why are you looking at me like that? Don't you believe me? All right, I did want the money. Even in those days I was after money. I never knew then how much I'd have one day. I've lots of money. Every minute I earn fifty pounds. And yet I'm so cold … Please, sit closer to me. How much do you want? Where's my cheque book? Holy God, where is my cheque book … ?" And she started to sob.

Then she calmed down noticeably.

I think I must have started quizzing her again about what had happened to the Earl. She told me what she knew, and I remember very clearly what she said—her words, her tone of voice. This part could not have been a dream. And yet … I also remember just as clearly what the gnome had said …

This is what she told me.

"As soon as we heard from Cynthia where he had gone, I went to see him. Now he couldn't just send a message that I wasn't welcome. He opened the door himself. I knew that once he saw me he would never have the strength to throw me out. It wasn't difficult to persuade him to go with me. He believed everything I told him. That I'd broken off with Morvin, but I was afraid and needed his protection. He got in the Hispano and came like a lamb to the slaughter. Please, don't draw back … I'm so cold … this whole night … never again while I live … Tell me, does the Devil really exist?"

I pressed her to continue.

"We came to this house, and imagine … in the very first room, Morvin. Just lying there. He should have been hiding. But he couldn't. He was dead."

She started to giggle.

"Why is that so funny?"

"I have to laugh when I think of him. Such an odd sight. His neck was twisted round; he was lying on his stomach and his head was facing upwards. I laughed then too. The Earl just stared at me, shocked by my response. He said I'd better be careful: it was how Maloney had died. But I was glad. I thought, now I'd be free of both of them. Now I'd have a bit more peace in my life. But that man … so much worse … oh, oh … You're a doctor. Tell me: what makes the body turn cold as ice?"

"Please continue. Tell me what happened to the Earl," I repeated, in my monomaniac refrain.

"Yes, yes, the Earl. I thought, this is no good; he can see Morvin's here, he'll start to get suspicious. He was sitting in a chair, with his head in his hands, like this … I took out my revolver, the tiny one I bought in Paris … it's so pretty, with white enamel … I thought I'd stand behind him and shoot him in the head, at the nape of the neck, where the skull is soft … Do you know, I once saw a man whose head had been shattered into pieces by a bullet. It was in Morocco … how warm it was there … and those women with their veils … We'll go to Morocco, won't we? But how can we ever get away from here?"

Oh, the contradictions of feeling! To hold in your arms some-one you yearn to embrace, whose body draws you like a magnet, and yet your trembling consciousness utterly abhors …

"What happened to the Earl?" I shouted at her.

"Don't shout, please; please, don't shout. I don't know what happened to him … That man was standing there. He took my revolver away. I couldn't move. He picked me up like a sack and threw me in a room … oh, such a room … I had no idea there were so many rooms in this little house, and so cold … Are you quite sure that man isn't the Earl of Gwynedd?"

"I'm not sure of it. How can we be sure of anything anymore? He may well be the Earl of Gwynedd. There have been so many of them. Eighteen. It could be any one of them. But you … Why do you think it was him?"

"His face. It was the same face. And yet different. As if it had been turned inside out."

She was seized by a renewed fit of ever more violent shivering and outbursts of sobbing. She was in a very bad way. To bring her round I had to rub her vigorously, as one does with people rescued from drowning. After that she fell asleep.

The bustle beyond the walls started up again, even noisier than before, and the smell of incense from the burner filled the room, covering everything like a fog. Outside the door, the door I couldn't see, the one Eileen had come through … was someone standing there, watching us? My terror mounted. I was feverish again. She whimpered and snuggled closer to me. We were like two animals in mortal danger, cowering together. Rather this guilty, wicked woman, who was at least human, than that presence beyond the wall …

Again I fell asleep.

When I woke, she was awake too. Her cloak had fallen open. On the black bedcover her white body lay in all its surreal and terrible beauty.

"Eileen … "

Her beauty enveloped me, like a cloud. The little seaport, at the end of the world …

She put her arms around my neck and kissed me.

I find the next bit difficult to relate. She was lying there in front of me. I threw myself on top of her and began to kiss her body, all over, with growing ecstasy and a passion I had never known in all my coldly conventional life.

"Oh, how wonderfully warm, how wonderfully warm your mouth is," she murmured. In the closeness of our embrace she was purring contentedly, like a kitten.

Had I nothing else to be thinking of? Was my ardour not chilled by my terror, the horrors I had lived through, or the danger hovering at the door? No. Nothing occupied me beyond the moment. I was at the end of the world, beyond my own life, just thirty seconds before everything imploded, light years away from all that was rational. Nothing remained but the desire of one body for another. In such a spiritual earthquake as this the deepest and most real layers of one's being are hurled to the surface. Perhaps I was trying to make up for every second I had failed to devote to my body? As a lover I had always been as silent as a butterfly, but now I was shouting out and gasping for breath. In fact it was no longer 'I', but a stream of pure life, utterly impersonal, cut off from its source and racing into extinction.

Suddenly, as if in response to some command, we broke apart. We quickly wiped our hands over our necks and faces, and got up.

The unseen door opened and we proceeded out, with slow, ritual steps.

Everything I did subsequently was done as if under orders. I never hesitated for a moment. I understood everything, how everything was connected; it was as if someone had revealed everything to me by some unknown, purely internal process.

I knew that she would be the sacrifice, on the sacred site I had prepared myself.

I knew too that she had to die in this particular way, her body soiled by lustful kisses, in mortal sin, for the sacrifice to be pleasing to Satan.

The strange thing is that I was not in the least afraid. I stood above and beyond everything human. My feelings were numb: they no longer existed. I simply went about my business. Later, I was glad it had happened this way. Who knows what trauma, what terrible damage to the nervous system, the stress of such moments might otherwise have caused?

We made our way through several empty rooms, all humming with some indefinable energy and life, as though a large furnace blazed nearby. And yet the rooms were empty, and nothing moved in them. There was dense smoke, and we went through a fog, as if over a nocturnal lake.

Then I stumbled on something, and glanced down. A man lay at my feet. He was dead, and his head was facing backwards. I knew it was James Morvin. I stepped over him and went on.

We arrived in the pentagonal room. Everything was just as I had arranged it, or appeared to have arranged it, in my dream: the concentric circles, the triangle containing the three smaller circles, the incense burner, the candlesticks, and the four symbolic objects—the bat, the cat, the goat's head and the skull.

We stopped.

The wall opposite us opened and the apparition stepped through. He wore a black robe and a black fur hat, and carried a curiously-shaped sword in his hand. His face was as devoid of expression as a man's could be.

Eileen continued towards him, her head bowed and her arms hanging by her sides. I leant against a column, incapable of further movement.

The gnome was once again leaping, flickering and sizzling before my eyes. At times his head was as high as the ceiling; at times he took the form of a dog. More and more his face came to resemble my own.

Someone had halted between the two black candelabra and spread her arms out wide: Eileen. Her hands touched the flames on either side, but she did not flinch. Could she not feel them?

The magus raised his curious-looking sword in the air. The gnome was trying, grotesquely and painfully, to balance himself over the incense-burner. Without a sound, the woman went down. The gnome scooped up the flowing blood in his hands and poured it, again and again, onto the marble slab.

The phantom stood above the slab … his arms wide, the sword in one hand …

The words of Satanic invocation … barbaric, incomprehensible words, as the sword drew figures in the air …

The smoke became ever more dense. I could barely make out

what was happening on the other side of the room. The words of conjuration reverberated in my ears, like the howling of wolves at prey.

Then a terrible scream, and the cry of a wounded animal beneath the pitiless stars.

The phantom flung the sword away and dashed out through the opening in the wall.

In that instant my nightmare, or vision—I have no idea what to call it—ended. I was suddenly as sober and sane as a person is often said to be when his life is on the brink.

It came to me in a flash that the Devil-conjuror must have seen some terrible sight that drained his courage, and made him throw down his sword and fly. He was fleeing from the horror he had called up within himself.

Now it was my turn to flee.

I darted out through the gap the apparition had used. In a trice I was in the open air, with the building behind me.

It was night. I was standing on the plateau that had been my last memory of the outer world. It was deserted. The rocks were so white it was as if the bones of the earth were protruding through its skin.

But I was free. I had made my escape.

I set off into the night, not minding which way I went. Nothing worse could happen to me now. I had escaped and would sooner or later be among human beings again.

Reaching the edge of the clearing I looked back, and saw the house on fire. I re-entered the woods, and made my way happily and steadily downhill.

After a while I lay down to sleep in a friendly meadow. When I woke, the sun was high in the sky, as in a children's story. I got up and continued on my way. I was extremely hungry, but in excellent spirits. Soon I reached a farm. The farmer's wife stared at me in astonishment. My clothes were crumpled, torn and filthy, and my face was disfigured by several days' growth of stubble. But she was a kindly soul, and for the money I gave her fed me copiously on cheese and milk. I was unspeakably happy to have pennies and shillings in my pocket, with cash again at the centre of things between man and man.

She pointed me the way to Abersych.

I must have been walking an hour or so, along a pleasant, sunlit road, when a large figure approached, waving his arms. As we neared I recognised John Griffith, whose medieval costume had so alarmed me that first night at Llanvygan.

"Thank heavens you've turned up, Doctor sir!" he boomed. "The entire staff and all the locals are out looking for you. There's a ten-pound reward for whoever finds you. It'll be mine, if you haven't met anyone else yet."

"No, Griffith, you're the first. Congratulations on the ten pounds. But what's happened to the Earl?"

"To the Earl, sir? Nothing, to the best of my knowledge. He's at home in Llanvygan. But we must get back to Abersych. We'll find Mr Osborne and the German lady there. They're also looking for you, sir."

And so it was. On arrival I shaved and sat down to lunch at the inn. But just as I was starting on the soup, Lene appeared and greeted me warmly. From her I gathered all the news.

By the time I set out on my strangely-ended journey, Osborne had already left by cart for Abersych, and from there he went on to the police station at Bala. The police of course knew nothing about Morvin or Eileen St Claire. Filled with desperation, Osborne had the sudden idea of telephoning Llanvygan. He was told the Earl had just that moment returned, safe and sound, but extremely nervous and upset, and had locked himself, as usual, in his rooms. Reassured, Osborne made his way back to Caerbryn and took Lene, Cynthia and the car home.

"We haven't seen him since. The word is, he's in bed with a fever. So of course nobody knows how his meeting with Mrs Roscoe went. We organised a search for you. The whole neighbourhood has been on the alert. For two days they've been scouring the mountains behind Caerbryn. But I haven't told you the strangest thing of all. The Earl came back with the little boy who vanished so mysteriously, the one who was abducted by a horseman. But that's all we know about it. The Earl sent the child back to his father before anyone could speak to him. "But oh, if you knew how hungry I am again! Mind you, I've already had my lunch. It must be because I'm so happy you've turned up. What shall I have? Do you know, I'd like a bit of Welsh rarebit. It's the best thing I've come across in this whole creepy province."

And she set about the toasted cheese with gusto. It is, after all, the national dish.

How happy I was to see her appetite, her glowing, puppy-like physical health. The entire, and very substantial, dish vanished in four mouthfuls –this is no exaggeration—and tears sprang to my eyes. Lene thumped me heartily on the back, but had great difficulty assuaging my grief.

At that moment Osborne appeared. He was pale and haggard, and the angle of his necktie outdid every previous achievement in its wild abandon.

"Hello, Doctor. So you're back. Thank God—I was really worried. Do you know what's happened?"

And he flopped down in a chair.

"Well, say something, you idiot!" Lene barked at him.

"The British Empire was built upon self-control, Lene. But that's not what I have to tell you. So just listen."

"Speak, or I'll murder you," she yelled.

"This morning the police found Morvin and Mrs Roscoe. Somewhere, on a godforsaken little upland near Betws-y-teg, the pair of them had had a peculiar little hut built, very hurriedly, in just a few days. It was a sort of cube-like structure, without doors or windows. The workmen were very unhappy about doing it. The old Welsh kings are said to be buried there, and Cwn Annwn, the red-eared dog, has often been seen in the area.

"This morning two policemen went up to the plateau to look for Bátky. And, can you imagine? … the hut had burned down. From what was left, they decided that it had happened quite recently … in the early hours of this morning in fact. Among the ruins they found the charred bodies of a man and a woman. There was just about enough of them left for the workmen to identify our friends."

"How can it have happened?" asked Lene.

"The most reasonable explanation would be suicide. You never can tell when knowledge of one's crimes might suddenly turn into a guilty conscience."

"So then," Lene remarked, "Llanvygan is safe, and I have come to the end of my mission. But it's all very strange. What do you make of it, Doctor? And by the by, you haven't said a word about where you've been gadding these past few days. Some little Welshwoman?"

"I'm saying nothing, Lene. I can't. There are some things that have an inner truth, but become nonsense when spoken. It just isn't possible to explain … We live simultaneously in two worlds, and there are two levels of meaning. One can be understood by everyone, the other is beyond words, and is utterly horrible."

"You're in fine philosophical mood today," she retorted. "And considering that you are a Doctor of Philosophy, your wisdoms are rather banal and dilettantish. But we won't pry into your secrets, or the little Welshwoman hiding behind your hocus-pocus."

Osborne smacked his brow.

"If Mrs Roscoe is dead, the Roscoe fortune, as far as I am aware, devolves automatically on the house of Pendragon. A tidy little sum. Even if Asaph had discovered how to make gold we would never have become this rich. Hm, Lene?"

"I'm not happy about it. I don't believe in large sums of money. It's not good news for you, Osborne. If you had no money at all you'd be a dear little chap. I couldn't wish for a better husband. It'd be such a joy looking after you."

Osborne telephoned instructions to call off the search, and informed Llanvygan that I had been found. Then we got in the car, and before long the outlines of the castle came into view.

I had a bath, changed and went down to tea. I found Osborne and Lene in the Chippendale room. Osborne had a sandwich in his hand, and was pacing up and down the room with giant strides, excitedly holding forth:

"The moment we have legal confirmation of her death I shall go to London to see Seton, on uncle's behalf. Unfortunately I don't have the appropriate technical jargon for the legal action we'll take, but the net result will be that the entire Roscoe fortune, the mines, the estates, the forests, the factories in South-East Asia and the whole God-knows-what will be in the possession of the

House of Pendragon. My uncle won't trouble himself with such mundane matters, and the running of the entire business empire will fall on my feeble shoulders."

His face was transfigured with joy. For the first time I became aware that behind his affected and effeminate manner lurked a downright, practical, dominant Englishman.

Lene heard him out with a face of sorrow, and then two enormous tears slid down her cheeks. She was thinking how much she would have loved Osborne as a poor and helpless little boy.

He suddenly stopped, deep in thought. He looked at Lene and his face brightened.

"Lene ... but you're an economist, and a good one at that! How would you like to be my secretary?"

She thought about it for a while.

"It's something we could discuss."

"But where's Cynthia?"

That in fact was the question I had being wanting to ask ever since I set foot in the castle. But a sort of lover-like bashfulness had held me back.

"She could well be in Switzerland by now," Osborne stated. "We packed her off the day after we got back from Caerbryn. She was a wreck: absolutely not herself at all. Our aunt, the Duchess of Warwick, came and took her away."

At just this moment the door opened, and there stood the towering figure of the Earl. But with what a changed face. There were black rings round his eyes, scored by who knows what dreadful tempests of the soul. His serene self-possession had vanished. Every line of his face was as sharp-set as those of the dead who have greatly suffered. The sight of him was so shocking even Lene dared not speak.

"Ah, Bátky," he said, very softly, by way of greeting. And he started to walk back and forth, with his long strides. His desolate footfalls commanded silence.

Then he stopped, and looked at us.

"You all know she's dead ... that they're both dead?"

"Oh yes, Your Lordship. I ... I ... "

But I fell silent. I had no wish to speak in front of Osborne and Lene about the visionary events I had been part of.

"János Bátky … where have you been? We have been very anxious about you."

"I shall tell you everything. But only you."

"Then come up to the Library."

From the depths of his vast armchair he listened in silence to the tale I stammered and stumbled out to him. He showed not the least surprise. From time to time he nodded his head, as if he had known all along exactly what would happen. Only the way he gripped the arm of his chair revealed his feelings. When I came to the story of Eileen's horrific death he stared at me fixedly for a moment, then his gaze fell away, like a meteor plunging to the bottom of the sea.

When I had finished he remained silent for a long, long time.

"And after that, you didn't see the … spirit … again?" he finally asked.

"No."

"No one has seen it. No one. It couldn't be otherwise … Bátky, will you come with me up to Pendragon? If we're quick we can get there while it's still light."

A few minutes later we were in the car, following the now familiar route, and before long we stood beside the ruins. We made our way quickly down, opening the hidden door by means of the rose cross, and the Earl led me directly towards our goal—down into the womb of the castle where the tombs of ancient Pendragons gaped, down along the corridors through which, speechless with terror, du Fresnoy and St Germain had followed Bonaventura. But I was not afraid. I had been face to face with the Impossible, and my standards had shifted. Thus the Egyptian priests must have walked the secret vaults of their temples, thronged with deities and spectres.

We now stood under the mysterious body of light whose rays illuminated the altar. The Earl raised the altar and lifted the slab of the tomb. We gazed down into the pit.

The figure was lying on the catafalque, dressed in black. His hands were folded on his breast, in the manner of the pious dead, and rings covered his fingers. His face was bloodless, lifeless, rigid … but this was not the serene rigidity of Nordic gods; it was bitter, tortured, unspeakably dark. Then I noticed it … the golden hilt of an antique dagger planted in the breast. The deathless horseman had slain himself.

A tear slid down the Earl's cheek. Then he closed the tomb.

We went up into the light of day. Twilight had begun, and the sun was setting in a blaze of colour. Below us, steeped in its glory, lay the mountains and valleys, the villages and farmhouses, the whole magical domain of the Earls of Gwynedd. And as night approached, the landscape became tinged from end to end with a gentle melancholy, a profound feeling of transience.

"I am tired," the Earl said, and we sat on a stone bench, green with moss.

We were there for some time. First the stars came out, then a kindly moon. Suddenly he started to talk. To this day I don't know what made him abandon his reticence. Perhaps it was his weariness, or the dreadful anguish of all he had been through; and because everything had come to an end.

"They were waiting for a particular moment," he began: "a rare conjunction of the stars, or some other sign we can't guess at. They called it the Coming of the Prophet Elias. It was the moment Asaph was also waiting for, lying in the tomb he had built for himself. Well, it came ... long after the last Rosicrucians had vanished, and a once-mocking world had forgotten them. It coincided exactly with my own ordeal. The midnight rider, the deathless dispenser of justice, had saved the lives of his descendants once again, but the Great Work wasn't proceeding according to plan. Only black magic and conjuration of the Devil could help, and that required a sacrifice. So he carried off the farmer's son. I searched for him, day after day, in the mountains. I was desperate. Eventually I found him, in the house Morvin had built. He made me choose. Either the woman would be sacrificed, he said, or the boy. It was a dreadful struggle. Anyway, I chose to save the little boy, the innocent child. I left the woman to her fate, and it found her. But the Great Work failed after all ... If it was as you describe it then the Devil did appear to him ... but we can't be sure about any of that. Only that he died in total despair. Come, Dr Bátky."

When we were back at the castle, the Earl addressed me in a very different voice. It was calm and perfectly objective:

"My dear friend, I have a final favour to ask of you. Would you go up to London once more, and call on Julian Huxley? He's Professor at the King's College Institute of Zoology. Tell him I shall be offering them the giant axolotls. And my instruments. And my tables of statistics. They can use them all, if they wish, and they can publish the results."

"You're going to abandon your research?"

"What is there left to study? Anyway my little experiments were laughable compared to everything the Rosicrucians knew, and with events that have taken place before our very eyes. I … believe in the resurrection of the body, and whether others do or not is of no interest to me. So, János Bátky … that is the end of my tale. All that's left are the years and months allotted to an old man, who is no longer consoled by thoughts of resurrection, but only of eternal death."

And with that the Welsh story came to its end.

The next day the Earl left for Scotland. Lene travelled back to Oxford, and Osborne and I to London. I contacted Julian Huxley, whom I had long admired as a great biologist and brother of Aldous Huxley, the cleverest and wittiest of all English novelists.

As Llanvygan's envoy, I became a minor celebrity among zoologists. They fêted me as if I had discovered the axolotl myself, and I revelled in it. After the historical nightmares I had endured, the natural sciences were as refreshing as an Alpine scene.

I saw Osborne regularly. A few days after our return to the capital he told me he had had a letter from Cynthia, saying she was now out of danger, and asking after me in the warmest possible terms.

I wrote back immediately, without revealing that I planned to follow her to Switzerland. As it happened, the trip was deferred again and again. Among my new acquaintances was a gentleman who invited me to accompany him to America to a conference on the history of natural science, where I was to read a paper on Lenglet du Fresnoy and the Alchemists of the Eighteenth Century.

The trip to America was extremely tempting. So far my travels had been limited to a single continent. Besides, common sense dictated that I should forget Cynthia. This love, or whatever it should be called, was quite hopeless. I could never marry her. My own snobbery recoiled at the thought of anyone so closely connected with the age of Shakespeare and Milton making herself the 'life-companion' of a so petty bourgeois a creature as myself.

And even if by some miracle she did become my bride, the marriage, I told myself, would not be a truly happy one. Cynthia as middle-class housewife would have lost everything I loved in her, the one quality she perhaps had never possessed at all—the proud, lofty inaccessibility of the legendary Lady of the Castle.

While I pondered and deliberated, the following letter arrived:

My Dear Friend,

It's extremely kind of you to think of me, especially as I've been reading a great many books, and I would love to have your opinion of them. Most of them are in French. It would be so nice if you were here, because there is so much I don't understand.

I am quite well now, and go out for short walks in the mountains. I wish I could write you a description of them, but I can't think what to say. Could you recommend a good book about the Engadin people and the Ladins in general?

I have excellent company here. My school friend Daphne FitzWilliam is here with her brother, who is a captain in the Navy. He's a very nice boy, and very intelligent. You would certainly find a good friend in him. Captain FitzWilliam has asked me to marry him.

I'd like it very much if you would write to me in detail about your plans for the future, and your work. In any case, never forget that I am, and always will be, your very good friend. Do write.

Yours,

Cynthia Pendragon

TRANSLATOR'S AFTERWORD

Antal Szerb's first full-length novel was the product of an enchanted year (1929–1930) on a postdoctoral scholarship in England, much of it spent in that cradle of learned eccentricity, the Reading Room of the British Museum. Already fluent in several European languages, Szerb was gathering material for his ground-breaking *Histories of English Literature* and *World Literature*. At the same time, though a committed Catholic, he was deeply interested in heterodox religious ideas and unusual states of consciousness, and in the late twenties Rosicrucianism and the Occult were very much in the air. The happy result of this conjunction was *The Pendragon Legend* (1934).

Into this, his first full-length novel, Szerb poured all his enthusiasms, many of them distinctly non-scholarly. In it he draws on, and quietly parodies, popular crime writing, gothic horror, romantic fiction, the regional novel, various forms of occult treatise and the historical memoir. The hero of the book is an unmistakable version of the writer himself, cruelly satirised. Most of the other characters are affectionate caricatures of the English (the category 'English' to include the Irish, Scots and Welsh), for whom he held an intense, if at times baffled, admiration. 'Continentals' such as the Hungarian anti-hero Janos Bátky and Lene, the sexually omnivorous Teutonic 'modern woman', receive the same irreverent treatment. The upshot of all this foolery is, against expectation, a highly original psychological study, with some intensely dramatic, and some delicately touching, moments.

Born in 1901, Szerb was an essayist, playwright, novelist, literary historian and academician. By 1934 he was Hungary's most respected writer: a small, shy, loveable man noted for his unfailing kindness and vast erudition, sweetened by an ever-playful wit. As the poet Agnes Nemes Nagy remarked: "Fifty per cent of what he said made you laugh, and ten per cent filled you with awe." But he was born into a deeply troubled Hungary, with his Jewish origins coming under increasing scrutiny, a disadvantage which he compounded by his consistently anti-fascist stance. His brutal death in a labour camp in 1945 was an unspeakable loss, not just to Hungary but to European literature.

For all its stylistic assurance, its almost post-modern virtuosity in playing literary genres off against one another to create a work of vital originality, *Pendragon* is probably not Szerb's masterpiece. That remains *Journey by Moonlight* (*Utas és Holdvilág, 1937*), a novel seemingly as dark and probing as *Pendragon* is light and flippant. But the two have more in common than meets the eye. Both are the record of a spiritual journey, thoughtlessly begun, that ends in significant failure. Bátky, like his counterpart Mihály in *Journey*, is a fatally shallow 'seeker' whose blunderings bring him up against profound truths the significance of which he never quite grasps. Both anti-heroes represent important aspects of Szerb himself, subjected to unsparing scrutiny. What the two books share above all is a particular irony, no doubt 'middle-European' in character but also distinctive to this particular writer. It is less a literary device than a mode of vision, in which a fiercely searching intelligence is balanced by a delight in humanity and an irrepressible playfulness. The Ego, as Bátky's progress reveals, is a pathetic, often absurd creature, a disconcerting mixture of ill-understood promptings and wild improvisation, always the prey of circumstance, and far less important than people imagine. Szerb has read his Freud, but the perspective here is closer to that of the mystic. As the narrator observes, in one of his wry flashes of self-insight: "What a shame that those moments when man is noble and pure and akin to the gods are so transient, so fleeting, while that complicated nonentity the Ego is always with us—of which one can speak only in terms of protective tenderness and gently irony". In that sentence lies the core of these endearing novels.

LEN RIX
May 2006

Other Antal Szerb titles published by

PUSHKIN PRESS

Journey by Moonlight
Translated by Len Rix

Oliver VII
Translated by Len Rix

The Queen's Necklace
Translated by Len Rix

Forthcoming

Love in a Bottle
Translated by Len Rix

www.pushkinpress.com